REVENANT

REVENANT

ANIMUS™ YEAR TWO BOOK TWO

JOSHUA ANDERLE

MICHAEL ANDERLE

DISRUPTIVE IMAGINATION

Thanks to the JIT Readers

Nicole Emens
James Caplan
Jeff Eaton
Kelly O'Donnell
Misty Roa
John Ashmore
Larry Omans

If I've missed anyone, please let me know!

Editor
The Skyhunter Editing Team

To Family, Friends and
Those Who Love
to Read.
May We All Enjoy Grace
to Live the Life We Are
Called.

REVENANT

The atmosphere at the market wasn't exactly what one would call bustling. Admittedly, though, an underground market that specialized in stolen tech, illegal weapons, and men who offered rather shady and often violent services was probably a place that wouldn't attract a very social crowd.

Despite the somewhat subdued undertone, a man hummed merrily to himself as he hurried along the fourth row of vendors, striding toward his destination with a firm but light step.

He stopped outside a shoddy structure comprised of what appeared to be crudely-cut ship parts and various pieces of metal hastily welded together to create a store-front. The man retrieved a tablet, looked down at it and back at the store, and smiled to himself. He put the device away and opened the door.

The sound of a pistol priming—a Dredd model by the sound of the charging core—immediately caught his attention. He focused his gaze on four men who stared at him with threatening scowls and flared nostrils. His smile widened when he saw the Dredd in the hands of one of the men, pleased to see he still had the knack of being able to identify a weapon simply by its sound.

He stepped toward the counter of the store, but one of the men stopped him.

"Can I help you?" he asked, but it didn't sound like he wanted to be particularly helpful.

"I'm sorry if I'm a little late," the newcomer stated and tapped the rim of his glasses. "The traffic was more of a catastrophe than I had expected it would be. You really have the riff-raff here in Florida."

Another man kicked a box over and spat on the ground, and the customer made a note to make sure to step around it. "Are you making a joke, punk?" he snapped.

The man tilted his head as he considered the question in silence for a moment or two. "I don't think so, but maybe humor is simpler down here. That's understandable, I suppose."

Before the aggressor's veins could throb any harder with his indignation, a door at the rear of the shop opened. The older gentleman who entered had long, curling hair, the black interspersed with strands of gray. He was dressed in a gray and blue bodysuit with a wraparound ocular device on his head. "Are you the five o'clock?" he asked nonchalantly, seemingly oblivious of the four goons.

"That I am," the newcomer confirmed. "It's good to finally meet you, Mr. Vinci."

"Likewise." He lowered his hands to signal the others to calm down. "Sorry about the greeting my friends gave you.

We've had some issues with new customers from the Red Suns. They are a little antsy."

"No worries at all." The man moved toward the counter once the guard in front of him had dropped his arm. "I can understand a degree of grandstanding. It takes guts to set up shop in a place like this, and it takes smarts to keep those guts inside you."

"Speaking of which…" A large hand settled heavily on his shoulder. "Don't think you are going in the back without getting frisked."

The man peered back, and the movement revealed glowing artificial eyes over the top of his shades, which thoroughly startled the guard. "How kind of you to offer, and on our first meeting, no less." He turned to the proprietor. "This is fantastic customer service."

Vinci chuckled as he took his visitor's tablet and placed it on the counter. The guard frowned but said nothing as the man turned and held his hands up. "Besides the tablet, I have two blades on my person," he explained as the guard began his search. "On the left is your basic Omni-blade, holstered inside its switcher."

The guard unclipped the device from the visitor's belt and examined it with surprise. "Look at this thing," he all but shouted and turned to show it to the other three. "This is unreal. It can produce up to a dozen different blade types, and it has a hard-light generator."

"It allows me to create hard-light versions of any personal blade I need, as well as adapt a few different qualities such as temperature and sharpness," the man bragged and folded his arms smugly. "Among other things. Nifty, right?"

"Put your hands back up," the guard snapped as he tossed the Omni-blade and switcher to one of the other goons in the front. "What else you do you have?"

"You'll find my pride and joy on my right," he responded and cocked his hip while he raised his hands once more. "I call her 'Macha.' She's been with me for almost a decade now. A piece of advice to you boys—get yourself a girl or guy that's as useful as she is, and you'll live a much happier life."

The guard took the knife from the other side of his belt and unsheathed it to reveal a curved blade with a line of jagged notches in it. "It doesn't look like much, especially compared to that Omni-blade."

"The Omni has its tricks, and is fun in its own way," he admitted. "But it's a fairly recent acquisition. I've only had it for about a year. Macha has been with me since I discovered my current passion. It's extremely difficult to find the right blade type, but it's damn sturdy and sharper than Likan fangs. Cleans easily, too." The guard replaced the blade in its sheath and tossed it behind him, then continued his search. "I've only had to change the blade out twice. Once was a few years back—wear and tear and all, quite literally in my case." The guard tried to block him out as he patted down his legs. "The other time was recently, though. I got it stuck in a hard place on a trip in the Amazon."

The guard stood to check his arms. "What's with the boots?" he asked. "They feel like they are made for heavy armor." He tugged at the man's arms. "And these gloves are super-tight."

"That would be because they are wraps, not gloves," he stated. "I could unwind them for you."

"Does you no good to hide a blade if you can't get to them if a fight broke out," he muttered. "This can't be all you have. You come down to a crypto bazaar with nothing but a couple of blades? Are you insane?"

"You don't deal with places like this often, do you?" another man spat. "There might be a general understanding between those of us who make our living down here, but you outsiders don't get the same treatment. You'd make an easy mark for a thief or merc looking for some liquor cash."

The man smoothed his jacket, adjusted his belt, and slid one hand into it as he leaned back on the counter. "I usually don't. I'm accustomed to finding what I need in other places or simply making it myself, but I needed something a little special." He pointed at Vinci. "And I heard that Mr. Vinci here could get me exactly what I needed."

"And I can't wait for you to see it, Mr. Sonny," the hacker said with barely restrained glee. "I'll get to the specifics shortly. Follow me into the back."

"Certainly. Assuming we are done here?" He looked at the guard, who studied him once more.

"Do you have anything else on you? If you try to pull a fast one, you can be sure we'll deal with you with our own personal touch."

"And I'm sure you'll really get those knots out." He chuckled. "As for weapons, nothing else but my arms and legs. I've heard I have an impressive punch, but unless you wanna take those wraps off, I can't say I have anything else."

The guard grabbed him by his jacket. "If you're playing us, that's exactly the first thing we'll do." He released him abruptly. "Get in there, and don't waste his time. He's not only a tech cracker but our division leader. His time is important."

The customer tugged on his jacket and nodded without losing his smile. "I won't take up any more time than is necessary." He clapped his hands in front of the guard. The sound was evidently much louder than the man had expected because he jerked his head back quickly. "I promise." He followed Vinci into his personal quarters.

As the door shut, the guard huffed and walked over to the others. "What a damn creep."

"He wouldn't stop smiling. I'd like to beat those teeth down his throat, myself," another one muttered and glanced at a third man, who looked away, his expression thoughtful. "Is something wrong, Mick?"

"Huh? It's noth— Well, I guess it's not nothing. Mr. Vinci called him Sonny. Is that name familiar to any of you?"

"I'm terribly sorry about those boys, Mr. Sonny," Vinci said in hasty apology and offered him a chair. "Like I mentioned, times have been somewhat tense, and they are still getting used to their duties. I had hoped they would be less green by now. I'm not sure if they had the slightest clue who they were addressing, or even if they are smart enough not to back talk if they did."

"No worries, good sir. And you can simply call me Gin," he stated affably as he sat and crossed one leg over the other before he leaned back. "Manners are nice and all, but I prefer friendly to formal."

"It's good to work with someone who's more relaxed," Vinci admitted. He took hold of a screen on a crane, pulled it down to the table, and activated a holoboard underneath it. "That's not the kind of clients who usually request my services."

"A pity. I don't have luck much either," Gin commiserated, leaned forward, and propped his chin on one hand as he looked at the screen. "Granted, I haven't worked for more than one person in the last several years, but back in my merc days, my superiors were drags."

"I don't have to interact with mine that much." The hacker typed on the keyboard. "Only a monthly status report and earnings and all that, and other than that, I might have to hack into the odd device or two. Otherwise, I run a stable operation down here."

"Meeting guys like you shows that life can be so beautiful sometimes," Gin mused. "You'd probably be a white-hat running ops for a corp or something if you didn't have that pesky record. It would've been a hell of a lot harder to find someone to handle my little project."

"To be honest, I'm not sure I would have taken the opportunity anyway. I prefer my freedom. Chains can be metaphorical or preferable if your choice is prison or working with some of those world council divisions."

"I take it you were given the offer?"

"And I laughed for weeks." Vinci nodded, a small smile on his lips. "I was able to get into the good graces of a Doxvod leader during my stint, which got me here. Much better, in my opinion."

"Except for the stooges, I would think." Gin glanced meaningfully at the door.

"If they give you any trouble, feel free to do what you must."

He raised an eyebrow. "Not too attached, huh?"

"Customer service. I can't have them making one of my new customers think this is a place that would allow such idiocy," Vinci reasoned and moved the screen to show it to his client. "Here are the schematics and the functions of the cracked EI you requested."

Gin leaned in closer, studied the screen intently, and whistled. "That's a lot of coding. You did this all in two weeks?"

"Would you believe this is one of the longest projects I've had in almost five years?" The hacker chuckled. "Most of the time, it takes hours, or a couple of days at most. You really gave me something to get my fingers tapping."

"I'm glad you enjoyed it. What do I owe you?"

"One million even."

Gin tapped a finger thoughtfully on his chin. "From our initial conversation, I expected more than triple that amount."

Vinci offered the other man his tablet. "It's a discount for giving me such an interesting project and being such a pleasant man to work with."

"I guess a little kindness goes a long way, huh?" Gin

took the tablet and transferred the money, his expression eminently satisfied. "This will work wonderfully."

"Don't do anything too naughty with it," the other man said in a knowing, playful tone as he unlocked a domed device. The two sides separated and revealed a chip, which he placed into a box and handed to Gin.

"You should know someone like me can't promise that." He pocketed the chip and stood quickly. "I mean, why would I order it otherwise?"

Vinci laughed as he made his way to the exit. "Good point!" He opened the door and nodded at Gin as he left.

Gin retrieved his tablet and placed it in his jacket as he made his way to the guards. "It's finished, boys. I'll take my things now."

"We don't think so," their leader growled, earning a curious look from the customer and a sigh from Vinci.

"What the hell are you doing?" the hacker protested. "He's paid in full and done nothing suspicious. Do you lot want me to report you?"

"This guy isn't on the up and up, Vinci!" another man declared, holding the Omni-blade up. "Look at this thing. There's no way he could have something like this. You can't even get one on the black market. It's way more advanced than anything I've ever seen."

"And I'm sure that your knowledge is vast," Gin muttered. "If you must know, I stole it from a tactical and security division tech development facility. Ironically, it's not that well secured."

"Tac-Sec? You broke into a Tac-Sec facility by yourself? Bullshit." The man scoffed. "We were thinking—"

"Congratulations."

"Shut up!" the guard snapped and grabbed Gin's neck. "You're a spook, aren't you?!"

"I can assure you he isn't. He's—" Vinci tried to warn them but stopped as Gin held up a hand.

"I suppose I never did properly introduce myself to you. My bad." He removed his glasses and the guards recoiled, unnerved by his eyes. "Perhaps I could give it another go so that we can be properly acquainted?"

"This guy is a damn idiot," one man gasped. "Boss, we can't have a guy like him with our tech? What if it gets traced back to us?"

"Do you think I'm that sloppy?!" Vinci barked. "Don't besmirch *me* because you are a bunch of paranoid idiots."

"Still, it's best to be rid of him. We have the money, right?" the guard said with a smirk and held Gin's own knife to his face

"You are really committed to this, aren't you?" Gin groused as he looked at both him and the blade in boredom.

"If you hadn't pissed me off—like you're doing now—I might have let you walk out of here," he stated. "Like I said, outsiders don't get the same treatment in the bazaar. You gotta be a killer to even set foot in a place like this and expect to leave."

"Oh, the irony." Gin snickered. He leaned back and tilted his head to look at Vinci with a broad smile. "You can go ahead and tell them if you want. See if it makes any difference. If not, I think I'll take you up on your offer."

The guards looked at Vinci, who returned their gazes with an expression of supreme indifference on his face. "I hope the next batch they send me isn't so stubborn."

"What are you—*herk*!" He grunted as Gin's hand lashed out, grabbed his throat, and crushed it with inhuman strength. The man took Macha back as he pulled the guard to him and whispered, "You really should have taken my arms."

"S-s-shoot him!" the guard croaked in a strangled, rasping tone. His colleagues drew their pistols and aimed at the man, whose gleeful smile turned into a wicked grin.

Gun and laser fire erupted in the hacking shop down the narrow lane. A few other merchants and buyers glanced that way, but most decided to leave well enough alone or were too jaded to respond. They expected to hear the thump of a body as it was thrown from the shop, but instead, they heard several guttural screams and shocked yelps, followed by a sudden silence. A little startled, a few more people looked toward the storefront as the door opened and a tall man dressed in a smart white suit sauntered through.

He smiled and donned a pair of hard-core shades as he stepped out. The stranger was covered in blood but didn't seem to care—or maybe even enjoyed it, if the expression on his face was any indication.

Calm and unruffled, he held the door open and looked back inside "I must get going now, Vinci. Sorry about the mess."

"If you don't mind, could you send a bagman this way on your way out? Tell them I'll need a disposal and clean-up. I'll be sure to tip them well. I have the creds for it now."

"Certainly. You always want to keep a clean shop," Gin stated cavalierly as he released the door and made his way out of the bazaar. The people in his way gave him a wide berth as he strolled along.

The door to Vinci's shop swung closed and only a couple of spectators managed to peek in, although they couldn't see much in that quick glimpse. Vinci returned to his private quarters and ignored the four bodies that lay on the ground. Two were missing heads, while another was covered in at least a dozen deep stab wounds, blood still trickling from each like a macabre fountain that had lost impetus. The last body was the leader's. His throat had been torn out and his chest and arms sliced through with massive incisions that gaped horribly and, in some places, revealed the organs within. His eyes remained fixed on the retreating figure of his employer as the shock and fear and faint vestige of life in them faded before the office door finally shut.

CHAPTER TWO

The first thing that annoyed Kaiden when he opened his eyes was that he seemed to be stuck under something. The second was the fire that burned around him.

"Can somebody get that?" he demanded irritably and used his free hand to shove at the piece of roofing that had pinned him down. "I'm a little preoccupied here."

"Certainly, friend Kaiden," Genos responded cheerfully, and foam fizzed as the Tsuna used an extinguisher close by. Kaiden was finally able to inch himself out from under the metal and exhaled a relieved sigh as he dropped the roofing sheet back to the ground. He took a moment to collect his thoughts and attempted to focus his concentration on his original objective.

He, Chiyo, and Genos were on their first long mission in the Animus, a single mission they had to complete within a week. It was too vast and complicated for them to manage in one sitting, so they had to save and load at different points. Their objective was to head to a pirate station and annihilate it. He made a more detailed examination of their surroundings and realized that what he had thought was a piece of roofing was, in fact, a section of metal ceiling. His gaze slid past Genos to a cockpit, and he frowned. It would seem that they had spawned inside a crashed ship for this mission leg.

That would make things slightly difficult.

Kaiden pushed to his feet as Genos extinguished the last of the flames. "Nice job, Genos, although the Animus seems to think you're not as good a pilot as you say you are."

"I believe this is a premade scenario, Kaiden," his friend stated as he brandished the extinguisher and searched for more potential fires. "Between my natural ability to pilot traveler and dropships and the three synapse points I have put into the skill, I do not believe the system based this outcome on my chances." An explosion of sparks erupted a few feet from the Tsuna's shoulder. "If it did, I will have words with the technicians to the effect that the system's readings for odds of success should be readjusted—or that the system appears to be mocking me."

"Don't sweat it. I know what you're capable of," Kaiden reassured him. He searched the small craft quickly, looking for their third teammate. "Chiyo! Where you at?"

"About one hundred yards to the west of you," she responded, her voice low and indistinct over the comm. He tapped his helmet in a futile effort to stabilize the feed. "Opening network connection." A small map appeared on his HUD and displayed a blinking white dot to the west.

Kaiden pressed a switch to open the side door of the ship, which broke from the wall and instead of unfolding, simply crashed onto the ground. He peered out cautiously.

They were in a jungle of some sort, but it didn't seem to be a jungle on Earth. The vegetation was definitely what he would call alien—tall trees with blue and purple leaves, and thin vines that crept along the ground with some sort of dark, bulbous seeds or flowers growing on them. Kaiden rapped his fingers on the hull of the ship and turned to the Tsuna. "How hosed do you think this thing is, Genos?"

"If you're asking if it is repairable or not..." Genos looked around as another sizzle of sparks erupted behind him, and some bounced off his armor. "I would say that given a few hours, I might be able to get it airborne, but without significant repairs, it certainly wouldn't be able to break the atmosphere. I would say there is a good chance that it would split apart in the air, even if I could get it off the ground."

"Not the greatest sit-rep but we'll make do," Kaiden said and jumped from the ship to the jungle floor. He looked up as Chiyo emerged from behind a line of trees and waved her over. "I guess they thought you would bail out. Do you like to roll those dice from time to time?"

She pushed past a large branch. "I believe the system simply has a number of predetermined spawn points—"

"Yeah, yeah. I had the same response from Genos," he interrupted and folded his arms in a show of mock annoyance. "I'm only trying to add a little character."

"So you think I'm the kind of person to abandon my team, then?" she asked casually as she walked past him to the ship.

Kaiden thought about it for a moment. "The system probably has random spawn points and stuff."

"I'm glad you agree." She jumped onto the ship and

approached Genos, who was studying some of the exposed wiring in the ceiling. "How does it look?"

"Hmm... It's more or less what I thought," he admitted and tapped his webbed fingers on his neck where his infuser would be. The visor of his helmet shimmered with the light of a scanner. "It seems that the scenario for the beginning of this mission was that we had to make an emergency landing. Most of the damage on the ship appears to be from the impact rather than from an assault. Although there *were* some fires," he added thoughtfully.

"Is it a lost cause?" she asked. Kaiden clambered back on board and leaned against a wall as the two more technology-inclined members discussed their situation.

"I told Kaiden that I could probably get it in the air." The Tsuna walked to the cockpit, and Chiyo followed. He used the claw of his gauntlet to open a panel beneath the pilot's console and fiddled around until power was restored—at least partly. Most of the devices still seemed to be inactive. "Viola, please check what systems you can and give me a status report."

The jellyfish avatar appeared on one of the working screens *"Understood, Genos,"* she acknowledged. Genos turned and leaned against the console. "There are a few containers of parts in the back of the ship, so I still believe that I can get it running, but for how long is, as the metaphor goes, up in the air."

They turned to Kaiden to see if he'd noticed the pun, but he seemed too preoccupied with something on his HUD.

"We'll have to find another option," Chiyo stated. "My guess is that there is an emergency signal we can send out, or perhaps a derelict vessel we can salvage from deeper in the jungle." She looked out the cockpit window at the world outside. "I don't think this is a place where we'll find much intelligent contact."

"You would be wrong, Ms. Kana," Kaiden chided. The two turned to see him stroll over to join them. "I had Chief take a look at the local fauna. It turns out we're on a colonized world called 'Ascension.'"

"Ascension?" she asked.

"A human- and Tsuna-colonized planet—the first one developed as a joint venture between the two races," Genos elaborated. "I'm not that familiar with it, though. The only planet I had seen outside of Abisalo before coming to Earth was our sister planet Bura."

"It's the reason for the campy name—to show it as an 'ascension' of human and Tsuna relations." Kaiden folded his arms. "Never mind that its name is an English word."

"It was actually chosen because of that," Genos explained. "It's similar to a Tsuna word, 'Azenton,' that translates as 'a bond of relations.'"

"Huh, neat. I'll have to remember it for trivia." Kaiden looked out the window. "Anyway, there are several colonies on the planet. My suggestion is that we scout and see if we can find the parts we need or a new ship."

Chiyo looked at the Tsuna, who shrugged and nodded. "It's a place to start, but we don't have any credits or much to barter."

"I can barter—in a way," Kaiden hinted and gestured to Debonair.

She sighed. "I know this is a simulation, Kaiden, but

JOSHUA ANDERLE & MICHAEL ANDERLE

you shouldn't always immediately resort to forceful means."

"In the real world, I would have credits," he countered. "But I thought that a colony would have a bounty board or gigs we could do in trade for what we need."

"Oh… That *is* possible," she conceded. "Where would we start, though? I didn't see any signs. Maybe I could have Kaitō see if he can trace any nearby signals—" Chiyo was cut off by the loud roar of ship engines overhead. The three ran to the open doorway as the ship soared over them toward the north. They expected it to disappear over the far horizon, but it began to descend and hover in place as if to land.

"What about over there?" Kaiden asked, and pointed in the direction of the craft. "I'd bet good credits that is at least a good place to start."

Chiyo was silent for a moment before she nodded. "I agree." She stood. "Should we all head out?"

Kaiden looked at Genos. "Not to leave you high and dry, but maybe you should hang back and work on the ship. If we can't find what we need, we will probably need the ship to fly to the next available port or colony."

"A wise deduction," Genos agreed and peered at the panel. "Viola has finished about seventy percent of her check, and I should be able to do what I need to in a few hours with her help. But we'll only be able to keep the ship together for about two hours and fly at a low speed and altitude. If you can find at least a small number of basic parts, it would be most helpful."

"Send us a list and we'll poke around." Kaiden turned toward the door of the ship. "Are you coming, Chiyo?"

She looked at the Tsuna. "Will you be all right alone?"

"From my understanding, this planet doesn't have many animals, and the ones it does have are herbivores for the most part." He walked past her to the back of the ship. "I should be fine, but I'll contact you if something happens. But do be careful. I've heard stories that it is home to some rather bothersome vegetation."

"Bothersome in what way?" Kaiden asked.

"The kind that devours you alive and digests you slowly," Genos stated cheerfully as he opened a container and rummaged through it.

Kaiden drew his rifle and primed it. "Good to know. Are you coming, Chiyo?"

Kaiden and Chiyo stepped out of the jungle into a clearing that held a small town that bustled with activity. Scientists —both Tsuna and human—talked as they walked, while others ran from one building to another. Several floating carts stacked with boxes or large cylinders headed down what might be defined as the main street. Kaiden looked around for any sort of marketplace or trade center, but it seemed to be an entirely science-focused outpost.

"I wonder how helpful this will be?" he muttered. "If nothing else, maybe we can find a ride to another town." Chiyo was silent as she observed the activity around them. Kaiden nudged her with his elbow. "Are you there, Chi?"

She shook her head as if she were trying to dislodge her stupor before she nodded. "Yes, sorry. I was simply admiring the authenticity of the map. It's nice to see that the Animus can realistically create spaces where we aren't immediately being shot at."

"It's a nice change of pace," he admitted as he holstered his rifle. "But it kinda makes me more anxious, really. Recently, it seems that anytime I go farther than Seattle, it's to shoot something or get shot at. And that's saying nothing about the dozens of times I've hopped into the Animus."

"Let's hope that we can have at least a couple hours of peace before we have to set off for our actual destination," she responded and finally wandered toward the outpost. He moved to follow and noticed a scientist in a mask stare questioningly at them. The man scurried quickly away once he realized Kaiden was looking at him.

"Yeah... Hopefully."

They walked into the outpost. Chiyo—definitely the more amiable of the two—asked some of the denizens if they knew of a place where they could find parts or a ship. Kaiden only paid minimal attention and instead, constantly watched the populace, who seemed to be skittish about their presence.

"No luck so far." She sighed and walked back to him. When she noticed that he was looking away, she tapped him on the shoulder. "Is something wrong?"

"Is it only me, or do these guys not seem thrilled to see us?" he inquired and gestured at two technicians, who hurried away from his gaze.

"I doubt they are used to travelers in a place like this— or at least ones who aren't on their schedule," she reasoned. "Plus a tall man in battle armor with a large energy rifle staring at them would make most people skittish."

"I suppose…" he mumbled and tapped on the Nexus symbol engraved into his armor. "But even in a simulation, you would think that we are tagged as an ark academy or potential world council member. I ain't asking them to hold a feast in our honor or nothing, but you would think there would be a little enthusiasm—or at least curiosity." He turned to her. "Did you run into any trouble?"

"They haven't been very forthcoming," she admitted, "but they appear to be working on secret projects here so I can understand them being standoffish. Again, they probably aren't used to heavily armed individuals appearing out of the jungle unannounced."

"You have a pistol and a submachine gun. It's adorable that you think that's heavily armed."

Kaiden couldn't see her eyes under her visor, but he could imagine her face scrunching in annoyance. "Either way, I don't think we'll find any parts here. At least none that we could buy or trade for."

He shrugged. "Well, if plan A is out of the question, let's go with plan B. If we can't get a ride out of here, we could at least try to see if they have a world map so we can find the quickest path to the next port." He waited for her opinion, but she paid him no attention. "Chiyo? What's—" He looked behind him, "Oh."

A group of four guards in white medium armor and carrying machine guns marched up to them. "I want to preemptively say that I didn't do a damn thing," he stated, reaching for his rifle.

Chiyo held out a hand to stop him. "Wait, we should see what they want. They could simply want to identify us and know why we're here."

"To be fair, we don't exactly know ourselves." He did, however, lower his hands reluctantly. "But maybe this could pan out. At worst, my guess is we'll be kicked out."

Three guards halted a few feet away, raised their weapons quickly, and aimed them at the duo. The fourth stood to the side, his hand on his pistol, "You have come onto this outpost unannounced and with no proper identification," he declared. "This is a world council facility. You will come with us peacefully or be eliminated where you stand."

Kaiden saw lights down the barrels of the guards' guns and glanced at Chiyo. "If it helps, between waking up and walking here, that was about an hour of peace."

CHAPTER THREE

The outpost guards continued to aim their guns with real intent, and Kaiden noticed that a couple of them tapped their fingers on their triggers. They seemed rather eager to fire in a place full of scientists and pedestrians. He looked to the side for a moment and confirmed that the locals had left hastily or taken refuge in one of the nearby buildings.

A quick glance at Chiyo reassured him that she didn't seem anxious or worried—more contemplative than anything else—but she hadn't moved her hands closer to her guns. "Are you gonna try to talk this out?" he asked in a disbelieving tone.

"We need to approach this as we would a real-world mission," she responded, remaining motionless. "Our days of merely shooting our way out of things will be at a minimum from now on." She gave a quick, small laugh as she turned to grin at him. "I would imagine that will be a harder issue for you than for most of us."

"Different strokes and all that," Kaiden retorted. "I'll

agree that our missions and scenarios will be more than simply straight-shooting galleries with objectives but look at the situation."

"I'm well aware of what's going on," she muttered.

"Hands up," the guard captain ordered. "Are you listening? I'm sure my men are more than willing to show you that we will go through with our threats if you do not comply."

"They are corrupt or paid off," Kaiden decided and continued to ignore the man. "There's no need for such a display in a place like this. They would put their own people in danger, especially if we were hostile."

"Perhaps, but look at it this way…they could take us to their hideout or command center. There, we could get more information on their employers or what has happened at this colony to make them so aggressive."

"I guess the term 'Occam's razor' is new to you?" he asked, which caught her attention. She glared at him from beneath her visor, the expression clear in the light of the planet's sun.

"Men, take aim and fire," the captain ordered. Kaiden sighed and reached for Debonair, but Chiyo stopped him.

"I already took care of it," she said. The guards fired—or, at least, tried to fire. They pulled their triggers fruitlessly, and a couple of them stopped to examine their weapons, confused and frustrated.

"Sabotage? Did you shut the systems down or something?"

"No, they aren't using very advanced weapons. I simply overheated them," she explained. "It won't last much longer, but it gives us a little more time."

"Well, look at you—discuss peace but make sure it can be enforced. Here I was, worried that all my teachings had gone over your head."

"I'm glad that I could make you so proud." Her words dripped sarcasm. "I'm still of the mind that we should let them take us in. We could gather important information any way this turns out."

Kaiden glanced at the guards, who had figured out the problem with their guns and now vented them. "That's one way. I say we take them out now and sort it out after. And before you say anything—" He flicked his hand and pointed at her before she could interrupt him. "I'm not only saying that because my trigger finger is itchy. Taking out a group of these guys is one thing, but we don't know where they will take us or how many others might be there. I doubt they will let us keep our gear."

"True, but there is one thing they don't know about, and even if they did, they can't take it."

"And what would that be?"

"Me, dumbass," Chief muttered. Kaiden glanced at the corner of his HUD, and the EI glared at him. *"Forgetting my birthday is one thing, but I'm right here."*

He placed his hands on his hips. "If you will recall, I was in the middle of a gig on your 'birthday,' which you seem to think is different from the day on which you were activated."

"That's our anniversary, sweetie," Chief retorted with mock sincerity. *"I was technically born a few months prior to that."*

"Technically, you weren't born at all," he countered with

a sigh. "All right, I see what you mean, Chi. But if this bites us, you will take responsibility."

"I believe that falls onto the ace," she said and looked up as Kaiden shook his head. "Pay attention. He's coming."

"Who is?" Kaiden asked and scowled when something pressed against his head. "Well, hello there."

"I should simply make a nice hole in your head," the captain barked and tapped the barrel of his pistol against Kaiden's helmet. "For not only trespassing on World Council property, but resisting arrest and tampering with our weapons."

"Three things," Kaiden said and held up three fingers to count them off. "One, this is a human and Tsuna colony, so it's not only under the WC's control. Two, you're merely security forces. Resisting arrest would mean you're cops, and trust me, I know the distinction. And finally," he pointed at Chiyo, "she was the one who tampered with your weapons, not me."

"Thanks for that," she huffed.

"Quiet!" the captain yelled and raised his weapon to pistol-whip Kaiden, who simply caught the man's hand as it was about to smash into his visor.

"Calm the hell down," he ordered as the captain struggled to escape his grasp. "We'll go with you. I imagine you have questions or something if you haven't already tried to blast us to bits."

He released the man's arm. The captain rubbed his wrist and scrutinized them carefully. "You'd be partially right," he acknowledged belligerently. "I couldn't care less who you are, but our superiors are extremely interested."

"Well, whoever wants to chat, let's go and do that,"

Kaiden said and began to walk away. "If they take requests, I'll have a beer when we get there. I prefer whiskey, but I don't wanna get too drunk when... What now?" He balked when he felt the captain's hand on his shoulder.

"Do you think we're idiots?" the man demanded. Kaiden was about to retort when he saw Chiyo shake her head. "You're not going anywhere with all that gear on. Strip!"

Kaiden turned to face him. "That'll cost you quite a few creds, buddy. I'm high-class goods." The unmistakable sound of guns priming confirmed that the guards behind him had their weapons functioning again. He was quiet for a moment before he placed his hands on his helmet to remove it. "But I suppose I'll work it for the crowd. Do any of you have music?"

They were led to a carrier, their hands in cuffs, dressed in nothing but their underlays. One of the guards slid the cases containing their confiscated equipment into a compartment on the underside of the vehicle. Chiyo stepped onto the platform at the back of the carrier and was led into the cabin.

Kaiden studied it for a moment before he turned to one of the guards. "Hey, my credit chip is in the compartment of my left leg's armor. Charge whatever when we make it wherever we're going in one piece."

The guard shoved him onto the platform, and Kaiden shrugged and went in. The doors closed behind him as he took a seat on a bench across from Chiyo. The interior was rather dark with only one light that worked above them. The others seemed to be broken. They heard two thumps on the side of the carrier, and it began to move. Kaiden crossed his legs and leaned back.

"Do y'all need some light?" Chief asked and appeared between them in a dimmed state.

Kaiden shook his head. "We should be good for now. I don't want to let them know about our little stowaway." He nodded at Chiyo. "Unless the infiltrator is scared of the dark for some reason."

"I'm fine," she answered, and Chief bobbed up and down before he disappeared again. "Chief should remain hidden until we're actually at the base or headquarters. Then we can see how best he can be used."

"Were you able to sneak Kaitō in?" Kaiden inquired.

She nodded, and her eyes flickered with an unnatural light in the darkness. Kaiden could see the faint outline of the EI's frame in her eyes. "They aren't very thorough. I expected to have to hide him within the drive on the back of my underlay." She tapped the back of her neck for emphasis. "But this will work much better."

"I hope this will work, plain and simple," he pointed out. "We've only got till the end of the month to finish this, right? I seriously don't wanna spend a couple of days in the pokey burning time."

"I doubt we'll be there very long. My guess is that you are right about them being on someone's payroll. I would guess it's the pirates we are supposed to eliminate."

"Do you hope to find the location of their ship?"

"It's a station," she corrected. "But yes. It would make it much easier to have a proper location than have to trace it through other means. If all goes well, we'll complete this in a few days rather than a few weeks."

"It's good to see you're looking ahead," Kaiden told her enthusiastically. "Still, we could have taken them at the outpost and interrogated the captain."

"They could have called in reinforcements or warned the others about our approach," she countered.

"Maybe, but that's why I keep you around," he said with a smile.

"To clean up your messes?"

"Your skills allow me to make a mess," he responded, his tone conciliatory. "They keep me from falling too hard, like that old parable in that story from the twentieth century, *Catcher in the Rye*."

"I'm not that familiar with it," she admitted. "But it sounds like a compliment."

"Maybe in a roundabout way," Kaiden said with a shrug. "I certainly intended it that way, but sometimes, the outcome is more important than the intention."

"A wise deduction," she said and a faint smile formed at the corners of her mouth. "Don't worry, I'm sure you'll have an opportunity to use your preferred way to solve things."

"I ain't worried about all that," he stated. "I have a gig tomorrow. I'll have my fill."

"A gig?" Chiyo asked and flashed him a quick glance. "What kind?"

"A dead-or-alive retrieval mission in Illinois." Kaiden studied his cuffs and wondered if he could or should break them. "I suppose it's more like a retrieve-or-destroy mission. Some sort of defense droid was stolen by a gang in the area, the Azure Halo. The dumbasses stole an experimental droid before it was finished, and it's missing important things like a proper threat detection system. If they are able to get the thing activated, it's likely to simply kill anything in the immediate vicinity. Obviously, no one wants that to get too far."

"There's something like that out in the civilian world?" Chiyo asked, flabbergasted. "And they are leaving that up to you?"

"Thanks for the vote of confidence," he snarked. "I'm simply the next in line. They've thrown mercs and guards at them, but they are stationed in a junker town. The gang owns the place, and it's turned out to be more difficult than they thought it would be. I think I'm the last one they will try before they request the WCM to go in there and take it. My guess is that they think a small group or a single person can get in and out easier. They hope to keep it as quiet as possible, although I'm sure a hacker gang like the Azures have already posted their catch on the gray net."

"I'll have to check once we get out," she said, lowering her head in consideration. "Kaiden…it seems rather soon."

"Soon for what?" he asked, his attention diverted from his cuffs.

"It's only been a couple of months since you were… When you fought that killer."

"You mean Gin?" he asked, and she nodded. Kaiden was quiet for a moment and rolled his tongue in his mouth as he thought. "Sure, but I can't think that I'll run into a universal threat every time I step out of the city. I took a couple of gigs in Tacoma already—simple ones to get back into the groove. Besides, taking droids out has become something of a specialty of mine."

"You shouldn't treat this any different than the Animus," she stated.

He held his hands up. "I get it, Chiyo, I do. But remember where I come from and what I did before I came here. Stuff like this has basically been my job since I was a preteen. I'm smart enough to know that I'll simply go in there and destroy the thing if it has so much as a flicker in its eye." He lowered his hands and brushed them over the underlay on his legs. "Besides, what good is staying at Nexus if I'm suddenly gonna crumble to bits every time I do a real mission? I would be useless. I can't say I have many skills that don't involve guns and armor anyway."

"You could start training to be a gunsmith," she suggested.

Kaiden looked at her quizzically for a moment before he chuckled., "I suppose that's a potential fallback option, along with the piloting, but come on. Do you honestly think I'm gonna be any good at the customer support part of that?"

She looked at him with real worry, but her demeanor changed slightly when her smile returned. "Yeah, I guess you wouldn't be able to stick with that for very long."

"I'm as likely to be shot doing that as anything else." He laughed. "I appreciate the concern, Chi, but you have to realize as much as anyone that for anyone in our group, the potential for death will be high in our lives. In a way, maybe it was somewhat fortuitous that my run-in with Gin happened since it really drove the point home." He leaned back and pursed his lips. "Fortuitous? I'm beginning to sound like Genos."

Chiyo's smile widened. "I'm not sure I would describe it that way, but it also showed that even with our dangerous lives, there is a chance we can make it home despite the dire circumstances."

"That's a good way to look at it."

She glanced up for a moment, and the artificial lights in her eyes dimmed. "Do you think there is any way I could help you?"

Kaiden's eyebrows went up in surprise, and he raised his cuffed hands to stroke his chin. "Well, I...not really. I don't think, with how good you are, that you'll run shady gigs like I do. Okay, maybe shady, but not dirty. Besides, I wouldn't want you to run with me anyway." His gaze darted to her, and she stared quizzically at him. "You know I don't mean that negatively," he said before she could retort. "I simply mean that... You know, I'm doing this to potentially buy myself out of my contract with the Academy by the time I graduate. There's no guarantee that I'll even make enough by that time, especially with all the repairs, ammo, and medical expenses I have. I wouldn't want you to be in harm's way when the payoff might not even happen. Besides, even if you convinced me to let you come along, there's a process you gotta go through to get your mercenary license. You certainly won't get it in fourteen hours."

"Maybe not by traditional means," she hinted.

Kaiden frowned at her suggestion. "This is not exactly the group of people you want to give the runaround to."

"Do you think they have the ability to catch me?" she

asked in a challenging tone. She glared at him, then sighed and leaned back. "It's all right. I won't burden you if you are that unsure, but I think there is another way to help you before you set out."

"And how's that?" he asked before he lost his balance and toppled at the sudden stop of the carrier.

"We're here!" one of the guards alerted them through the speakers. "Hands up and prepare to disembark."

CHAPTER FOUR

When Kaiden was led out of the carrier, he immediately saw that they were back in the jungle, and probably fairly deep, considering the drive. They had arrived at a nondescript building a few stories tall and maybe several hundred yards long, with a faded gray exterior and a few token windows to break the monotone walls.

"I guess they make sure you guys live easy out here, huh?" Kaiden remarked to the guard who led him to the building. "It's not exactly a pleasure palace, but I'm sure it has enough closets and rec rooms for you guys to take some time out to get to know each other, right?"

"Keep quiet," the man ordered brusquely.

"I'll try. Not hard, though. The ride was rough, and I'm curmudgeonly." Kaiden glanced over his shoulder as Chiyo stepped out of the carrier. The captain of the guard gave orders to the others, and two men returned to the carrier to retrieve the cases with their gear while the other one flanked Chiyo and led her forward to Kaiden.

Once she stood beside him, the guard told her to wait as he filled the other man in. The captain walked past and barely acknowledged them.

"So, how do you think your plan is shaping up so far?" he asked mostly sarcastically, but if she had something up her sleeve, he was more than willing to hear it.

"I'll let you know more when we actually get inside," she answered and pushed some of her hair out of her eyes.

"I have a feeling that it'll be a little harder to talk when they interrogate us," he pointed out. "I know it hasn't really come up, but I'm shit at charades."

"And on top of that, they will probably separate us." She glanced quickly at him. "I'll be out within half an hour once we get inside. I assume you'll be able to find your own way out with Chief's help, but if not, hold out until I can reach you."

"Don't worry about me. I'll save the damsel thing for a night when I feel like roleplaying," Kaiden quipped.

"Do you want me to bring up a catalog? I found a dress in white I think you would look divine in."

"This is not the time, Chief," Kaiden muttered in a low tone. "Besides, good luck finding something to fit over my hips."

"All right, you two," one of the guards growled as he walked up to them. "You'll go through a checkpoint before we deal with you. If you have any other contraband on you that you wanna give up right now, I recommend it. We would feel rather disappointed if you kept anything from us."

Kaiden held his cuffed hands up. "I'm clean unless you

wanna take the underlay. But I should warn you that my personal weapon is quite dangerous in the open."

"Then to be safe, maybe we should cut it off."

"I'm sure that would make a great trophy for the office," he retorted with a smirk.

The guard gave an exasperated grunt and turned to Chiyo. "You?"

"You didn't take my optics," she stated as she raised her hands to her eyes and carefully removed them. "I assumed you didn't so that I could see, but I don't want to risk potential issues arising from a bad guess."

"You need these to see?" the guard asked as she handed him the lenses. "You haven't gotten them fixed? What about trading them out for digital eyes?"

"I have a condition called 'Biological Xenoaphobia.' My body rejects augmentations," she explained. "As for Lasik or visual correction scans, I've read reports that they can go rather poorly. I've been too frightened to try since I was a child."

"And yet you ended up with a job where you run around with guns and fly off to distant planets?" the guard snorted. "Maybe you should give it a shot sometime."

Kaiden somehow managed to keep his face neutral, but he had to admit to himself that he was impressed with Chiyo's ability to lie so easily and thoroughly.

"I'll keep these for now," the man said as he found a small box and placed the contacts within. "But I will say it was smart of you to hand them over. It will spare you from having something unfortunate happen." He spun and addressed the other guards. "All right, boys, let's take them in so we can get down to business."

After another pat-down and a trip through a scanner, both Chiyo and Kaiden were cleared to enter the facility. He expected it to resemble a jail or a barracks, but it looked more like a reconfigured business center. For one thing, they passed a spacious lobby on the way to the elevators that had a statue of a devil bird in the center. He grimaced involuntarily. It seemed that even in deep space, he couldn't get away from those things.

"I can see you guys live a spartan life out here," Kaiden commented. One of the guards looked back and mumbled harshly, but the others tried to tune him out. "Nice atmosphere and all, but I know you guys have to deal with the harsh stuff, and probably only get lobster on Fridays and beds with sheets that are only one thousand thread count. It's gotta be the pits."

"You should shut that smart mouth of yours," the irate man warned. "We've had to deal with things you probably couldn't begin to understand."

"Oh, I'm sure the scientists get uppity from time to time, asking for you to hand them microscopes, lenses or fetch samples and all that. Real man's work." He could see another guard bristle. If they intended to waste his time, he would have a little fun. "I also heard about the man-eating plants. You must have guns filled with poison or plasma garden shears. You can't go out and deal with such a menace without the best equipment, right?"

"I'll have you know that we've lost good men to this damn jungle," the third guard retorted.

"Well, you know, we will all be food for the plants one day. I guess your boys were more proactive. Tree-huggers, probably."

The man turned, snatched Kaiden by the front of his suit, and glared at him through his visor. He returned the menace with a disinterested stare. "You know what? I expected you to lose your shitty little attitude once you realized where you were."

"Yes. The mood lighting and clean floor have really instilled the fear of God in me." He pulled back, and the guard's grip tightened.

The man addressed his colleagues. "You boys take the girl to the interrogation room. I'll look after this one."

"How kind of you. Could you get my bags?"

The guard dragged him farther down the hallway before he kicked a door open and hauled him in. "Good idea," he yelled over his shoulder. "Make sure to have Capers bring up the case with this guy's goods. I wanna talk shop with him."

With that, the door closed. The other men looked at one another and shrugged. One instructed Capers on his comm to take the confiscated items to what he called the treatment room. Chiyo simply sighed and shook her head.

The guard shoved Kaiden onto a metal slab and pushed a button on the side that cuffed his arms and legs to it. The ace observed the various devices and pointy things aimed toward him. "I take it this is the suite?"

"Of a kind." The man's tone seemed more jovial, and even morbidly excited. He walked over to a console and pressed a button, and the devices over Kaiden came to life. With a grin, he pressed another and leaned forward. "Send the doctor in asap," he ordered. His expression smug, he leaned back and folded his arms. "So, allow me to be a gracious host."

"You've done great so far," Kaiden mocked and managed to give an okay sign with his entrapped hands.

"This is our treatment room. It's where we bring people when the normal stuff doesn't work," he explained and gestured to various instruments. "When one of our guests needs a little extra pampering to make them more cooperative, they spend a little time in here. Usually, it takes a few days before we resort to this, but I decided that you needed this treatment right away."

"I'm sure that was kind of you," Kaiden responded and examined all the various painful-looking prongs and prods above him. "Maybe we could work something out. I have my own questions, after all."

"So now you're suddenly not such a smartass," his captor scolded, placed his hands on the console, and tilted his head. "I didn't bring you in here to shoot the shit. You *will* answer me."

"If it's how I get my hair so nice, I use a shampoo with selenium sulfide. It makes it shiny and flake-free."

"I want to know why you and your little gal pal are here on our planet," he demanded brusquely and slammed the console for emphasis.

"We already told everyone who would listen that we

didn't want to be here. Our ship crashed, and we came to the outpost looking for parts," Kaiden reiterated. "If you won't pay attention, what's the point of me bothering to tell you anything?"

The man cursed but cut it short when a door slid open behind him. He looked back while Kaiden craned his neck to look over his shoulder. A woman wearing a dark coat with a gray blouse and pants walked in. Her dark hair was wound in a bun, and her hazel eyes glimmered with EI lenses. She was followed by an autonomous trolley with a case on top of it.

"Hello, Wilson," she greeted the guard. "I ran into Capers on the way here, and he asked me to bring this to you since I was headed to meet you."

"Nice to see you, Doc. I have a patient here you need to look over." The man walked past her, opened the crate, and rifled through it before he removed Debonair. "Hopefully, you don't break him too badly. I wanna try out *my* new gun on a live target."

She took a seat at the console, looked at Kaiden, and waved playfully. "And how are you doing this afternoon?"

"It's been a rather exhausting half-hour," he admitted. "So, do we talk about my feelings, or will you give me a checkup?"

"I'm not that kind of doctor, dear," she stated calmly and placed a finger on one of the screens. In response, one of the instruments slid closer to him and placed its forked prongs on the right side of his chest. It emitted a sharp sound, much like static, and immense pain followed as electricity surged through him.

"I know much about the body, but that's what makes me so good at torture," she explained as she raised her finger and stopped the device. "That part of your chest is mostly muscle. It's quite painful, of course, but it won't compromise your internal systems. At least, not without a few more amps."

"Now that's a good snippet of trivia." Kaiden wheezed. He tried to remain aware, but the shock seemed to have clouded his head. He needed to hurry to steer the conversation to get what he was looking for. Otherwise, this would swing quickly in their favor. "I told you that we aren't here to invade or steal anything. What do you want to know?"

"We originally thought you were mercs, but you flew WC marks," the guard stated and twirled Debonair with his finger.

"Yeah, and you keep saying this is WC space, so why are you acting like such a bastard?"

"Juice him again," the man ordered, and the doctor slid her finger over the screen again.

"Oh, come on. No—*humph*—" A bar slid over Kaiden's mouth to muffle his cry as another shock was administered. When it was done, the mouthpiece was removed.

"The truth is that this place is WC territory only in theory. We received a rather nice chunk of creds and equipment from a local operation—a mom-and-pop joint. They're called the Dead Space Crew. Maybe you've heard of them?" The guard stopped twirling the gun and aimed it at Kaiden. "Because they are looking for you."

"Word…gets around…I guess," Kaiden said between staggered breaths. "The scientists are in on this too?"

"Ha! They weren't consulted about it, but what the hell are they gonna do?" Wilson chortled. "We control all the safety systems, and to send a message to even the closest off-world station has a four-minute upload time. We can catch it and stop it in half a minute. This place is basically our playground now."

"At least until I report it to the WC. I'm sure they'll respond well to knowing that their own people betrayed them. The Tsuna might want a couple of words as well," Kaiden reminded him.

The doctor looked at the guard, who simply placed his free hand on his waist. "That ain't gonna happen. We're doing this to get whatever info we can out of you and the bitch to hand over to the pirates. Anything else beyond that is up to us. Maybe we can get some good cash if we put you up for sale."

Kaiden leaned up as much as his cuffs would permit. "Funny you would call my partner a bitch because that's probably what she's making your friends down below." Kaiden gave a sly smile. "And what I'm about to make you."

The lights in the room flickered, and both the doctor and the guard looked around for a moment in confusion before it went dark.

"What's going on?" the doc asked, and her tone betrayed real anxiety.

"I don't know. Hit every button and kill him before he — Why isn't this gun working?"

Within the darkness, the scientist heard something heavy crash repeatedly into the console. She fell out of her chair and backed away along the floor. When the lights came back on, Kaiden held Debonair. He had his back to her, and the guard lay unconscious on the floor.

"Did he really think there wouldn't be a lock on my gun?" he muttered and placed his thumb on the backplate of the weapon until a green light appeared and the weapon primed. The doctor tried to stand in order to sneak away, but he grabbed her arm quickly. "Let's not be so hasty. I still have questions, Doc, and your buddy is…" Kaiden glanced at the guard on the ground. "He's indisposed, so let's chat for a while. But this time, *you'll* be in the big chair."

"I had my EI sneak into the systems through the console, which gave him control of the lights and the devices and all that. Y'all really need stronger security. He was able to get inside within ten seconds, and I only have two talent points in remote hacking." Kaiden finished his explanation as he put on the last of his armor, placed Debonair in its holster and his rifle on his back, and took his helmet in his hands.

He walked over to the console. The doctor was strapped to the table with the mouth bar active, and he leaned against it. "Now the console isn't in the best shape now considering your buddy's head ran into it a few times, but it's working well enough that Chief can still operate all the little doodads above you." Two of the prongs snipped at her for emphasis, and she flinched visibly. "Now then, I have a few minutes before I have to leave, and like I said, there are a couple more things I want to know before I head out." The mouth bar was removed as he pointed to the instruments. "So will we do this the nice way? Keep in mind that I don't know the specifics of the human body like you do, so I'll have to spin the wheel and see what happens."

CHAPTER FIVE

"Hey, Chiyo, are you there?" Kaiden asked once he'd put his helmet on. He began to leave the room, the doctor still strapped to the table and gagged.

"You remembered to open a private line this time," she responded. "I'm happy to see that you are learning as well."

"Fits and bursts," he conceded. He tried to activate the pad to open the door, but to no avail. He pointed at it so Chief could get it open. "How long did it take you to take care of your guys?"

"Only a couple of minutes. They weren't very forthcoming with intel, so I borrowed an idea of Genos' from his coop test. I locked their helmets and turned their oxygen supply off."

"Ah, classic." Kaiden looked at the panel, where a red light blinked. "Have you already done your thing, Chiyo? Chief can't get into the door."

"I've accessed simple systems and tried to get into the defensive systems, so I may have temporarily deactivated some switches in their base. I'll get them working in a moment," she explained. "Once I'm done, I need to grab my gear. I have a map of the building, and I'll send it to you with a rendezvous location and a pathway."

"You have all the goodies." Kaiden flipped a hand to tell Chief to return to the HUD. "What do you think you can do to this place? Do they have a group of bots you can take over?"

"Sadly, nothing so extravagant," she stated. "They don't have much in the way of interior defenses except for the staff. I'll make sure that they don't send the place into lock-down, but there aren't many turrets or any bots around to use to our advantage."

"On the plus side, that means less to worry about, I suppose," he reasoned and drew his rifle as Chiyo's map appeared in his visor. "Why is your path so roundabout? It tells me to take the back door. If I go through the front door, I can cut across the hall and go up the stairs."

"Yes, but if you do that—" Kaiden hit the pad as Chiyo tried to explain herself.

The door opened, and he was greeted by four guards who aimed rifles at him. "It's all right, I got the picture." He pushed on the pad again and slammed the door shut. After a moment's thought, he shot it to lock it in place as he turned to go out the other way. Blasts struck the door from outside as he left.

Chiyo sighed as she overheard Kaiden's blunder. She

continued to work on the systems while her EI looked for any information in the database that might prove useful.

"Kaitō, when you're done, would you please contact Genos and give him our location?"

"Certainly, madame. This is almost complete. Do you think he will be able to meet up with you on foot?"

"It's doubtful, but he can start to make his way here for us to pick him up."

"Pick him up?"

She nodded. "They have a hangar with two ships capable of space travel. We can take both, or sabotage one and take the other. Then we can get off this planet and start the real mission."

"Ah, I have good news on that front," Kaitō stated. *"I am still searching through the last batch of files, but I did find communications between these guards and the Dead Space Crew, a pirate clan in this system. They are the ones you are pursuing. I was able to find details on their station and its location."*

"Well done, Kaitō," Chiyo complimented as she deactivated the lockdown sequence and froze it while she disarmed the outside aerial turrets. "That will be a big boon for us."

"I am glad to be of service, madame, and will finish in thirty seconds." With that, he disappeared as Chiyo pressed a button to unlock a safe behind her. She walked over and withdrew the case within, unlocked it, and retrieved her armor. After she put it on, she looked at a large vent in the room with a resigned sigh. Ever since she had started working with Kaiden, she had climbed through more of these than she would ever like.

"You guys can stop now, really!" Kaiden shouted at a group of guards as they fired down the hallway at him. "This is why I think negotiation is bull."

"You haven't exactly made a good case," Chief chided.

"That's not my strong suit either. And no, I'm not gonna put points in it." Kaiden felt in his grenade holder and removed one of the explosives. "Oh, a thermal. Good thing we don't have to worry about collateral damage." He activated it and held the switch down to let it cook for a moment before he rolled it along the floor under the guards' laser fire.

"Look out! Explo—" The man didn't manage to finish his warning before the thermal went off, ending the guards' assault, and allowing Kaiden to continue. He ran past another defender, who attempted to raise his rifle, and he stepped on the wounded man's helmet and shoved him down as he increased his pace.

"According to Chiyo's map, you'll meet up in a room right next to this building's hangar," Chief informed him. *"It looks like we have a ride."*

"Speaking of that, I wonder how Genos is doing? Do you think we should get in touch?" He slid to the corner of the wall and peered cautiously around it to see two guards sprinting in his direction.

"He's too far to link him into the private channel, but it looks like Chiyo already hailed him."

"She's on the ball on this mission." Kaiden knelt and leaned out into the hall to fire two blasts from his rifle. One struck a guard in his chest and created a smoldering crater in his armor as he fell to his knees. The other landed at the feet of the second guard and knocked him into the window. The glass shattered, and he fell to the jungle floor below. The first man's body toppled into the opposite wall. "This is a damn good gun."

"That's the one Wolfson got you, right?"

"Yeah, it's called an HIII-BXG, but that doesn't really roll off the tongue. I think I'll simply call it 'Sire.'"

"That certainly has a respectable sound to it," Chief agreed.

"I'll call it that since the ones who are shot by it can't." He chuckled. "Where to next?"

Chief widened the map on his visor. *"It looks like she's updated it with guard placements. Unless you wanna hold her up, you should head to the stairs on the right down the hall."*

"I'm tempted to get some extra points, but I'm sure there will be plenty of opportunity at the station," Kaiden reasoned, albeit a little regretfully. "Let's get going."

"Kaiden, are you there?" Chiyo asked, her voice slightly blurred over the comm.

"I'm here. Almost to the map's waypoint," he responded.

"Do you mind if I change it?" she asked.

"Is something wrong?" he asked. His visor blinked red on his left, and he spun and fired instinctively. The blast eliminated a guard who came around the corner.

"I ended up on the first floor. Can we meet in the elevators?"

"What? How did you manage that?"

"I climbed through the vents, but my path only allowed me to drop down," she explained. Kaiden could hear a tinge of embarrassment in her voice, and his spontaneous chortle of amusement likely did little to help.

"Do you have a thing for vents, or what's the deal there? It's like every other mission for you."

"I wouldn't have to resort to them so often if you wouldn't make going into the halls such a nuisance," she retorted. "Plus, I don't have any defensive options other than my guns, and the second floor is crawling with at least twenty guards."

"I can meet you wherever you need me to," Kaiden assured her. "But the elevators? Won't we trap ourselves in what would essentially be a moving coffin?"

During the few moments of silence that followed his question, Kaiden wondered if he'd lost the connection. Finally, she sighed and responded. "I have a plan for that."

The captain of the guard burned with rage, but his mood had begun to lift. He and his men had been played like fools by these two off-worlders. If they were able to get back to space and contact another outpost, the World Council would knock on their doors in a matter of days.

And he did not intend to be the one to explain their little deal with the pirates when the powers that be asked the inevitable questions.

Now, however, he saw the opportunity to eliminate them. He and a dozen men stood in front of the elevator doors to the hangar. He had seen on the surveillance—one of the few things he could wrest control of away from that damned infiltrator—that the two had met up and were taking the elevator to this floor. He had thought they were elite agents, but such an idiotic decision proved they were simply mercs who'd had one lucky break. That would end. Now.

"The elevator is arriving, sir," one of the guards informed him, and the rest readied their weapons.

"As soon as it arrives, blast it apart," he commanded. The men were silent as they waited for the hum of the ascending elevator to stop and the light above to flash with its arrival.

Ding.

The guards opened fire before the doors had even opened, and it exploded beneath a volley of both kinetic rounds and laser bolts. Smoke kicked up from the blasts, and chunks of the doors and interior careened away like giant pieces of shrapnel. When the firing ceased and the smoke began to clear, the captain chuckled. "Bring out the bodies. Maybe we can salvage their equip— What the hell?"

"I guess I owe you a hundred creds." Kaiden sighed with his arms folded as he and Chiyo stood atop the elevator. "I can't believe this worked."

"Show some faith with that pride," she chided as she knelt to grab the handle of the hatch. "Besides, do you really think it's any different from something you would suggest?"

"Okay, I won't say no," he admitted as he removed his grenade holster and depressed the button on top to activate all the thermals within. "But I will counter that by saying that you would think it was stupid if I did it."

"I won't say no," she responded, then opened the hatch

as he threw the container down and over to the feet of the guards in front of the elevator. A massive eruption drowned out the shrieks of the unsuspecting victims. Kaiden drew his rifle and nodded to Chiyo, who activated a stealth generator and became translucent before her armor created a mirror-like surface to hide her and she disappeared.

Kaiden vaulted into the elevator and immediately opened fire. He picked off several guards as Chiyo rushed past him to commandeer one of the ships. He eliminated two other guards as they tried to recover, and turned as a door opened in the far corner of the hangar. Another group made their way in, but the doorway throttled the press of bodies. Kaiden fired two more shots before his rifle overheated, but with the defenders so bunched up, the shots he had managed to fire effectively decimated those in front. He vented his gun, placed it on his back, and drew Debonair.

After a deep breath, he surged forward to get closer and dodged a few shots before he rolled up beside a metal crate. The laser blasts from his adversaries began to melt through the container and his makeshift shield, but it would hold for long enough. He leaned to the side and delivered three shots to the stomach of one guard. At this range, it took only one shot to penetrate the armor and another to finish the kill.

With two men remaining, Kaiden rolled out from behind his cover and fired. A bullet penetrated one man's visor, and another two in the leg brought the second guard down. He fell, which allowed Kaiden to fire a perfect shot to his head. With only two more shots, the last of the defenders went down.

The ace stood and glanced around quickly. Chiyo decloaked and waved him over. As he began to make his way to her, he recalled that he hadn't seen the captain, yet he could have sworn he had heard him when they arrived.

When he felt a wind rush around him, he whirled and stopped as one of the fighter craft hovered and turned slowly toward them.

"You won't get out of here," the captain bellowed over the speakers in the hangar. "I am the judge on this planet, and for everything you've done, I sentence you to death."

As ominous as the fighter was, what Kaiden saw behind it galvanized him into action. Adrenaline kicked in, and he sprinted away from the craft as its cannons began to prime. The captain's laugh held both mockery and triumph, distorted and amplified by the speakers.

A flaming wreck of a ship barreled in and the captain barely caught it in his peripheral vision before it slammed into his fighter. Both exploded, and the force hurled Kaiden to the floor. Crates, ship parts, and other items in the hangar rolled past or sailed over him. He flipped over and stared at a massive fire on the other side of the hangar where the two crashed ships burned.

"Good Lord! What was that?" Kaiden demanded.

"A rescue...of a sort," a familiar voice answered over the comm.

"Genos?" he asked and peered around for his teammate. "Was that you?"

"Indeed, but if you don't mind, could you come to the front of the hangar?"

Kaiden scrambled to his feet and rushed forward. Genos dangled from the lip of the hangar entrance. "I could use some assistance if you please."

Kaiden grabbed the Tsuna's waiting hand. "Crazy, dude. I've rubbed off on both of you." He chuckled and hauled his friend to safety.

"I received Chiyo's distress beacon, and I was able to get the ship airborne but not in the best shape," he explained as he dusted himself off and checked his gear. "I wish you could have held off getting into danger for a couple of hours longer."

"It really wasn't our intention. I mean it," Kaiden assured him and flicked a thumb at the ship Chiyo had activated. "I'll explain once we set off if you like, but for now, do you think you're steady enough to fly that?"

Genos looked at the ship. "Certainly, and maybe the system will realize I am a far superior pilot than it believes me to be."

"So it *did* bother you, then?" he prodded.

The Tsuna simply gave a curt nod as he passed. They made their way to the ship, boarded, and closed the door. "Best we get out before any more guards come in."

"Agreed. Good to see you made it, Genos." Chiyo greeted him from the co-pilot's chair as Genos took his seat.

"With aplomb, too," Kaiden pointed out.

"Once we make it into space, what will our next move be?" Genos inquired as he completed the preparations Chiyo had initiated for take-off.

"I have coordinates for the station. It should be a

straight path, but there's a fair amount of flying without a warp gate or high-grade thrusters," she stated.

"Then I guess we'll save it and take it on later." Kaiden rubbed the back of his neck as the ship began to depart. "I have a date with a killer robot in about nineteen hours."

CHAPTER SIX

"A re the tests finished?" the lead technician asked his subordinates.

"Yes, sir. We've completed the trials," one of them said enthusiastically. "With this, we can advise Axiom that the device will be completed on schedule."

"Wonderful," the lead said with a smile. "I appreciate all the work you've done in support of this, gentlemen. We will tell them they will have it in their hands in seven days' time."

Gin paused the video and looked past the techs at the device they spoke of. It appeared to be such a simple thing —a slim square box, featureless with the exception of a hole in the middle that contained a scanning device. From what he understood, it wouldn't even function properly without a top-grade mirage system linked to it.

Which happened to be one of a number of things he had acquired in his travels, so he certainly had no concerns there.

The killer tapped a finger on his chin as he considered

his options. How should he approach this? It seemed it would be easy enough to simply go in and take it. Thanks to the access he had through his benefactor, it wouldn't require too much to hide from prying eyes. Perhaps he could make it part of a night's work quickly completed.

He mulled it over for a moment before he decided against that. Although this particular company, Eton Inc., wasn't a part of Zubanz's little organization directly, it did work for Axiom, whose owners very much were. Given that connection, it was probably for the best that he didn't stir the pot too much.

He sighed and scratched his head. It truly was most inconvenient to work for others and have to factor in things like allegiances and who was pandering to whom. He would much rather not have to deal with the politics. It wasn't like they wouldn't know someone had been there when a special classified device had been removed directly from the factory. He sighed and told himself to focus on the toys he would play with later. The fun he would have would be so much greater after a job well done.

It appeared that it would be the stealthy way, then. He checked the date on the record—three days ago. That still left more than enough time, but he didn't want to risk them handing it off early or possibly transferring it to another location due to safety concerns. Well-founded safety concerns, perhaps, but it would still be a nuisance. He turned the video off, took the chip from the table, and flipped it in his hand as he approached a massive oil painting in his sponsored abode.

Gin traced his fingers over the lines of a bleeding-heart flower in the middle, which was entwined around a pale beauty. The painting shimmered with a dull white light before it dissolved to reveal his armor, weapons, and tools hidden behind it. The table that held the suit moved away from the wall and descended at an angle in front of him. He smiled as he traced his hand over the front of his chest plate before he lifted it to retrieve his helmet and placed the chip inside.

He wondered if perhaps his plan was too elaborate to snatch a single target. It was an honest question, but then he thought of the prizes—both the boy and the tool he would create.

With these, he would not only take care of one of the few who got away, but he would have access to the Nexus Academy whenever he wished, both in the real world and inside their celebrated Animus.

"Are the security systems in place?" the night watch captain, Bellerd, asked his subordinate.

"Yes, sir. Everything is locked down, and defenses are active. I don't think anyone is in here except the night shift guard," the man answered.

"Good, but you would be wrong on us being the only ones in here," Bellerd stated. "Professor Lumiya is still in his office."

"This late? It's past midnight," the guard spluttered. "Isn't he a new father? You would think he would want to spend time with his family."

"This is his last big project before he takes an extended vacation," the captain explained. "The man is a workaholic.

He's as excited about his baby girl as anyone could be, but he's also the lead in this project. He gotta make sure everything works right, or his vacation might be spoiled if he's called back in."

"Fair enough." The other man shrugged. "I guess I'll go take point at the main entrance. I promised Darvish I would take over so he could get some caffeine in him."

"I'll join you after I make another round on level four," Bellerd promised. "The sensors there still aren't aligned right, and I constantly receive silent alarms if so much as a bolt knocks against the ground. The brass knows that, but I would still get reamed in reports if I didn't go and record the area."

"Understood, sir." His subordinate saluted and made his way to his position.

The captain sighed as he watched him go. He'd known Ovid for a few years now, and the man would probably make lead in a few more years himself. He was a good man, if a little uptight. While he respected that his subordinate knew protocol, they could relax a little in this job. The systems did most of the work there, after all.

"I thought he would never leave," a low, mirthful voice muttered. Bellerd instinctively grabbed for his shock baton, but his hand was snatched and forced against his back. Something jabbed into his neck, and he saw only black before he could make a sound.

Gin held the night watch captain up and dragged him over to the door to the main development lab. He used the guard's keycard to activate the console, and opened his eye for the scanner to read him. Eye readers were tricky. He couldn't simply remove the eyeball since then it wouldn't read life signs. Even tranquilizers or sedatives had to be administered with extreme care. Otherwise, the eyes flickered or some shit and the scanner would register them as asleep. That was certainly a good way to trigger an alarm.

The door opened, and Gin dragged the man inside and placed him behind a table for now. He closed the door and made a mental note to come back for him before he left. A quick glance at his surroundings confirmed that he recognized most of the area from the videos he had watched. He checked the map in his HUD. The device should be here. He took a few more steps and noticed an enclosed dome on a station in the middle of the room. Well, if that didn't look fancy!

He sauntered over, and his scrutiny revealed laser triggers around it that would trip if he got too close. The dome was reinforced, so he probably couldn't blast it open with a hundred thermals. He smiled. Normally, this would be a pain. Doable, but he would have to work on it for a couple of hours. However, now seemed like a good time to recoup some of his investment in the new bauble he'd received from Vinci. This would be a single demonstration of its varied uses.

The killer held his hand out and activated the command in his HUD. The scanner washed over the display for a few seconds, and he saw the interior of every device in his vicinity. In the next second, darkness appeared on his HUD and seemed to swallow all the wiring, not only around the dome but any device in his view. The lasers died, and the dome opened as several other machines turned off.

Gin smiled with smug satisfaction. It was very sensitive,

but he could tweak that, no problem. He would have to give Vinci proper congratulations the next time he saw him. This had exceeded his expectations.

Maybe he should kill him so no one else would get it? Would Vinci sell out like that? He didn't seem like that kind of man. This was a program written to his specifications, after all, and one of a kind. The hacker had best hope it stayed that way.

He picked up the device and admired it for a moment before he slipped it into a container strapped onto his leg. The time in his visor indicated forty-two minutes and twenty-three seconds since he'd made his way in. Not a personal best, but not too shabby, given that he'd had to wait for that idiot guard to wander off.

A gun primed behind him, and his experience identified it immediately—Altair model, a slim but efficient energy pistol. He turned quickly. The lead scientist from the videos stood behind him and brandished a pistol—an Altair, just like he'd thought. At least he hadn't lost his touch.

"Who are you?" the man demanded. "How did you get in, and what are you doing with that?"

"I'm taking it," Gin stated calmly and leaned back against the desk. "For all those smarts, you aren't very wise, are you?"

"Fool! Do you even know what that is?" the scientist demanded. "That's a—"

"New type of hologram system. It combines hard-light creations with replicant software and bio-transfusion chems to perfectly replicate another person," the killer finished for him. "I believe you named the project 'Worm-wood.' I like your sense of style, Mr. Lumiya."

"Are you merely a burglar, or is this corporate espionage?" he asked.

"Neither, really. Plus, espionage would imply that I'm looking for schematics or something." Gin patted his leg. "I'm taking the whole thing."

"You idiot. That is a device ordered and funded by Axiom. They won't simply allow you to keep it. You'll be hounded until they catch you and get it back, and they will make you disappear when they get their hands on you."

"That wouldn't change my life much, honestly," he admitted. "And I'm good enough to disappear on my own, although I don't suppose you would know that. I really need to work on my introductions a little more." He straightened, and the professor continued to threaten him with the gun. Gin bowed mockingly. "My name is Gin Sonny, collector of only the finest shiny things. I'm also an intergalactic killer, but I usually leave that out. It tends to ruin the mood."

"Gin…Gin Sonny?" the professor stammered. "What are you— No, enough talk. I will not allow you to take that device or live to kill anyone ever again." He fired his pistol, and the interloper simply held up a hand. A small barrier formed, blocked his head, and absorbed the shots. The man changed his aim to direct a few shots at his chest, but the armor's barrier flared to life and deflected the blasts.

The pistol overheated and burned Lumiya's hand, and he dropped it with a curse.

"Those Altair models are stylish and have decent punching power, but you should have sprung for the new model. It rectifies the rapid overheat problem. You should know that the overheat on those things is one of the worst in the pistol department, especially without gloves." Gin walked forward and the professor backed away, clutching his burnt hand.

Lumiya's gaze found a nearby panel, and he wondered if he could reach it and trigger the alarm.

"I'm enjoying our talk, Professor." The killer stretched his hand casually toward the panel. It and all the devices around it deactivated, including the nearby lights, and they were immediately enshrouded in semi-darkness.

The professor retrieved the pistol with his other hand and vented it. "You will not—"

"I hear you are a new father, Professor," Gin commented as he tapped his fingers on his Omni-blade.

The man's eyes widened in rage. "Don't start that. You will not threaten my daughter."

"I'm not. That is honestly not how I do things. I will simply offer you a choice. Either way, I'll walk out of here, but I made it a personal goal—or maybe a game—to not spill a drop of blood." Gin looked at the table beneath which he'd hidden the guard. "I guess that technically I already broke that since an injection would pull out a literal drop of blood, but considering what I normally do, I'm still clean."

A crisp click sounded as Lumiya slid the vent of his pistol closed with his shaking burnt hand and aimed it at the intruder once again.

"When you take up a weapon, your life is in play," the killer stated coolly. "'Kill or be killed' is the more common phrasing, but you're obviously new to this. I'm willing to overlook your little stunt—"

"When you threaten my family?"

"I said I'm not. Not directly, anyway." Gin removed his helmet and stared at the professor with his artificial eyes. "You're a new daddy. An exciting time, isn't it?" He placed his helmet on the table. "There's the initial excitement, but once that's over, there's the future to look forward to. The first time she walks, talks, rides a hoverboard. Those father-daughter dances and the like."

"Quit taunting me."

"Tell me..." The killer's smirk disappeared, and he stared at the other man with an expressionless façade. "Is it worth giving up all that for some knick-knack? To rob both you and your daughter of that potential happiness?"

"I don't want to live in a world you inhabit!" he declared, and a single tear hovered on his lashes.

"I don't usually come to Earth. I'm here for a special reason, so there is no need to worry about that." Gin straightened to emphasize the large difference in height between him and the other man. "This might be a foolish question, but do you believe in an afterlife, Professor?"

Both of Lumiya's hands shook visibly. "What a-are you t-t-talking about?" he stammered.

"I've never come to a conclusion myself, but the basic gist is you're supposed to meet your loved ones after you pass on, right?" The killer pondered this for a moment. "Tell me, if I kill you here, when your daughter eventually passes on, and if there is an afterlife in which you meet, what will you tell her when she asks why you weren't there? Why you had to die?" He didn't move the dispassionate, inhuman gaze from his victim's face. "My guess is that you will have to tell her that you felt that this device and being a company man was worth more to you than she was."

Lumiya lowered his gaze to the floor, and his legs trembled as the Altair pistol fell from his hand. A few tears dripped onto the weapon where it lay at his feet. Gin placed a hand on his shoulder. "This isn't a threat, merely a fact. There is no point in being a hero. I've killed many heroes." He leaned in so close that his mouth was just to the right of the professor's ear. "If you wanna be a hero, make sure you are her hero."

The man remained motionless and silent before he slowly nodded his head. "J-j-just go," he muttered.

The killer nodded, picked his helmet up, and walked past Lumiya. "There's a guard under that desk. You simply need to make up something about falling asleep." He placed his helmet on and turned back to the man, who still trembled, his face ashen. "No one needs to learn what happened here. I froze all the cameras, and even if you could convince them to find me, many have tried and failed." He opened the door leading out of the lab. "Hopefully, this is the last time we see each other. Don't do anything foolish, Professor." With that final warning, he activated his cloak and the doors closed. The scientist fell to his knees with both sadness and relief.

CHAPTER SEVEN

"I'm here for a gig," Kaiden told the dealer, who looked up from her tablet, her eyes darkened and hazy from either a long shift or the use of stimulants. Probably both.

"What is the name and—"

"The job title is 'Crash,' and my merc number is 909-117," he informed her. She nodded, turned to her console's screen, and typed it in.

"You were almost late. Seven more minutes and we would have cleared the transport for takeoff," she admonished and frowned at him. "We would've passed your gig on to another merc in the lobby."

He turned to scrutinize about twenty mercs who loitered in the area, shook his head, and gestured at them with a thumb as he turned to her. "I'm sure you would have had plenty of biters for a job that has you chasing after a machine designed for heavy combat. Look at that lot. Do you think they would last one round with a few decently-armed defense droids?"

She studied him and raised an eyebrow at his long

jacket and boots. "You don't exactly look like someone geared up and able to take one on either, unless you think looking like a sub-flick action hero will strike terror into an unfeeling robot."

Kaiden opened his jacket to reveal his armor. "It's more likely that I'll deal with a group of hackers who grew too big-headed for their own good. Besides, the idea is to take as little fire as possible, so this'll suffice," he explained as he closed the jacket once more. "I didn't think it would be a good idea to walk around Chicago in full armor."

"As long as you keep your merc tag on and don't carry your weapons in plain view, you're fine." She pointed to the other mercs. "Do you think they arrived here dressed casually?"

"I'm not even sure that any of them bathed." He sighed and waved a finger under his nose for emphasis.

The dealer chuckled and shook her head. "I imagine that most of them hope their missions are downwind." She scrutinized him once more. "Are you prepared? I don't see any weapons."

"They're in the case." He pointed to a silver carrier on his left, and the woman peered at it for a moment before she nodded.

"Very well. If you're all set, here are your details." A small chip popped out of her console, and she took it and handed it to him.

He drew his oculars from his pocket, slid the chip into a compartment on the side of the frames, and put them on. Quickly, he read through the information as it appeared onscreen.

"You've cut it a bit close, so here's the important stuff,"

the dealer offered and he lowered the oculars down his nose slightly to look at her. "Your ride is in bay three, pad two. You're assigned to a pod-zep. I'd get there quickly. The pilot is known for his punctuality, not for his nice demeanor."

"I don't think I've ever ridden in a zep before. Wait, a pod-zep? That's a one-way transport."

"Yep," she said in a bored tone. "You should have been aware of this when you took the job. What's the problem?"

"The gig said the company would provide transport. How will I get back from the middle of nowhere?"

"Leg it, I guess," she suggested unhelpfully. "That's what the contractor paid for. You seem resourceful, so I'm sure you can figure something out."

"My target is a junk town owned by a gang. I doubt there'll be a carrier station nearby," Kaiden muttered, which merely earned a shrug from the woman.

"Contact them and bitch. I can't do anything. You'll have plenty of time on the ride there. Zeps are stealthier than most dropships, but that sacrifices speed." She looked at her monitor. "By the way, you have about two and a half minutes before takeoff."

He rapped his knuckles on the counter and shook his head as he grabbed his case and walked off. "Cheap bastards."

"Are you trying to hold up this entire op, kid?" the pilot snapped as Kaiden boarded. "If you had gotten here earlier, you wouldn't have to holler at me like that."

"I still had a few seconds, and you were closing the door," he countered as he placed his case on the floor. He cast a quick glance around the ship and saw a long hallway with four doors on either side. "What's your hurry? All you have to do is fly us over our spots and drop us off. Do you have a hot date you're picking up on the way or something?"

"I gotta take my zep in for repairs at the next stop. I ain't gonna have the mechanics up my ass because you took your sweet time."

"Well, with that in mind, thanks for using some of your precious time to yap at me." He removed the chip from his oculars and handed it to the pilot. "Also, thanks for letting me know I'm riding on a busted flyer. Should I start making my peace with God when we take off or wait until we crash?"

The man took the chip and slid it into a notch on his tablet. "Calm down. This baby is perfectly functional. She simply needs a little TLC." He looked at Kaiden with a wry smirk. "Maybe next time, you won't be so cheap and go with the default option. You could spend the creds to get your own transport."

"Maybe, but then I wouldn't be able to meet wonderful people like you," he sassed and looked back to see a door open on the left. "Well, it's easy to guess which compartment is mine."

"I would hope so. Special assistance like that isn't part of the package," the other man snarked. When Kaiden looked back to glare at him over his oculars, he removed the chip and handed it back to him. "You might have been the last one on, but you'll be the first one off. You'll be dropped off at the southern edge of the state near the borders of Indiana and Kentucky."

"Is that so? When I'm done, I might get me some moonshine to celebrate," he quipped. "About how long until the drop?"

"A little less than a half-hour." The pilot moved past him into the corridor.

"That long?" he asked incredulously. "I know these big bastards are called zeps in reference to zeppelins, but don't you think the flight speed is too much homage?"

"This craft is built for stealth drops and to withstand all sorts of mayhem. The tradeoff is speed and maneuverability." He sounded like he was reading the information from a pamphlet. "Which is all the more reason to get going, so get into your pod, get comfy, and shut the hell up."

Kaiden picked his case up and made his way to his pod behind the other man, who evidently headed toward the cockpit. He grabbed the door handle and turned back as he entered. "I guess I'll kick back and enjoy my ride on the SS *Flying Turtle*, then. Try not to make it too bumpy."

The pilot stared at him for a moment, and he half-expected him to get in one last dig. Instead, his expression was bemused, which worried him more than sarcasm would have. "I recommend that you hold on," he warned. "The ride *might* be bumpy, but the drop? That'll be a hell of a lot more than bumpy." With that, he pressed a button on the wall as he strode into the cockpit. The lights in the cabin dimmed, and the door above Kaiden begin to slide down. He hastened into the compartment, and after it shut, dim blue light illuminated his surroundings as he heard the zep activate.

"Nice guy." Chief chortled, and Kaiden shook his head as he removed his oculars and hefted his case to slide it into a compartment above. He paused and thought about it for a moment before he lowered it, removed his helmet, and placed it on the chair before he finally pushed the container away. "It might be a good thing he won't come back."

"Do you really think it was smart to mouth off to the guy who'll drop you to earth? He's responsible for where you'll land, so you might end up in the middle of the junk town."

"If he does that, I'll give him a seriously pissed-off review," he muttered, then picked his helmet up and examined it as he took a seat. "Two stars, minus four for dropping me into the middle of a battle zone, but I crushed two hostiles on landing so plus one for a nice shot."

"Next question: do you really think we'll only have to deal with the Azure Halo members?" the EI asked and appeared near the door to study him. *"You're the fifth attempt at this point. A couple of the previous gigs actually involved groups. I doubt a gang known primarily for their hacking would be able to take on a few battle-hardened mercs."*

"That's probably what Tessa Labs was thinking, which would also explain why they've been so frugal with everything." Kaiden pondered the ramifications for a moment. "Not paying for incidentals, shoving my ass on this zep with no way back… At least they didn't skip on the payout." He flipped his helmet and put it on, folded his arms, and leaned back as the HUD came up. "A million credits. I'm getting the big bucks already."

"Two things," Chief intoned cautiously as he slowly floated closer. *"It's a million credits if you bring it back intact.*

My guess would be that it's pooled from the payouts of the unsuccessful gigs. Keep that in mind."

"Noted. Next grievance?"

"Purely so that you don't walk around enemy territory with an overinflated head as a target, I should remind you that you weren't offered this because of your notoriety. You took a gig no one else wanted."

"Their loss, my gain," Kaiden retorted and stretched his arms along the back of the seat as he fixed his gaze on the glowing orb. "Are you trying to insinuate that my decision wasn't because of confidence and grit but because of something like idiocy?"

Chief rolled his eye. *"I would feign politeness and say something like, 'Perish the thought,' but I've worked on a pet project to prove that all your decisions are at least ten to twelve percent idiocy, so I'll let that lie."*

Kaiden chuckled with real amusement. "Only ten to twelve? Have you gone soft on me?"

"I'm talking about something you should want at zero," Chief countered and floated lazily in the air. *"But I haven't given up on you. I'm sure we can bring it down, although I should add that I'm hoping for a bump on the head to speed things along."*

"Did you actually have a second point, or was that only a ruse for you to prod at me?"

"No, I do, but keeping your ego in check has been updated to a primary function, so priorities and all that."

Kaiden made an "okay" sign with his hand. "Bang-up job, Chief."

The EI's eye narrowed *"My point was that the gig had no takers because it was a risk level of seven-point-five. It started at five but had to be updated—you know, because of the aforementioned horrible deaths of the last guys who tried it."*

"It's on a scale of one to eleven," he countered. "Besides, we don't know if the deaths were *horrible* per se. They might have simply been 'unfortunate' or 'would rather have not.'"

"Should I also remind you that the gig on which you ran into Gin was a risk level of five?"

"Unforeseen circumstance." Kaiden waved airily. "The Azure Halos don't work with anyone other than themselves. They supply devices or hack things brought to them. They're more an illegitimate business than a real gang."

"I'm merely saying, considering what happened, that you should be—"

"I'll get it done, Chief," he stated, his tone heavy and stern. "I'll get in there and get that droid, and I'll live to get drunk off my ass when it's done." He looked squarely at the EI. "I won't let him win."

A long and almost uncomfortably silent pause hung between the two before Chief looked away slowly. He suddenly seemed to find the wall rather interesting as he shifted to a dim white hue. *"So, uh, have you looked over those upgrades Chiyo made to your HUD? What do you think?"*

Kaiden's gaze roamed around the HUD and studied the new display and additions. "You popped in to look at them when she gave it back to me. Don't you have an opinion?"

"Oh, they are good. Surprisingly good. When she said it was only a firmware upgrade she found on the Net, I expected a new background and maybe the option to add filters to any pictures you take, but we could get some use out of these."

"That's close to what I thought," he admitted and scrolled through the options in the display. "The scanner had the biggest overhaul. I wanted to ask where she got it, but I imagine that would probably make me liable or an accomplice in the right court."

"It's the gifts that could get you five to ten that show you how much they love you," Chief intoned cheerfully. Kaiden looked up and tilted his head in query. *"Potentially sharing a cell shows they like being around you, at least."*

"I'm reasonably sure co-ed prisons aren't a thing—at least not ones where they intermingle. It might work, though. More opportunities to blow off steam."

"I'm sure the annual Sadie Hawkins Dance would be a huge hit among the criminal crowd."

"That's not quite what I implied, but we can go with it."

"I'm not programmed for dirty jokes."

"Oh, bullshit."

Kaiden and Chief continued to talk and joke as they awaited the drop, which was announced by a shift of the room's light to yellow.

"There she glows." Kaiden straightened in his chair as a safety bar came down across his chest. He slid the safety belt around his waist and held on. "How long until the drop?"

"The yellow light means two minutes until ejection, so counting down from one minute and forty-one seconds now," Chief stated and disappeared from sight before he appeared in the HUD. *"Also, that was a terrible pun."*

"Not my best, I'll admit—" A loud hiss distracted him just before the pod shook, dropped a few feet, and tilted at an angle. "What the hell was that?"

"The hiss was some of the latches disengaging." The EI glanced around quickly. *"Activating x-ray. Oh, not good."*

"What?"

"There are barriers that hold the pod in place before launch, but the one on the left isn't in place."

"What does that mean?" Kaiden asked and immediately looked for a way to contact the pilot.

"It means this ship needs something more thorough than TLC," Chief grunted. *"Also, it means that instead of a perfectly vertical drop... Did you ever do one of those experiments in school where you put an egg in a basket and dropped it from a tall building to see if it cracked?"*

"Get me the hell out of this thing," he fumed, and shook his harness.

"That would be inadvisable at this time, buddy. Hopefully, this has orientation jets or safety chutes. About that making your peace with God thing? You might want to make a deal instead."

Before he could respond, he heard three quick clicks, then gravity took over and sent him into a spiraling descent.

"That bastard will get one star!" he swore. His curse became a yell as he careened helplessly to the hard landing that waited below.

CHAPTER EIGHT

Kaiden kicked the door of his pod, but it took several hard blows before the door righted and slid open. He crawled out and rolled his neck and left shoulder as he peered upward to watch the zep fly away in the distance.

"Chief, put him on the list," he muttered as he turned to retrieve his container from the pod.

"Which one, specifically?" the EI asked, and his eye blinked in and out. *"The hit list, the jerk list? You have so many. Most of them are negative, now that I look at them."*

"Pick one. I'll sort the details out later." He grunted, heaved the case out of the compartment, and tossed it on the ground.

"It's a good thing you put the helmet on," Chief noted. *"It's also a good thing the pod did have orientation jets, although they could have activated a little sooner. If it had landed with the door facing the ground... Well, considering that the only people around are those you're potentially here to kill, it would make for an awkward introduction."*

"I may not have to kill them. I could simply avoid a full-on confrontation and try to steal the droid back," Kaiden pointed out as he popped the case open and drew Sire out to check it for damage.

"Saying you're not going to do this violently while spit-shining a big-ass gun makes it seem like it's not your primary concern," the EI commented. *"And about that droid... How exactly will you carry it back? We might not have the specific measurements and weight, but even the lightest Defense and Battle droids clock in at a few hundred pounds. This thing is supposed to be the latest in wartime nightmare machines. Whatever they might have done to make it more maneuverable and all, that is probably partially undone by whatever firepower is strapped to it."*

"I won't carry it," Kaiden replied as he attached Debonair to the magnetic strip on his belt before he loaded his thermal and shock grenade canisters. "You'll drive it."

"Come again?"

"The droid's OS wasn't finished, so they used another Defense droid's coding to fill in the gaps until it was. Since it was stolen, that didn't happen." He clipped the canisters to his belt. "I ain't a technician or engineer, but I know a little about the process. The makers of these things usually use a series of chips or an older model 'brain' from a different droid to house the OS while they test it. That way, they can work on the chassis and weapons and the programming simultaneously. It's different divisions and all that."

"And this relates to me how?"

"You're the brains, smartass. I'll cast you into the droid when we find it. If this thing had whatever fancy OS they were planning to install... Well, they could probably simply have activated it when it was stolen in the first place and killed all the Halo members before they even left the room. But my thought is that if they used an older model, you'll have an easier time getting into it before whatever defenses it might have in place to try to keep you out." He finished his statement by strapping a box of medical items to his leg.

Chief looked into the corner for a moment in thought. *"A rather well-formed plan. I'm impressed, but I see a slight issue."*

"And that would be?"

"Do you really think they didn't install updated internal defenses as soon as they could power the thing on?" he retorted. *"Sure, they might have used older devices to hold it in place until they got the shiny stuff to work, but if they already had some of it in place, the firewall and security measures would be the top priorities."*

"Well, if the Azure Halo hackers haven't already fucked with it, I did hope for incompetence on the creators' part, considering how they lost it in the first place," Kaiden confessed. "They made it capable of firing but didn't install a proper threat detector?"

"They have droids hooked up directly into their computers during the creation process. It doesn't make a move without proper input and is basically a glorified puppet for months or years," Chief explained.

"So this thing might not even be functional?" he inquired. "That would make this way easier."

"Assuming the hackers didn't mess with it. If they gave it a power source and command chip, it's perfectly functional."

Chief's color became a worried blue. *"And also the technological equivalent of psychotic."*

"Faaantastic," Kaiden muttered. He turned his attention to the terrain, which was mostly rolling hills, with only a few scattered trees. In the distance was the junk town the Halos called home. Even from there, Kaiden could tell they hadn't done much—at least on the outside—to dissuade anyone from thinking it might be anything but trashy.

"You know, we didn't exactly land with grace."

"Not even thinkin' liberally."

He continued his scrutiny of the town and rested his rifle against his shoulder. "You would think they would want to know what the hell just crashed in their backyard."

Chief's eye widened and the scanner in Kaiden's HUD activated to trace the horizon. *"I can't pick anything up, not even a Scout drone or some bastard with a pair of binoculars."*

He tapped his fingers on Sire. "Well, then we're lucky, or they are waiting for us, or…"

The two were silent for a moment as each considered the implications. Chief's eye widened and looked directly into Kaiden's. *"It looks like all that planning might get tossed out, huh?"*

"It's moments like these that make me tune out when Chiyo or Jaxon try to lecture me on the importance of working on things like strategy and subterfuge." He sighed, slid his rifle off his shoulder, and grasped it with both hands. "I'd usually say something like let's have some fun, but that would require knowing what we're up against."

With that, he set off toward the town and hoped that for once, his enemies were on the smarter side. If not, that might make things more complicated than he wanted.

As Kaiden reached a point only a few hundred yards from the town, he saw a ramshackle wall and a gate on the perimeter. He walked up to the door, alert for guards or bots, but nothing approached. He moved closer but paused when he saw a terminal near the door. "Hey, Chief, could you get in there and open this thing for me?"

"I can try, but if they have it trapped or bugged, we could potentially set off an alarm or any hidden defenses," he warned.

"Maybe, but even if we did, I almost feel like no one would come," Kaiden said quietly, with another furtive look at their surroundings. "Besides, the wall seems to encompass the entire town. I can't jump over it, and I don't have any scorpion wire or claws so I would have to blow my way in anyway."

"You could use explosives instead."

"Get in the damn box," he ordered. Chief glowed an amused pink before he disappeared from the HUD. Kaiden tapped his finger lightly on Sire's trigger guard and looked around once again. Aside from the wind and a few distant cicadas, he couldn't hear anything coming from behind the walls. He glanced at his gun and the energy within, and the sight reassured him somewhat. He had seen the damage it could do, and knew it could evaporate flesh and metal with ease. At full power, it was essentially a miniature version of a Tesla cannon. Even Marlo was impressed. Despite that, he began to wonder if he needed something even more visceral.

"I'm in. Opening the gate," Chief announced. The doors slid apart slowly, and Chief once again took his place in the

HUD as Kaiden walked toward them. He stood at the entrance and surveyed the scene ahead of him. Dozens of shacks, some tents, and several buildings left from when the town was abandoned filled the area, but no bodies littered the streets. He felt more unease at this than if lasers had fired on him as soon he walked in.

"Are we in the right place, Chief?" he asked as his confused gaze scrutinized the vacated space once more.

"According to the mission location, yes," the EI answered, and his eye shrunk. *"But from the looks of things, you would think this town was washed."*

"The whole point of sending mercs in was the hope that they wouldn't have to do something like drop an organic incinerator bomb on the place. That's not exactly a good look." Kaiden took a few steps inside and listened intently for movement or any sound of life. This time he didn't even hear the cicadas. "Although, to be fair, that would seem like the kind of thing the WC would do in this situation. I'm not sure it would be cheaper than sending in a TAC team, but it would provide an opportunity for them to use their weapons catalog."

"I agree with the sentiment, but if you're knocking someone else for taking joy in destruction, it does seem like calling the kettle black."

"At least I have enough tact to be personable, even if it's only for a few seconds," Kaiden countered. He continued down the street and peered into some of the buildings and shacks. It quickly became apparent where the Halos spent all their money. While the exteriors of the buildings were questionable, the interiors of many were filled with tech and equipment. He identified an enormous variety of stolen tech, weapons, devices, armor, and parts for droids and ships. Consoles and holoscreens hummed faintly within some of the structures, but it only made the scene more unnerving since no one actually manned them.

"Kaiden—blood," Chief stated, and an arrow on his screen pointed him in the direction of what the EI had found. He walked cautiously to the entrance of one of the buildings—one a few stories tall that had probably been used as an office at one point. The glass at the entrance was shattered, chunks of linoleum were scattered along the street, and interspersed with everything were a few spots of dried blood.

"Oh, hell," Chief rasped, and Kaiden looked up.

"Wha— Good God!" He yelped and staggered back reflexively as he looked inside the building. He saw only three bodies, but dozens of *parts*. The only light came from the sun outside. The interior was dark, but what he could see was enough to classify this as a massacre. The bodies that were whole seemed to have fallen to either laser or gunfire, but the various appendages and mutilated bodies seemed to have been torn apart by physical strength.

"It doesn't look like a retrieval mission anymore," Chief cautioned unnecessarily. *"Keep your gun close."*

He walked inside and activated the lights on his helmet as he approached one of the more intact bodies to examine the wounds. "These are wounds from an energy projectile —plasma or electric." He turned the body and studied the front of the wound. "Definitely plasma. If this is the droid, its weapons are working."

"Who or what else could it be? There aren't any mutants in this area."

"It could have been the previous mercs. They had to have made *some* headway." Kaiden looked around again and frowned. "But unless the company hired Psychs or let loose a bunch of Neurosiks, I don't think they would have taken the time to do this—or would have even been capable of it."

"If its weapons are working, it would have been more efficient to simply shoot everything in sight," Chief stated. *"This is probably the most macabre math I've ever had to do, but counting all the body parts, it ripped apart at least seven people in here. That's over twice the number it only shot."*

"Maybe it's an issue of power," Kaiden suggested. He noticed a stairway in the corner and shuffled carefully around the viscera to make his way to it. "According to the mission briefing, the robot shouldn't have had anything more than a small cell—enough to turn it off and on. Whatever they used to give it more juice might not be enough for it to use its weapons for more than a few shots at a time."

"That might be lucky for us," Chief conceded. *"But look at the damage and...everything. There are weapons on the ground, so they fought back, and yet it still went in for close combat. Unless it was stuck with a Fodder droid command chip, it would know to either retreat and bait them out or take one of their weapons if its own were compromised."*

"What are you trying to lead me to, Chief?" he asked as he began to ascend the stairs

"I think this droid is a literal killing machine," the EI clarified. *"And before you ask if I'm making a pun to cut the tension, no. I think they have designed this thing to be a killer. A Battle Droid is a mechanical soldier; take out the target and move on. This thing is trying to make a statement."*

"Don't fuck with me?"

"Don't fuck with who bought me."

Kaiden reached the top step and turned, immediately greeted by another gory scene. He ignored the violence and scrutinized the rest of the room. In the middle was a table surrounded by wires and cables. A number of them were ripped apart, several monitors and consoles were smashed, and pieces of the ceiling were cracked and lay on the ground.

"This is where they must have worked on it," he deduced as he approached it. "Chief, jump around to anything that's working and see if you can find anything useful."

"Acknowledged." The EI vanished as Kaiden continued to search for signs of what the hackers were doing with the droid. His foot struck something, and he looked down to see a small gray sphere. It was a power core, he decided as he picked it up and examined it, one used in most Defense droids. He glanced to the side to see a table with a couple more on it, different types for different droids. It looked like they tried to activate it, but they didn't take any care. More like Frankensteining it together.

"Kaiden, I have something."

"Details?" he questioned, tossing the core to the floor.

"There are some logs, but not much information. I would guess they kept that somewhere else. But they installed a tracker on the droid."

"Where is it?" he demanded as Chief appeared in the HUD again. "Has it left the town?"

"No, which is odd. I rewound the time on the tracker, and it began to move forty-two hours ago. But it hasn't moved for

seventeen hours." He added a dot to Kaiden's map that identified the droid's position.

"Did it deactivate?"

Chief shook from side to side. *"Also no, otherwise the tracker wouldn't be live. It's powered by the droid's core, so it's simply idle. Without a specific directive, I think its only command was to eliminate hostiles, and with that busted threat detector, everything was hostile. My guess is that it's killed every one of the Halos it saw and the rest ran off, so now it's waiting for a new target."*

"So it'll wait there until we get to it?" Kaiden asked. He hefted his rifle as he walked to the far side of the room to look out the window. "Then I'll take care of it before it has a chance to see me."

"I don't think it's only using sight. It probably has some sort of radar or detector that lets it— Kaiden, it's found us."

CHAPTER NINE

"It's sure is taking its sweet time, isn't it?" Kaiden grumbled irritably. He stood at the top of the building and looked through Sire's scope as he waited for the approaching droid.

"While I can appreciate the gung-ho attitude, maybe you should use this time to find a more advantageous position than a rooftop," Chief suggested. *"It might not have your precise position. It might only have picked up a life sign and is now searching for it. The tracking signal shows it meandering around at the moment. We really don't know much about this thing, do we?"*

He sighed and lowered his rifle. "No, we don't. The mission statement simply said there was a stolen droid that needed retrieval or destruction but didn't say much else. I only know the backstory thanks to some digging by Julio."

"It makes you wonder if you're really supposed to destroy this thing." The EI sounded thoughtful. *"Maybe this is some sort of training or trial run for the droid disguised as a gig. That's a thing, right?"*

"Yeah, but that's usually done by black markets or gangs who don't have the millions of creds required to properly test things like this. Julio did a hell of a lot of leg work before he handed this off to me. He still feels a bit guilty about the whole Gin situation," Kaiden explained. He surveyed the town again and shifted his gaze between the horizon and the map in his visor. "Besides, you would think, if that was the case, they would have had more than enough data, considering this thing presumably took out most of a gang and at least a couple of merc groups."

"Do you have any other plan besides shooting it?"

"It's all I can do until we figure out what it's capable of. Although, if you want to take a look around and see if there are any defenses left that we could potentially use, I'm all for it."

"There are none in the immediate area that I can detect," Chief informed him. *"If you wanna take a quick walk around and a gander, that could bring something up."*

"I think I'll pass on that." He looked at the tracker signal. "It's stopped moving again. Do you think it's busted or something?"

"I saw an old Havok Mk. II in the room full of bits downstairs," Chief stated. *"These Azure Halo guys obviously had some firepower, even if that's not their usual deal. It's possible they were able to damage it somewhat. But it's still functional, so my guess is that it can take a beating."*

"Then I'll be the one to finish— It's moving again, and has turned down the street." He crouched and looked down the street to the corner of a building. "It's four blocks away now. Assuming it doesn't start charging through the buildings, it'll come up the street soon."

"Your rifle is midrange, so even at full charge, the round won't travel fast enough to hit from here. I doubt it's braindead enough to simply stand there and take a glowing energy blast from a few hundred yards away."

"I'm simply observing," Kaiden explained. "I'll take the shot when it's closer. At full charge, Sire can break shielding, disrupt barriers, and melt through heavy armor. I may not eliminate it in one shot, but I should do some damage, and we can go from there."

"And what's the plan if it turns out we can't hurt it?" Chief asked.

He remained silent for a moment, then tensed and whispered, "It's here."

The droid cruised slowly into the street. It stood a little over normal human height, perhaps seven to seven and a half feet tall. Contrary to all the different visages Kaiden had imagined it having, it was rather plain. A pure silver body with chunks missing, either from not being complete or lost in combat, revealed black and gray wires within. Long, cylindrical gauntlets encased its forearms, and five slender fingers opened and closed rhythmically on each hand. Its head moved slowly from side to side, its face featureless with the exception of one wide, round compartment in the middle—possibly an eye or an emblem of some kind.

"You know, it kind of looks like how I would imagine you would look if you were a droid," he remarked.

Chief's eye narrowed, and his body flared to an annoyed red. *"I don't appreciate the comparison."*

The mechanical took a few more steps. Kaiden noted its tripod-like feet with two long talons in front and one at the back, which indicated that it could probably climb the sides of buildings with no issue. He primed his gun when the droid took several rapid steps, possibly because it had detected him. However, it stopped again and resumed what seemed to be a scan of the area.

"Something's up. It's closing in, but it still can't find us." Kaiden frowned and shook his head. "Its long-range detection might be crap, but its visuals seem to be fine, considering that it stands still and bobs its head around like a muskrat. He squinted and focused hard. "I don't see anything that could be a sign of shielding or a barrier."

"There is something, though," Chief informed him.

"What have you seen?"

"I'm not entirely sure," Chief said in a puzzled tone. *"I'm using the scanner. The normal readings show nothing, but that upgrade Chiyo got us added a few new options and readouts, and it's picked up a trace amount of some sort of energy. It would be more accurate to say minuscule amounts of several types of energies."*

"Meaning what, exactly?" Kaiden asked and raised Sire again as the droid began to patrol the street ponderously. "My guess would be that it's reading the power source and maybe traces of residual from weapons fire."

"I already calculated that. Besides, if this thing hasn't attacked anything in almost a day, that would have dissipated by now." Chief's eye pulsed in thought. *"It's like something is powered on but not in active use. Whatever it is, it has a similar structure to a shield and a barrier."* His eye stopped glowing as the rest of his body dimmed. *"Kaiden, I have a suggestion."*

"What are you thinking?" The droid was now within

firing range, but he held off from pulling the trigger. "Make it quick, Chief."

"If you fire a fully charged shot, you'll have to vent immediately, right? Even with whatever upgrades you and Wolfson slapped onto that thing, it's at least eight seconds for a full cycle."

"Yeah?" he answered, wondering what the EI had in mind.

"Fire at half—no, a third of a charge," Chief ordered. *"Even a quick burst is enough to compromise medium armor, and a slightly charged shot should be sufficient to hit it quickly from this distance. Aim for a weak spot—one of the areas that is vulnerable to internal damage. That way, we'll see if it's hiding any sort of defenses, and we won't be completely caught off-guard when it comes our way."*

Kaiden tapped his finger on the trigger guard as he considered the instructions. "If it doesn't have any sort of defenses outside of the armor, a fully-charged shot might not destroy it, but it wouldn't be in any condition to fight."

"If it does have defenses, you will have to wait to recharge, and it will know where you are and be as pissed as an unfeeling automaton can be," Chief countered.

With an understanding nod and a heavy sigh, Kaiden balanced his rifle on the edge of the wall in front of him and aimed at the bot, now immediately across the street and looking into the opposite building. He chose a weak section on its back where he saw a patchwork composed of small sections of metal spliced together to cover the area rather than to act as armor. Exhaling a slow breath, he pressed his finger on the trigger for two seconds and watched as the circular light in the scope filled up to the marked point to indicate a third of a charge before he fired at the droid.

The charge rocketed forward for only a second and almost connected with the target, but as it drew near, a flash of blue light erupted from the mechanical body and dissipated before it struck its mark.

"What the hell was that, Chief?" Kaiden gasped.

"That was a shield," the EI stated. *"As I deduced, it's not always active. It seems to respond and flare up when the droid is in danger. From what I can see, it acts like a pulse. That must be a way for the droid to remain undetected and conserve power when in the field."*

"I saw it break." Kaiden took aim again and charged another shot. "It won't have time to recharge. I'll take it out." He fired another shot, this one slightly stronger. The droid turned toward him, and its eye narrowed as the blast hurtled toward it. Instead of moving out of the way, it walked forward. When the shot came close, there was another flash. The blast erupted to create a cloud of debris around it, but it was unharmed.

"It doesn't create a constant shield, Kaiden, only one that's strong enough to block your attacks," Chief told him. *"I don't think you'll be able to get through with those shots."*

Kaiden retrieved a thermal from his belt, activated it, and threw it at the droid as it bent in preparation to leap at him. It saw the thermal and grabbed it. The blue light of the shield enveloped the droid's hand as the explosive went off with a muffled blast, and a stream of smoke puffed from the clenched appendage. Once again, it remained undamaged.

"Oh, this is turning out poorly," he muttered, venting

his gun as he backed away. He took a shock grenade from the other container.

"Quick! Before it gets up here, we need to—" Chief was interrupted by a rush of air as the droid sailed overhead and crashed onto the rooftop. It remained unmoving for a moment before its arms stretched out to its sides and it looked up into the air, then down at him.

"Is it...posing?" Kaiden wondered and eyed Chief in his visor. "You can't tell me that that's something you wouldn't do."

"Really? You're being snarky at a time like this?"

"Keeping my spirits up and all that," he retorted as he activated a shock grenade and threw it at the feet the mechanical. It didn't even acknowledge it as it went off. Streaks of electricity consumed its body, but before Kaiden's confidence could swell, his mouth dropped open when his adversary whirred alarmingly. The electricity began to dissipate, and the light in its eye grew brighter.

"What in the—"

"It has some sort of generator that absorbs the electricity and converts it into power for the droid," Chief stated. "You gave it the equivalent of a hot meal."

"It has something like that? Unfinished, my ass!" Kaiden snapped as he shut the vent on his gun.

"It lacks a paint job," Chief pointed out. "And you'll note that it hasn't tried to tear your arms off yet. Maybe it— Oh, I think I jinxed us."

The droid extended one of its arms, and the fingers folded back against the gauntlet as a bright white light issued from the appendage. Kaiden held the trigger of his rifle, but instead of firing at the droid, he jumped up and fired at the ground a few feet in front of him. The blast knocked him back as his attacker fired a stream of energy at him. It missed as he tumbled across the rooftop, and instead of being stopped by it, hurtled over the wall. He snatched at it as he fell and instinctively began to pull himself up. At the unmistakable sound of the droid's approach, he hesitated and looked down to see which was the better option.

It looks like it can only take one shot at a time," Chief informed him as readings began to flash rapidly in the HUD. *"But considering the energy you gifted him, it'll be able to fire in only a few seconds."* More loud thuds confirmed the droid's continued approach. *"But from what we've seen so far, that doesn't seem to be this guy's style anyway."*

Kaiden looked down again and thought frantically. He was at the top of a seven-story building. His armor did have force dampeners that would enable him to survive the fall, but it wasn't built for that purpose, and it would hurt like a bastard.

He looked up as one of the droid's tri-clawed legs clunked atop the wall. The sight aided the decision to take the fall. He shoved his rifle quickly onto his back and let go as the mechanical arms swung over to grab him. Kaiden flailed in an effort to correct and braced himself as the ground approached rapidly. He landed and rolled and ignored a burst of pain in his legs and hips as he pushed to his feet to sprint along the street and put distance between himself and his attacker. It didn't appear to be able to move very quickly.

Another rush of air caught his attention, and he grimaced as he glanced over his shoulder. The mechanical had leapt off the building and now soared effortlessly over him. Oh, right, it *could* do *that*.

It brought its cannon to bear again and took aim. Kaiden drew Debonair and turned to fire in the hope that he could sink a shot into the cannon. He managed to get off a couple of shots, and while it didn't cause the weapon to backfire as he had hoped, it did do something. The blast wasn't as powerful as before, and it only fired a short burst that knocked the droid back to land some yards away.

Kaiden turned a corner into an alley, then leaned against the wall and took a moment to catch his breath as he thought about how to approach this.

"I think it's obvious I won't outrun this thing," he muttered. "When it prepares to fire seems to be the only time I can get a clean shot, but with a beam like that, it can trace me if I try to run or roll out of the way."

"I was able to get more info," Chief interjected. *"As we thought, it doesn't have a proper power source to run everything at full power, but it micromanages the hell out of the power it has. Things like the pulse shielding and the concentrated bursts of fire show quick spikes in energy, and it jumps to cover distances instead of running because it uses less power. If we can somehow overwhelm it, you can finish it off."*

"That's something, at least." Kaiden acknowledged. "But right now I'm too vulnerable, and we don't know the extent of what it has available. If we could get it into an enclosed space or distract it somehow, I could—" A group of *somethings* rushed by outside the alley, and he squinted at the drones that had materialized in the air. "Are those his buddies?"

As if in answer, they began to fire—but not at him.

Instead, they fired down the street at the droid. Voices yelled and shouted commands before volleys of lasers came from behind the drones. He looked at the mechanicals again and zoomed in on them with his visor.

They were tagged with a blue halo composed of ones and zeros—the symbol of the Azure Halo gang.

CHAPTER TEN

"*They're still alive?*" Chief asked, seemingly as shocked as Kaiden was despite his usual air of aplomb.

"I guess so," the ace mumbled as he inched closer to the wall of the opposite building. He peered out, careful to remain out of sight of the drones. A group of about fifteen men and women in various distressed outfits with at least one article in the dark-blue hue of their organization's main color were focused on his enemy. "Did they come back from somewhere? I know I was a little busy, but I didn't see any ships in the sky."

"*I didn't pick anything up either. In fact, I don't pick anything up on the scanner at all.*"

"They're right there."

Chief's eye narrowed in annoyance. "*I can see that, idiot. My guess is that they're using some sort of device to mask their readings. They've probably been laying low this whole time.*"

"I guess all the ruckus brought them out," he reasoned as various beams and orbs hurtled past him at the killer droid. "They are really laying into it."

"It looks like we have the distraction we needed," Chief observed. "So, did you actually have a plan, or were you simply talking nonsense?"

"I was dreaming something up," he admitted and ran down the alley to the other end. "Right now, we need to see what's happening. It might be preoccupied with having to deal with them. If I can sneak around and get behind it, I might be able to take a clean shot at its back and do some damage."

"It wasn't ready for you the first time you fired on it," Chief reminded him. "Your plan is to beat it through bug bites?"

Kaiden turned into the empty street and another large building, this one in much worse shape than any he had seen thus far, caught his attention. He stopped running for a moment and observed it as a new thought popped into his head. "I think I'll make that my plan B," he said, then hurried over to the building, and retrieved his container of thermals.

"What are you thinking?"

Kaiden put Debonair away and gathered his remaining grenades. "That I'll take this thing out with a bang."

"Keep firing. Kit, are you able to crack it?" Janis, the current leader of the remaining Halos—or what amounted to their leader due to natural succession after a pile of bodies had amassed—yelled.

"Nothing doing, Jan!" Kit answered. "It's completely blocked any sort of remote port. I'll have to get— Shit, *look out!*"

Janis saw the droid step forward, leap, and snatch two of the seven drones out of the air. The others banked out of the way, but once it landed, it spun and flung the captured fliers at two others. They collided with each other and dropped in a broken heap. The remaining drones regrouped to fly in front of the droid. Their light lasers rearmed and fired, and a dim blue shimmer showed that they struck nothing but shielding.

"Keep on it!" Janis instructed as he raised his Tempest machine gun and fired at the mechanical. "Needle it down. What were you saying, Kit?"

"That I can't do a damn thing unless I have direct access." She deactivated her holoscreen, drew an Acolyte pistol, and charged a shot. "After what it did to the others it got close to, I ain't volunteering for that!"

Janis' Tempest overheated, and he sighed and motioned for Fitz and Shala to move up as he vented his gun. "I guess we'll have to go with the heavy option. Where the hell are Zeek and Dobi? We need those cannons if we're gonna punch through."

"They sent a message a few minutes ago. They are on the way," Rani informed him as he vented his rifle. "I'm not sure how fast they can move in that heavy armor."

"Get the rest of the drones on the attack," he ordered. "Keep it distracted so that when they do come it won't— Everyone, *get down!*"

The droid stood tall, both its arms outstretched and formed into cannons. The Halo members scattered quickly or dropped to the ground as the weapons primed and fired, destroying the remaining drones in a swath of bright light.

The beams hurtled over Kit's head, and she flattened herself instinctively to avoid them.

"I guess it can still see us," Fitz groaned.

"Smart deduction, idiot," Janis barked and knelt to activate a holoscreen and summon the last of the drones. "The covert drives only mask our vitals. Even if it was visually impaired, we're still shooting at it."

"Jan, it's getting closer," Kit warned. She could hear it stomp toward them and the hum of its cannons as they charged.

"It's about to fire again," Rani called. "I thought there was a twelve-second cooldown period before it could fire again?"

"The energy reading is stronger than it was an hour ago," Kit stated, her hand against her helmet as she studied her HUD. "How did it get juiced?"

"Here come the drones!" Janis yelled. A dozen flew in, and a mixture of light lasers and kinetic rounds flew at the droid. It looked up and aimed at the invaders. The hacker leader took manual control of ten of them and used one finger each to control them on his holoscreen. He moved them around to try to avoid the blasts.

"Rani, give me an update on Zeek and Dobi. The rest of you keep firing," he ordered.

The remaining members of the Azure Halos took their positions or pivoted around the walls and barricades they used for cover and fired at the droid. It released intermittent waves of shielding to block the fire, but a few shots got through. Slowly, they were wearing it down.

"They are two hundred and thirteen meters away," Rani shouted. "They'll be here soon using the jump jets."

Janis nodded and ducked as the droid fired to eliminate a couple of the drones before it lowered its cannons. Curses and pained cries indicated that it had taken out at least a couple more of his friends.

"If Dudley was still alive, I'd kill him myself for bringing this thing here," he declared as he set the drones on autopilot and grasped his Tempest. "And Mara too, for bringing it back online. Whatever amount of creds we would have gotten for this was not worth it."

"It was close to fifty million," Fitz said and fired from beside Janis as the leader took aim and continued to fire. "I still say we should salvage what hardware we can and see what we can get on the UGM."

"We'll worry about that when it's in pieces," Janis told him. "But I'll comb through every log we have to see who requested this thing, then we're gonna raid their accounts for every cred they have."

"We should probably have done that in the beginning," Fitz said tartly. "The droid isn't so tough. It's easy to dodge the beams when it telegraphs them so obviously."

As if the droid had heard him, the fingers on its right side formed back into a hand. It lurched toward one of the members in the front and grabbed him by the neck to crush him with a sickening crack, then whipped the corpse at a nearby Halo member. The heavy boots knocked against his head to drive him back into a wall. The mechanical then aimed its cannon directly at Janis and Fitz.

"Shit, that thing can move like that?" Fitz barked.

Janis dropped his Tempest and grabbed the other man by his arm. "Everyone, get back!" he ordered, flinging himself and Fitz into an alley as the droid fired. Instead of the expected beam, an orb passed them, and his eyes widened.

The projectile impacted and exploded, followed by a wave of force. It was an offensive attack, but he guessed that wasn't the main objective as light enveloped his vision. "Look out, it's coming!"

Janis' warning came too late. Shouts of confusion and shock mingled with the droid's rapid movement as he waited for his vision to clear. Fitz grabbed him and hauled him to the side and through a doorway into the building beside them.

"Janis, open your eyes. Are you all right?" he asked.

"Where's the droid?" he demanded, blinking rapidly to clear his vision. Fitz dragged him out the other entrance of the shack. "Where's the droid?"

"Where do you think, man?" his companion answered through clenched teeth. "Tearing up the rest of the gang. If we don't—"

"Janis, are you there?" Zeek asked over the comm. "Dobi and I are around the corner. You guys need to get away so we can—"

"When you see it, *fire*," Janis ordered. "It's tearing everyone apart anyway. Smoke it."

"Not a problem." He signed off.

"Janis! Fitz!" Kit called. They looked up as she skidded behind a desk through a hole in the wall of the building in front of them.

"Get down. Zeek and Dobi are about to…" Janis' words were drowned out by the scream of two blasts that roared through the street beside them. The impact was deafening.

Fitz and Janis sprawled on the floor and covered their ears. Eruptions of red and blue energy flared, followed by a static shriek and a swirl of smoke and electricity.

Fitz slowly lowered his hands and opened his eyes. "Did we get it?" he asked Janis, only to see their leader race out into the street.

Zeek and Dobi, in heavy armor and wielding cannons, approached Janis. He looked at the area of the impact, hoping to see the scattered remains of the droid.

Instead, he saw a glinting white light among the dark smoke.

"No! No way could it still be alive."

"It's what?" Zeek asked.

Janis turned to warn them, but Kit and Fitz tackled him as the droid blasted a beam through the smoke. It tore into Dobi's armor and panned to the left to bisect Zeek before either could utter a word. The top halves of their bodies dropped clumsily, followed by their lower sections.

The three hackers stared as the droid approached. Its body crackled with blue light, pieces of its armor had fallen off, and electricity sputtered along one of its arms, but it was still moving. Kit's and Fitz's eyes widened in horror, but Janis seethed in rage. Transfixed by their helplessness, the three could only await their inevitable fate.

The mechanical brought its claws out as it came closer and clicked them together dramatically. As it raised one of its arms, a blast of green energy struck it from behind and forced it to its knees. Janis looked up to see where that blast had come from, hoping to find some other Halos alive. Instead, he saw a figure in dark armor venting a rifle.

Before he could ask either of his teammates if they

knew who it was, they grasped him under the arms and hauled him away as the droid spun and fired a blast at the stranger. The armored figured ducked into the alley they had been in and avoided the blast as the droid lurched after him.

Kaiden nearly stumbled from the blast behind him but managed to right himself before he fell. He continued his sprint, and the now-familiar rush of air warned him that the droid was preparing to leap. That confirmed that he had its full attention.

"Are you ready, Chief?"

"I am," the EI stated calmly. "But you know that for this to work, it's all on you, right? I simply have to press a button. You have to avoid about ten different ways to die."

"That's usually the average." Kaiden chuckled and glanced back as the mechanical landed on top of the shack. He almost laughed as it crashed through the roof while he readied another shot, then backpedaled as he aimed and fired. It crashed through the wall into the blast. A shield flared up, but it was still knocked onto its back. Apparently, the cannon shots from the Halo members had finally caused some real damage. His plan looked less foolhardy and more like overkill.

Assuming it worked.

He made his way to the shoddy building he'd seen before, ran through it, and primed a shot that he fired at the wall in front of him to create an opening. The building shifted around him.

"Come on, you piece of junk," he muttered as he turned to the entrance and waited for the droid. "Get in here."

Kaiden saw nothing and wondered if it was trying to bait him instead. Chief flared in the HUD. *Kaiden—energy spike above!*

"What?" he barked and glanced up at the ceiling.

Move anywhere.

He jumped back as a beam melted through the ceiling above and scorched the ground where he had been. It began to sweep the floor, and he backed away as it drew closer. When it stopped, he heard loud thuds and a crash above. "Sneaky bastard."

It's in the building like you wanted. Time to do the thing.

Kaiden nodded and ran out of his makeshift exit as the droid continued to descend. "Blow it, Chief!"

Get some more distance. We don't know which way—"

"I'll keep going. Blow it!" he demanded. Chief dimmed as **Activated** flashed across his HUD. The thermals he had scattered around the pillars in the building exploded behind him, but he didn't look back to see if the droid had been caught in the blast. That would have simply been insurance. He focused instead on the unmistakable sounds as the building began to topple and collapse in on itself after its supports disintegrated.

The implosion of stone, glass, and metal kicked up a wall of dust that enveloped Kaiden. He peered back to make sure the building wasn't falling toward him. It looked like it was being swallowed whole by the earth as it collapsed into itself. He slid to a halt as many tons of rubble shifted and thundered—hopefully onto the droid.

The ace scanned the surroundings for readings of

power among the dust and debris. Finding one, he grasped his rifle and went back in.

"What's it doing, Chief?"

"It's in there somewhere, but I don't read anything that resembles a shield or laser fire. It looks like it's focusing its energy."

He raised his rifle when he identified the outline of the droid in his visor. It was stuck under literally tons of rock and metal, but it somehow held the top half of its body up. The arms shook under the weight, and although he couldn't see it, the silhouette of its energy reading showed it looking up at him as the energy began to condense in its chest.

"Kaiden, it's trying to—"

"I know," he stated, charged a full shot, and fired directly toward the massive chest. The blast evaporated the droid's armor and power source, and the head popped off and rolled down the pile of the building's remains as the debris the droid had held up collapsed. The thud generated a gust of wind that scattered the dust around Kaiden and cleared his vision. The head rolled along the ground, and he stopped it with his foot.

"I've seen Genos do that plenty—trying to overcharge its core to self-destruct." He rested his foot on the droid's head. "A malicious, sneaky, and dirty bastard." Kaiden holstered Sire as he bent and picked up the mechanical's dusty skull. "Good riddance."

CHAPTER ELEVEN

Gloomily, he examined the head and contemplated how much of a bounty this would qualify him for, considering that he would, at best, bring in about a tenth of the mechanical. Kaiden's thoughts were distracted by someone running up the street. He placed his hand on his belt, ready to engage, as a trio of Azure Halo members approached him.

"Who are— Wait, is that the droid?" the one in front asked, a tall man with tanned skin and dyed blue hair worn in a short mohawk style. His voice was hoarse but still quite loud. He was flanked by a pale girl with a brunette bob hidden under what appeared to be an ancient aviator-style cap and a lanky blond man with sunglasses whose lenses had cracked during all the commotion.

Kaiden looked from them to the droid's head. "What's left of it." He balanced the head in the palm of his hand for a moment before he tucked it under his arm. "The rest is under there somewhere." He pointed to the mound of what had once been a building.

"Man, I know this town ain't much to look at, but do you really think we can simply destroy buildings when they become an eyesore?" the lanky one asked as he scowled at the pile of rubble.

"I am neither in construction nor décor," Kaiden said easily. "The damn thing wouldn't die, and I don't have a nuke or EMP to detonate on a whim. This seemed to be the best option to make damn sure it stayed down." His grip tightened around the head. "It did try to blow itself up before going down. Would any of you nerds like to guess how much damage that would have done?"

The one with the blue mohawk frowned, but the girl spoke quickly. "Considering the core we used was an Axiom model and the amount of power that the droid could have condensed, it could probably have leveled at least a couple of blocks."

Kaiden sighed at hearing the corporation's name. "Even when I'm not on a mission for them, they somehow find a way to screw me over," he mumbled heatedly under his breath, "So which one of you thought it would be a good idea to activate an unfinished assault-slash-battle-slash-serial-killer droid?"

The blue mohawk man stepped forward. "None of us. The one who stole it and the one who turned it on are both dead."

"Well, I'm sorry they lived long enough to make a such a monumentally stupid decision," Kaiden retorted sarcastically. "What exactly was y'all's endgame here?"

"Who the hell are you?" the man demanded. "Why are you here? Are you some sort of WC operative?"

"No, but they were next," Kaiden admitted. He moved

the head out from under his arm and spun it in his hand. "I'm here on a gig to retrieve this thing and turn it in. In a weird way, I guess it's a different kind of luck for you. Otherwise, I would probably have had to mow you guys down to get it instead."

"You're another merc, huh?" the lanky one interjected as the leader tried to speak. "We've had to deal with you assholes ever since we took that thing."

"Yeah. If you steal a piece of equipment from a corporation that really wants it back, that is the usual outcome," he pointed out.

"We've stolen plenty of things before, and hacked into some big-time databases too," the girl stated. "We never had to deal with as many problems as that droid gave us."

"Take it as a lesson to keep to your lane," he advised and tossed the droid's head into the air. The trio watched it move up and then down before Kaiden caught it. "You're a hacker gang. Why branch out when you have a good thing going?"

"What do you know about being a part of something like this?" the leader asked as he drew a pistol and aimed it at Kaiden. "Do you know how many of my friends I've lost in the last two days?"

Kaiden held a finger up and then pointed at the ground. The leader didn't bite, but the other two looked down. They tried to jump back, but the three were caught in a discharge of electricity from one of his shocks and were hurled to the ground, where their bodies contorted in pain.

"I threw that down when I tossed the droid's head into the air," he stated as he placed the head back under his arm and walked up to them. "Neat trick, huh?"

The three were too busy spasming to reply.

"Anyway, I'd go ahead and get out of here, but I'm in something of a tough spot. I have no transport outside of my own two legs." He looked at the three and waited for their motor functions to return to something resembling normal. "Would any of you be willing to help me out?"

"F-f-fuck y-you," the leader hissed through chattering teeth.

Kaiden sighed as he drew Debonair and aimed it at him. "I have to admit, it's impressive that you still have your pride after all this, but now would be a good time to show a little humility." He looked off to the side for a moment. "To extend an olive branch. It's something I've only started learning myself."

"You c-can h-h-have my j-jet bike," the girl stammered. Kaiden turned his attention to her after a last look at the leader before he holstered his gun.

He stepped over the man and knelt beside her. "And where would that be?"

"Go down the s-street. Take a l-l-left and go down three blocks, and i-it'll be in a rack with f-five others," she explained. Her mouth still trembled from the shocks, but she seemed to have calmed a little. "Take the sensor—o-on my hat. It'll activate it. The bike is black and w-white. It's fully charged."

Kaiden nodded and took a small circular device from her cap. "Much obliged." He nodded his thanks, stood, and walked away from the downed trio, but stopped after a few steps. "For what it's worth, I do know what it's like to call a ragtag group of misfits friends and family. I can be a little cynical, and yeah, your friends made some stupid decisions that cost all of you, but I mean this." He looked back for a moment, and the leader rolled his head to look at him as Kaiden opened his helmet's visor to reveal his downcast eyes. "I am sorry you lost so many." He closed his visor and turned away. "Mourn them, and make sure it doesn't happen again."

With that, he left them to recover as he went to get the jet bike and leave this town with another job completed.

Gin sat on a plush couch and glanced around the abode provided for him by his benefactor. He had been rather busy over the last couple of months, so he hadn't had time to appreciate his current place of residence.

It was certainly a few steps up from the derelict ships and abandoned labs where he usually laid his head, but it lacked their ambiance.

He stood, and the silk robe he wore dragged on the floor as he walked up to Macha and took the blade into his hands. It occurred to him, as he examined it keenly, that he needed to take the time to have a night out with her. The event in the underground had been the last time she had received any use, and he realized that he'd allowed other distractions to render him a little idle when it came to his preferred pastimes.

Tracing his finger lightly along the blade, he recalled one event about a year or so ago when a soldier had demanded to know why he was a killer—why he felt the need to kill. To him, it was hypocrisy that a *soldier* of all things had admonished him for his occupation, hobby, passion, whatever one would title his actions. If this soldier could kill under the belief that he did this in defense of his loved ones and the ideologies of his homeworld, why could he not do the same for his own philosophies? Along with having a bit of fun, of course.

Granted, he also remembered being too enraged by the question to engage in civil reasoning. If he recalled correctly, his reply was, "If you were better at it I would be dead, not a killer." Which was true enough, but it wasn't usually like him to be so flat when a chance at conversation presented itself. He hadn't even given the soldier a chance to retort before he'd thrust Macha into his eye.

Gin set the blade down and tapped a finger on his chin as he thought. Perhaps he should use the opportunity to add another branch to his legacy. After all, he was good with many more things than blades. That was how he had gotten his current job—an honest one that required almost all of his unique talents and probably the first "honest" piece of work he'd had in about a decade.

His thought was interrupted by a ringing sound. His communicator blinked, and considering that the only one with the number to it was his current benefactor, he decided he should probably answer it.

He sauntered over to the screen and accepted the call, folded his arms, and adopted a lazy smile. "Good evening, Zubanz. How are—"

"What do you think you are doing?" the businessman snapped. A vein throbbed visibly on his forehead as his wrathful eyes stared from the screen.

Gin's smile fell, replaced by a quizzical frown "I would ask if this is a bad time, but you called me."

"Two nights ago, one of my partner's labs was broken into and a device was stolen," Zubanz growled, and his eyes continued to bore into Gin. "A device being worked on for another one of my partners. No one talked until we injected serums into the lead technician. One for anxiety, one for mental clarity, and one for stimulation. Through his drug-addled haze, he said you were the one to take it."

"A device…" He hummed and played coy, then snapped his fingers in mock realization. "Project Wormwood? So dead Professor Lumiya is doing well, then? How's his daughter?"

"Don't get cute, Gin," Zubanz warned. "The professor was so afraid of telling us what happened that even with the drugs, he collapsed in fear when he finally admitted that you broke in and stole it. He had to be rushed to a hospital." After a few heavy breaths, Zubanz did what he could to compose himself and leaned back from the screen. "What were you thinking?" he hissed. "I gave you the job of sneaking into Nexus Academy and taking that experimental EI. It's been months since then. What is your game?"

"My game is your job," the killer stated equably, seemingly oblivious to the chairman's rage. "And I'm playing by my rules. Even someone like me can't simply waltz into the top ark academy in the world like I could, for example, break into a lab developing a new type of stealth technology."

Zubanz clenched the fist on his deck, and his nostrils flared. "I told you, if you needed something we could provide, to contact the broker I set you up with and we would handle it."

"I did. It took him three days to get back to me, and he told me it would take several months to get the device." Gin leaned against the desk behind him. "He had to wait for tests and all that to complete, then had to make up a cover story for where it was going. I figured that was far too long to wait. I assumed you wanted this done as quickly as possible, so I decided to take care of it myself at no extra charge."

"You could have caused an incident," Zubanz pointed out and slammed his fist on the desk. Ice rattled in the glass beside him.

The killer's fingernails dug into the wood of the desk, and his eyes narrowed at Zubanz's accusations. "But I did not. Since you said you did your research into me, you should know that I usually handle such situations very differently," he reminded the man. "I did that as a favor, thinking it would mean we could avoid having a discussion like this."

The chairman went silent and looked at his desk, but his hand clenched and unclenched to the rhythm of what Gin assumed was the man's heartbeat. "Never do anything that affects the organization. Ever," he finally stated unequivocally. "I should remind you that no matter how good you are, you are on a planet where millions of soldiers, officers, bounty hunters, and mercs are searching for you—not to mention what I alone could do to end your little escapades."

The killer said nothing as he stared at Zubanz, who continued to avoid his gaze. "If you want to think of this as a game, know you are nothing more than a pawn. One I am paying, which means I control you. You will do what I say and get this done." The chairman looked up at last and stared at him once more with angry eyes. "Never bite the hand that feeds you, Gin. If you do, that hand will grip your jaw and tear it off." With that, he raised a finger and ended the call.

He stood motionless for a moment, except for a single finger that tapped the desk. Finally, he straightened and disrobed before he wandered over to the compartment with his gear. There was something else he needed and he would have taken the chance to ask Zubanz if he could make it happen, but the man had been uncouth and hadn't given him the opportunity. He pressed the switch to open the compartment, and his armor was revealed. After a moment's thought, he turned and picked Macha up and twirled the blade in his hand. He contemplated Zubanz's warning. "Don't bite the hand that feeds lest you get your jaw ripped out."

That simply meant he would have to bite through the hand and sever it before it had the chance.

Gin glanced at Macha and caught his reflection in the blade. He wanted to smile, but all he saw was his grim façade. He would usually take care to maintain the same requirements as he had at the previous lab. Now, however, that was pointless if Zubanz wouldn't acknowledge the obvious goodwill he had demonstrated. Instead, he would simply have to show him what could have happened.

He took Macha's sheath from the compartment and slid her in. With deft movements, he took each piece of armor out and put it on. After he was done, he was sure that his benefactor would make another call, but he didn't like how impersonal that call felt.

When he had finally obtained the last item on his list, he would allow Zubanz to speak of his grievances in person.

Then, the chairman would see that he was *not* his better.

CHAPTER TWELVE

K aiden gazed out of the window of the carrier into the early afternoon light as Nexus Academy came into view when the transport turned onto the mountain access road.

"You, uh, gonna keep ignoring those messages?" Chief asked. He appeared on the ace's lap and looked up at him.

"I'm gonna be there in ten minutes," Kaiden retorted and continued to stare absentmindedly out the window.

"Well, I tried to tell you on the flight back to Seattle."

"I find messaging impersonal."

The EI gave him a quizzical look. *"More impersonal than not responding?"*

"Are you my caretaker now?" he asked and glared at him with an expression of real displeasure.

Chief shrank his artificial body and floated to his shoulder. *"I worry sometimes. Plus, you haven't had a proper sleep or eaten your veggies."*

"Spare me," Kaiden said flippantly. "My head still isn't on completely straight at the moment."

"I told you four bottles would be over your level," the EI mocked and turned an amused pink.

"Celebration knows no limits," he defended. as he rubbed his temple.

"Not when you leave dignity with the coats." Chief chuckled.

He looked out the window again, his stare fixed on the fish that jumped out of the water. "I completed a level-seven mission and got a good deal on that jet bike." He crossed his legs and leaned back. "A double win."

"You know that Halo chick probably had some sort of tracker on that thing."

"Hey, it's not my property anymore." Although Kaiden didn't look, he could visualize Chief's eye-roll.

"Technically, it was not yours to begin with," he grumbled. *"All for a little R and R after a gig. But you did burn through more than your allotted time. You're gonna have some workshops to make up."*

"Yeah, that'll probably take the rest of my day." Kaiden sighed. "All for the better, I guess. I'm not sure going into the Animus with the last of a hangover is the best idea."

"You managed to fly back in with a hangover all right."

He raised a hand and tilted it from side-to-side. "Kinda. It was a test of willpower and abdominal fortitude."

"Remember when Luke and Cameron went in after a night of partying?"

He laughed heartily. "Yeah, that was probably one of the few times they went into the med bay that wasn't because of me."

"I'm reasonably sure you should probably not say that last part so nonchalantly," Chief prodded.

Kaiden shrugged. "They know what they're signing up for when they jump into the pods with me." He glanced up again as the Academy drew closer. "By the time I check in and put my weapons and armor away, it will be around lunchtime. I should probably meet up with everyone and see how they're doing on their tests."

"Probably farther along than you are," Chief chastised. *"Between getting to the mission, completing it, then 'celebrating' before you returned, you've burned through three and a half days of the allotted time."*

"We'll be good. We still have two weeks left," the ace pointed out.

"Eleven, or rather ten days, actually, if you consider the fact that you'll probably spend the rest of the day and most of tomorrow catching up and heading to classes." Chief popped a small screen open and acted as if he was reading it instead of simply bringing the files up. *"I won't go through the whole thing, but the* CliffsNotes *are that Genos and Chiyo both sent roughly a dozen messages asking about your whereabouts and which days they should schedule to complete the long mission test."*

"They need to have more faith in the team."

Chief scoffed, *"Oh, that's rich."*

"Or at least in me."

"There we go."

The carrier drove up the long road to the entrance of the Academy and waited for the barrier to lower. Kaiden stroked his chin. "I'm serious, though. We got off-world, and in a matter of a few hours, we found a location for the base—ship, station, whichever. All that's left is to get in, blow it up or otherwise compromise it, and then get the hell out of Dodge." Kaiden clapped melodramatically. "Done and done. If we don't finish it the next time we drop in, it'll be done the time after that, no worries."

"I'm inclined to agree, for the most part," Chief said as he floated up to the window and twirled around. *"But you should also agree that the missions and training sims you've gone on have definitely stepped up this year—and the ones last year weren't exactly a cakewalk."*

"I make things look good, not easy," Kaiden retorted. "Sometimes both happen, but only occasionally." He straightened, stretched, and prepared to disembark as the barrier around the Academy lowered. "It's more than only me, Chief. I have a damn good team who know what they are doing, but as I said, they need more confidence." He looked at the small orb. "That includes you, by the way."

"Aw, well, ain't that sweet," the EI chirped, and returned to its normal golden hue. *"So how much of that was hot air?"*

"Hot air? None, of course," Kaiden stated and folded his arms sternly before he looked off to the side. "Cockiness? Fifty to sixty percent."

"That's about what my bullshit meter detected." Chief chuckled.

"Just remember…" Kaiden began as he stood and hauled his container from the compartment above him, "that means the rest was honest."

───

Hundreds of students were walking around during free time or lunch when Kaiden left the office and looked at the plaza. He remembered feeling overwhelmed the first few times he saw the hordes of soldiers, techies, medics, and the like, but now it was oddly comforting.

"All right, Chief, set me to active on the network and let's see where the others are."

"Doing it. Bringing up a map on your oculars."

He whipped the shades from his jacket, put them on, and immediately identified a few green spots some yards ahead near the cafeteria. One in particular was in a familiar location.

"Well, let's go and greet the guys and gals. I'm sure they've felt ever so lonely," he said with a smile before his stomach rumbled demandingly. "But first, sustenance should probably be procured."

"I've heard it does wonders for things like continuing to live."

He set his tray down on the table, sprawled in the booth, and smiled at Chiyo across from him, who poked at a piece of fish. "Howdy. Things suddenly feel a little brighter now, huh?"

She continued to poke the partially-eaten fish and completely ignored him.

Kaiden lowered his oculars and blinked a few times. "Is she seriously doing this?" he asked Chief through the clenched teeth under his smile.

"I told you that you were being a dick," the EI chided.

"Yo, Chiyo, are you there?" he asked and waved a hand in front of her.

She looked up, expressionless. "So now would be a good time to answer you?" she asked. He heard annoyance under her affected monotone. "I wondered if you had taken up a new lifestyle that involved no conversation or replies to messages."

"Oh, this might go somewhere fun." Chief chortled, and a small translucent popcorn box appeared beside the avatar.

"When the hell did you get *that* installed?" Kaiden asked, and glared at the lenses.

"Don't look at me. You are my entertainment now."

Kaiden removed the oculars and placed them on the table. "I didn't mean to make it look like I was ignoring you or Genos—or Jaxon or Flynn, come to think of it." He tapped his chin. "Will I have to go through this a few times? I should probably send cards or something."

"They are on their way," Chiyo informed him. "Well, most are. Others, like Flynn and his team, went to the Animus Center to continue their missions."

"Right. Right, I'll get to them," Kaiden stated. "But back to the first thing. I didn't mean anything malicious. I'm sure I've mentioned that I don't really do messaging. It seems too impersonal, you know?"

"More impersonal than not replying?" she questioned.

Even with the oculars off, Kaiden heard a deep laugh from Chief in his head.

"I was coming back, and I was a little preoccupied," he said. "Okay, I was dealing with morning-after problems, but I didn't message y'all the last time I went on a far-off mission."

"That would be because you were bleeding out in the Amazon," she reminded him, and took a mouthful of her meal.

Kaiden was silent for a moment as the mental gears

turned, then the realization hit and his grin dropped. "Oh... Oh, wow! I'm a dick."

"At least you came to the right conclusion quickly enough," she mumbled as she finished a small bowl of glazed carrots.

"Uh, yeah..." Kaiden fumbled for words. "The upgrade you gave me was very helpful."

"I'm glad," she stated and wiped her mouth with a napkin. "The mission was a success, then?"

"Yeah. Yeah, it was." He nodded, and finally felt easy enough to eat his own meal. "I didn't manage to retrieve the droid. Had to destroy it and return what scraps I could, so I ended up with only the head."

"What happened to the rest of it?"

"It's probably still under the building I dropped on it."

Chiyo finally showed some emotion. Her eyes widened in surprise and she looked at him with a mixture of confusion and suspicion, then returned to normal as she sighed. "If nothing else, you come back with interesting stories." She placed her utensils on the tray, folded her hands together, and rested her chin on the backs. "How did you manage that?"

Kaiden's grin returned. "Well, the droid had been activated by the gang members and it had this weird shield, so my normal attacks didn't work. Eventually—"

"Hello, friend Kaiden!" Genos called. Kaiden and Chiyo turned as Genos, Jaxon, Silas, Izzy, and Julius walked up.

"Hey, guys." He waved and quickly finished a piece of tri-tip. "How are ya?"

"Happy to see you," Genos said merrily. "Kin Jaxon was

worried, although I'm sure seeing you has relieved that stress."

Jaxon pressed a hand to his face. "You needn't tell him that, Genos," he muttered, moved the hand away, and raised it in greeting. "It is good to see you back, Kaiden. From what Genos and Chiyo told me, we expected you in yesterday morning."

Kaiden rubbed the back of his head. "I got a little caught up with basking in the glow of victory and all that," he said sheepishly. "I'll, uh…" He looked at Chiyo. "I'll work on messaging in the future."

"Good to know." Julius nodded. "I don't see you that often anyway. I kind of hoped you would have some injuries I could treat for practice."

"I wanted to say that we don't seem to run into each other enough." Kaiden chuckled. "But if that's what it takes, I think I might focus on staying acquaintances."

"We've learned that it's his kind of small talk." Izzy laughed and placed an arm on the biologist's shoulder. "Ever since the Deathmatch, he keeps asking Silas how his foot is even though he damaged it in the Animus."

"Keep in mind that once the Synch ratio gets higher, physical harm will be the norm," Julius pointed out. "Even if it's a foot blown off in the Animus, it will lead to a sprain."

"We *do* have a medbay," Silas said with a glance at Julius as he walked over to Kaiden.

"I could be running it one day," he retorted.

"Considering that I know the daughter of the current lead, I doubt that." Silas chuckled and offered a hand to Kaiden. "Good to see you in one piece. After the last time, I wondered if all your stories of running gigs as a kid had been your imagination."

Kaiden slapped his hand against Silas'. "Even after seeing me in the Animus?"

"I figured she had hacked in and made you look good," he said, nodding at Chiyo.

"She still does, but those kills are all mine," the ace responded.

"So what were you guys talking about before we interrupted?" Izzy asked.

"Kaiden apparently dropped an entire building on a droid," Chiyo said. He watched with amusement as almost all of the present party responded the same way she had, although Genos, for his part, merely blinked and nodded.

"That does seem to align with the normal way Kaiden handles situations," he remarked. "Although it is a new one." He held a hand out to the ace. "Congratulations on your ingenuity when it comes to destruction."

Kaiden smiled and took the Tsuna's hand as Chiyo shook her head. "Genos, you're encouraging him."

"What was that, friend Chiyo?" the mechanist asked.

She waved him off. "Nothing. On to a more pressing matter." She looked at her teammates. "When can we continue our test?"

Kaiden let go of Genos' hand and turned to her. "I have a few things I have to catch up on, but after I get them done, I should be free."

"When do you believe that will be?"

"Tomorrow afternoon sometime. I have a workshop after lunch, but I'll be free after that."

Genos tapped a finger on his infuser. "Ah, right, that

reminds me. Officer Wolfson wished to see you. He said that you haven't been 'grounded' in some time." Genos looked at Kaiden's feet. "You seem to be fine, however. Gravity is affecting you normally."

Kaiden frowned, "Honestly, I'd prefer physics to whatever he might be thinking," he mumbled. "Okay, I have that too. But after that, I'm free."

"Then we'll plan to meet tomorrow in the early evening at the AC?"

Her teammates nodded, and Kaiden glanced at the others. "How're your tests going so far?"

"Pretty well, all things considered," Jaxon told him.

"That's it?" Kaiden asked.

"He's being modest," Silas answered. "He's done most of the work. We started in a cave, and would probably still be stuck there if he hadn't been able to find the exit using a droid's internal tracking system." He looked at Izzy. "It sounds like something a scout would come up with, but what do I know?"

She threw her hands up and rolled eyes as she walked over to Silas. Julius coughed to clear his throat. "Mack, Otto, and I have progressed well. I would say we're over halfway complete, but Otto is a little reluctant to continue."

"Why's that?" Kaiden asked.

"We're on a space station looking for a specific specimen to recover. Otto thought he'd found it, but it turned out to be some sort of fungal growth that attached to his arm. I was able to remove it, but they started to implement allotted time slots to deal with the influx, and we were kicked out before I could administer the pain relievers and all that. Since we were saved in that position, he'll have to deal with it when we first get back in. He's worried I won't be able to heal it fast enough once we start."

Kaiden chuckled at the image. "Most people prefer to not know when the pain will hit. It makes them anxious when they know it's coming."

"Well, I won't fail because of his white-coat syndrome," Julius huffed. "We'll go back in tomorrow as well."

"Maybe we'll see you guys there."

"Well, that could have been more thrilling. It was all right, but I'm not one for sappy friendship episodes," Chief muttered.

"You don't wanna come out and say hi?" Kaiden asked.

"Considering that I am the one who handles your messages? Chiyo might have some words for me, so no," Chief stated flatly. *"But if you don't wanna fall behind any more than you already have, I suggest you finish eating and get to your Ace workshop. It begins in fifteen minutes."*

"Ah, right." Kaiden looked at his meal and began to wolf it down. "Sorry, guys. I gotta get going soon, and I'm famished."

"It's about time we all went to our next workshop," Jaxon agreed as he turned away. Silas and Izzy followed. "Good to see you back. Hopefully, we can go on another mission together once we complete these tests."

"We're in the same Ace class, Jaxon. Where are you going?" Kaiden called after him.

The Tsuna stopped and turned. "To the workshop. I can take my time setting up," he explained. "See you there, Kaiden."

"Brown-noser," he muttered and flashed a quick glance at Genos. "Although Tsuna don't technically have noses. What would the equivalent be?"

Genos stared at him in bewilderment. "I do not know."

The two regarded one another somewhat awkwardly for a moment. "Uh…sorry, Genos, it was kind of a rhetorical question," Kaiden admitted.

"All right, then. I hope you find your answer eventually." Genos nodded. "Today is a free day for me. I'll head to the library for now."

"Same here. Do you mind if I accompany you?" Julius asked.

"Certainly. Perhaps we can become friends. That's where I became friends with Chiyo," Genos explained as the two walked off.

"Uhm, neat. I would like that." Julius continued to chat as they set off.

Kaiden smirked at the pair as Chiyo picked her tray up. "I'll head off as well." She looked quietly at him for a moment. "I'm happy you are safe and that my upgrade was helpful. I'll see you tomorrow."

"See you— Hey Chiyo!" he called as she began to walk away. She paused and looked back. "I'm…sorry if I worried you."

She gave him a small smile. "You did, but apology accepted. Get some rest and be ready. We should be able to complete our mission soon if all goes well."

"I thought the same thing," Kaiden agreed. "I'll be ready."

"I hope so. We have to make up for your lost time," she reminded him before she walked away.

Kaiden sat quietly for a moment. "Is it just me, or has she gotten a lot more snarky lately?"

"I dig it," the EI responded with real approval.

CHAPTER THIRTEEN

The trio opened their eyes as the last trails of light faded away, and the ship's interior took shape within the Animus. Genos took a few moments to blink and regain his composure before he looked at his teammates. "Has everyone adjusted?"

Kaiden nodded, but tilted his head and pointed commandingly at the Tsuna. "I'm all right, but I'd be better if you would take control of the ship right quick."

Genos' eyes widened behind his helmet before he spun in his chair and grasped the flight stick. "Right. Yes. 'Controls before manners' is probably a solid piece of advice."

"Well, considering that the first time we booted in, we were in the aftermath of a crash, it's nice to be back to normal flying for a change." Kaiden watched through the cockpit window as the ship left the final traces of the planet's atmosphere. He glanced down at one of the screens as numbers changed to indicate that the interior of the ship adjusted to being in free space. "But please don't crash into any asteroids or debris, or you'll prove the system right."

Genos responded with a disjointed mutter along the lines of the Animus not taking ingenuity into account or offering to allow Kaiden to fly. Chiyo patted his shoulder before his reaction distracted him too much.

"You are a great pilot, Genos. Kaiden simply tried to deflect that we are supposed to have made greater progress than we have because he was too busy killing brain cells over the last few days."

"After taking out a killer droid that took down most of a gang," he defended. "Although, yes, some brain cells gave their lives in the aftermath. That was better than me going down instead, right?"

"Personally, I don't mind. It makes more room in here," Chief chirped and appeared in the center of the cockpit. *"I've thought of adding a patio."*

"See, Chief is happy," Kaiden pointed out. "And he's never happy."

"I look at it as making the best of a bad situation," the EI countered. *"But we can play it your way. Hopefully, we don't learn that SXP gains are lowered by cell count. Otherwise, you'll need the extra gains simply to be at normal capacity."*

The ace nodded, silent for a moment in thought. "You know, I have a couple of talent points left. I was saving them to get the final point in mutant knowledge, but considering that we're about to raid a pirate station on our lonesome, perhaps I could stick them in one of the more martial talents?"

"That is a possibility," Genos agreed and glanced over his shoulder. "Although I would like to add that you are quite skilled with guns and explosives. I can't see how being able to replicate moves and actions from those martial arts films I have seen would be of great benefit to you—or us, really."

"Style points?" Kaiden responded jokingly. "Fair point. I'll look and see how my weapons talents are. I could probably get more use out of my blade or gauntlet."

"You should always keep your talents up, certainly, but for now, I recommend keeping the points. When we have a better look at the station or anything else along the way, it would be an advantage if at least one of us has the chance to take a skill that might help us surmount a potential obstacle."

"Sounds good. Wait, neither of you has spare points?" Kaiden inquired.

"No," Genos said with a shake of his head. He returned his attention to the front of the ship. "Since I have taken on the designation of pilot, I have had to use additional points to make up for the lack of skill so that I can fly any potential craft we may need to use." He took a moment to glance at his gauntlet. "And, of course, as an engineer, the rest go to furthering my class skills."

"And I'm the only hacker in our whole group outside of Otto," Chiyo added. "I may be gifted, but I can always be better. I developed a list of required talents and have followed it since last year." She looked at Kaiden and made a zero with her hand. "I'm fresh out. I was able to get barely enough SXP to have three points and add another tier to my sabotage talent."

The Tsuna pressed a couple of buttons on the console. "Chief, would you mind returning to your device?"

Chief shrank, floated to Genos, and widened his eye. *"Too much glory to behold, periwinkle?"*

"I'm not sure I can comment on that," Genos responded in an honestly curious tone. "But in this case, it's because I activated the admittedly meager stealth functions on the ship since we will now fly directly into enemy territory. Therefore, we need to lower any energy signatures we can, and while you use your holographic form, you give off an energy signal. It's quite weak, but it is unique, so we could be compromised."

"What a fair and balanced argument you made there! It's quite refreshing." Chief looked at Kaiden. *"I'm used to having orders barked at me, sometimes followed by not-as-witty-as-he-thinks insults."*

Kaiden raised a hand and beckoned Chief with a finger. "Get back in the box, smartass."

The EI rolled his eye before he vanished, and loaded into Kaiden's visor shortly after.

"Did we actually take the time to look around the ship before de-syncing last time?" Chiyo asked.

"We didn't even wait to break the atmosphere," Kaiden mused. "Do you think there are any goodies lying around?"

"Potentially, this is more of a shipping cruiser than a combat craft. If we procured it before they made a delivery or after they stocked it for any reason for trips, there could be items of value on board," Genos reasoned.

"Well, I'm not doing anything at the moment, and leaning against this wall makes my arm fall asleep, so I'll scout around." Kaiden stood, stretched, and turned to walk away before Chiyo called to him,

"Kaiden, take this." She tossed him a small drive. "It's a device you can use to unlock any doors or activate anything that you think might contain something interesting. I loaded Kaitō into it so he'll assist with anything that has a safety rating of five or higher."

Kaiden looked at the device, then flipped it and caught it in the air a couple of times. "That's neat. What's that? Chief says he can handle anything up to a safety rating of six."

"I understand, but this is Kaitō's main function, and he requested to help with anything he can on the mission. Right now, I have nothing for him," Chiyo explained. "I should also point out that Kaitō can deal with devices with a safety rating up to eleven on his own."

"Eleven? I thought the highest rating was ten," Kaiden questioned.

"That's what most corporations want people to think. It's a trap, actually, because currently, the unofficial rating scale goes up to about twenty."

"Damn. How high do you think you can go when it comes to breaking into a system?"

Chiyo pondered it for a moment. "On my own, comfortably around twelve. With Kaitō, I would say maybe sixteen? I haven't had to do so under stressful situations, only during training games and simulations. The highest I had to do in a mission so far is ten."

"That certainly ain't bad. What? No, I won't put my points into remote hacking right now. It's not a necessary skill. The highest we've run into is five. I thought you were over your one-sided squabble? The fox isn't saying anything. He's in the drive, not my helmet!" Kaiden sighed and waved at his teammates. "I'm off. The bright light is getting into his feelings." He walked out of the cockpit, bickering with Chief as he went.

"You know, although I am in awe of Chief's technology, I'm not sure I would trade Viola for him," Genos stated and glanced at Chiyo. "She is much more…agreeable."

"Were Tsuna given a choice of their EI's personality or were you all given pre-mades?" she asked.

"We went through the setup process, although from my understanding, it was not as in-depth as what you went through," he recalled. "We had fewer options, although it was only a couple of years prior that they could actually get the EIs to function for us."

"Why did it take so long? Not all EIs are like Kaiden's. They are simply a piece of software within a device, not integrated like Chief."

"It mostly came down to language," Genos clarified. "As you probably know, Tsuna speak a dialect that is more unique sounds than words. After First Contact between humans and Tsuna and the establishment of the galactic nations, translators were one of the first things worked on for both species. From what I was told, the Mirus were quite vital in the early days due to their ability to communicate with any species."

"Interesting, but what does that have to do with the EIs?" Chiyo asked, trying to keep Genos from going off on a tangent.

"Oh, it was only that the translation software was a little slow at the beginning. Since the EIs were a human creation, they were only programmed to correspond to human languages. Any Tsuna or Sauren who used an EI had a delay between their commands and them being executed, which was not ideal in a battlefield."

"It certainly doesn't sound that way," she agreed.

"Couldn't they have developed the EI software to adapt to the race's language until the translators were updated?"

"That's actually what they ended up doing." Genos nodded. "Though it took some time, and from there, they were able to use the information collected by the EIs to further improve the translation software. It's almost one-to-one now."

"I see." Chiyo looked out the window and back to the screen on the console. "We should hopefully be there soon. At our current speed, it should be a little over two hours, but that's not factoring in any problems."

Genos didn't respond but remained focused ahead.

"Genos?" Chiyo asked, "Are you all right?"

He twitched slightly and glanced at her. "Hmm? I'm sorry. I was lost in thought, you might say."

"Thinking about EIs and translation software?" she asked playfully.

"I thought about Chief, which made me think of Kaiden," Genos explained. "He is an...interesting character."

"You've said as much several times before, but you've never seemed so pensive."

"Chiyo, might I ask something of a...dark, question?"

"In what way?"

"Do you think Kaiden will live to see graduation?"

Silence fell over them, and Chiyo glanced away as he looked out the window. "I ask because last night, I corresponded with Kaiden about his mission. He had Chief send me a message containing the details. When I looked at them—the kind of missions that he goes on—they would be operated by half-marked warriors or greater on Abisalo.

I'll go over the details at another time, but warriors who are half-marked have seen combat for at least the equivalent of twenty of your years or distinguished themselves by defeating a great enemy."

She remained silent but gave a brief nod.

"I don't doubt Kaiden's abilities. He has proven himself, certainly, so I don't mean for this to come off as thinking him weak, but it's—"

"I understand," Chiyo muttered. "You're worried about a friend."

"That certainly, but I suppose I also wonder if I worry about him more than he worries about himself."

She laughed weakly and nodded once again. "You said you weren't a part of the warrior clan on your planet, right? But that you had close ties to it?"

"Yes. I trained in the ways of the warrior, but it was not my forte. I was part of what you would consider to be the 'science' or 'alchemist' clan."

"But you trained to be a warrior as well. That's what led to your designation as a mechanist here, right?"

The Tsuna nodded. "Indeed—something I was rather concerned about, although Kaiden helped calm my doubts back then."

Chiyo folded her legs onto the chair and drew them against her chest. "It was a similar situation for me. I spent most of my life training for one thing—for a position of power in a place I thought would welcome me—but had to look for a different path once I came of age."

Genos glanced at her for a moment before he returned his attention to the blackness of space ahead of them. "I don't recall you telling me much about your past."

"I don't believe I have." She opened her visor. "Sorry. You've been so open with your life, and I never reciprocated."

"I never wanted to pry," he assured her. "Although I suppose I do wish to know what this has to do with my question about Kaiden."

She sighed and focused on the stars ahead of them. "Kaiden did the same thing for me as he did for you—helped me feel that the choice I made was the right one. When I think about him as a person, I see much stubbornness and confidence, but also someone with a good heart, if not a right mind." She chuckled lightly. "I guess I bring this up because unlike you or me, he doesn't see other choices. He was also like us in a way. His life took a turn and he adapted, and he will seize it for all it's worth."

She took a deep breath. "Do I think he'll die before graduation? It's a possibility, but when I think of how high or low that chance is and how lucky he was to live after that one mission—he told me a bit more about it later, how Gin was the first opponent he felt was too far above him. I remember him saying that he felt that he didn't care about dying in the field if he took as many people with him as possible if it came to that. But with Gin, he felt it was the first time he fought someone he couldn't even touch—like he wasn't a soldier anymore, more like someone desperately firing at whatever came out of the darkness."

"That is quite…harrowing coming from someone like him," Genos muttered.

"I heard anger in his voice as well as a tinge of fear, but after he finished talking, I remember him looking up and smiling." She smiled under her helmet herself.

"Smiling? About what?" His tone sounded confused but curious.

"He said that he might have gotten knocked down a few pegs, but that one of the men he had worked with told him to not let Gin 'win'—in this case, the mental victory. Wolfson also helped him get back on his feet, and he said that you, me, and all of us in our little group helped too." She chuckled again, and merriment returned to her voice. "Yes, I do worry that he might not return one day. I also know that may come even after we graduate. Who knows what our lives will be then? But seeing who he is, what he's done… I think…however it may sound, I would be more broken if he stopped altogether, to see that part of him fade away." She looked at her companion and wondered if he could understand.

Genos nodded. "There's a saying among the warriors—translated, it would be something along the lines of 'The best weapon is your will, the greatest armor is your conviction. Only you can wield them or let them shatter.' Do you think it applies?"

"I believe so," she agreed. "But despite all of that, I would still like him to message us more when he leaves."

"Yes, he said something to the effect that you 'grilled' him on that subject."

"Did he now?" she muttered.

As the two continued to talk and their craft flew deeper into space and closer to their target, something approached them—unseen and not on their radar, but they were in its sights.

CHAPTER FOURTEEN

Kaiden pushed open the fourth locked door he had found so far in the shuttle to reveal only a few crates hidden in the far corner of the room. He walked over and undid the straps that held them together before he pried open the top one and looked inside.

"Do you see anything good?" Chief asked.

"Can't you see what I see?" he asked as he peered inside the crate with real disappointment.

"I'm making small talk. Everything is bupkis so far. This is the only way I can entertain myself."

"Aren't you supposed to be making that patio?" He shut the crate and opened the others to take quick peeks before he sighed. "This one has a few pistols in it, and the others had some rifles. Certainly nothing worth trading our weapons in for. Maybe Genos can use them to make a torpedo or something."

Chief's eye skewed in the HUD. *"I don't think that's possible."*

"I was exaggerating, although to be fair, if you'd played

it right, I would have totally believed you if you said it was possible." Kaiden let the top of the crate crash to the floor. He dusted his hands off and looked around. On the other side of the room, a few shelves ran along the wall. He hurried over to examine a couple of cylinders with white markings on the side, picked one up, and shook his head. "Hey, Chief, what are these?"

"Explosives of some kind. Hold it up and let me scan it."

He raised the device to his visor and a white line flared across his screen. *"It appears to be a type of swarm grenade similar to the ones Genos and Cameron use from time to time. It looks like they seek out anything with an energy source and attach to it before they drain the energy from whatever they stick to."*

Kaiden rolled it around in his hand. "That sounds nifty, but if the seekers search things out indiscriminately, it's basically a crapshoot if they attack anything useful."

"That's why the ones who usually use them are engineers or techies who have devices that allow them to control the devices a little better. But in this case, the top of the grenade has a little dial. Take a look."

He flipped the grenade and looked at a small dial with white marking beside it. Without thinking, he took the knob between his fingers and turned it once. The white marking at the knob and on the side of the grenade changed to blue. "What did I do?" he asked and nearly dropped the grenade. "I didn't just kill us, did I?"

"As hilarious as that would be, I wouldn't let you do that," Chief huffed. *"Even in the relative safety of the Animus, I have some sense of self-preservation."*

Kaiden looked at the device once more, turned the

knob again, and changed the color to red. "Okay, so my guess is that it's a color-coded system, and each color means a different type of target for the seekers to attack?"

"Good guess. White is neutral, so they go after whatever is nearby. Blue is for electricity, purple is plasma, and red is heat."

"Heat?" he asked, surprised. "As in, only heat-seeking, or can they actually drain body heat?"

"I would typically blast you for suggesting something so silly, but in this case, you are right. These are experimental grenades made by our now good friends at Tessa," Chief explained. Kaiden's eyes narrowed in annoyance as he continued, *"They were developed about three years ago, apparently a prototype for use by soldiers to circumvent that whole 'these things are really complicated' problem they had with other seeker grenades. Fun fact: they earned the nickname 'nerd grenades' because of this difficulty. Apparently, they had limited tests on Earth but sent batches out to other colonies and outposts where they could have different targets and experiences. Also anywhere they really lacked engineers. That's probably more important."*

"I guess Axiom can't make all the pain-in-the-ass doodads." He sighed and took the other grenade from the shelf. "It's hard to see where they could benefit by using them on a planet that was such a hostile jungle that the plants wanted to kill you, especially since you would be the one with the most power flowing. You could literally throw this thing sixty yards away and still have it blow up in your face."

"My guess is that they were either supposed to be used in testing, procured from another ship, or were 'gifts' from the pirates for doing their dirty work on the planet."

"If we did this for real, we could have made some

money off them. Corporations and the WC have a turn-in value for devices like these if they are found in the wild." He clipped both grenades to his belt. "For now, I think I'll hang onto them."

"There's only that one room on the left still to check. I looked through the ship's blueprints and didn't find any smugglers' hatches or secret doors."

"Well, that's disappointing. These guys don't even know how to run a proper operation." Kaiden left the room and sauntered to the remaining door, Chiyo's drive at the ready. "Either the Animus is getting lazy, or these guys were based on galactic yuppies."

He pressed the driver into a slot on the door's access panel. "Wanna place a bet on what's in there? No peeking with the scanner."

"Yes, because there's no place for such deviousness in gambling," Chief chided with a roll of his eye. *"My guess is provisions. We haven't found any so far, and you would think they would have some aboard."*

"I'd bet on cleaning supplies. Maybe I can at least get my gear shined while we're twiddling our thumbs." He snickered. The light on the access panel turned green, and the door opened. He took one step, and his eyes widened at what was within. "Oh, this is way better than either of those things. Wait, do I even know how to use one of those?"

"Good thing you saved those points, huh?"

"Are there talents I can use to let me have a little fun with that?"

"Maybe not a specific one, but with the points you have left,

we could invest them in a couple of different ones, and that should be enough to— Kaiden, brace yourself!"

Without hesitation, Kaiden dropped and braced himself against the frame of the door. A blast rocked the ship and tilted it to its side so steeply that he almost slid into the room opposite. He tightened his grip on the frame and used both hands to hold himself steady.

"What's going on?"

"We're under attack!" Chiyo shouted as she righted herself in her chair and stared at the screens.

"I agree." Genos banked sharply away and pressed a few buttons on the console. "No need for stealth at the moment."

"Who or what is attacking us?" she asked, staring at the displays. "Moderate damage to the shields. Another blast or two and those will be gone. Kaitō, get back here!" In less than a second, the fox avatar appeared in her display.

"I am ready, madame," Kaitō acknowledged. *"What do you require?"*

"I'm sending you into the ship's systems. Activate cyberwarfare suite, and make sure they can't access us." Another bolt of energy roared toward the left side of the cockpit, barely avoided by a quick tilt of the controls from Genos. Chiyo drew a plug on a cord from her gauntlet and inserted it into the ship's console. "I don't think they plan to attack us that way, but to be safe, after that, see if there's any way we can access their systems."

The fox nodded. *"Understood. I shall inform you of my*

progress momentarily." With that, Kaitō disappeared, and Chiyo opened a holoscreen,

"I'll see if there are any auto-guns or turrets on the ship we can use. If so, I'll set them to fire all at once on them to break through their shields."

"I'm not sure that's an option," Genos confessed. "Like I said, this ship is more along the lines of a supply ship. It doesn't have many offensive options." He looked at the stick in his right hand. "This controls the front cannon. That may be all we have to fight with. I turned off the stealth drive so the shields will gain power, but that doesn't mean we can take more than a few strikes before it tears into us."

She balled a fist. "Dammit, you're right. There's nothing." She sighed but laughed almost immediately.

"Is something amusing, friend Chiyo?" he asked as he made a deft turn to try to bring the enemy ship into view. "I could certainly use something to make the mood more joyous."

"I simply thought we should try to finish this before Kaiden is able to get back in here. My guess is that he would volunteer to be shot out of a torpedo tube at the ship so he could infiltrate it."

"That's actually pretty close." She looked over her shoulder as Kaiden stumbled into the cockpit, a hand on either wall to steady himself as he approached. "Since you seem to be so attuned to my way of thinking, I guess I won't have to argue much."

"Kaiden, we don't even have a torpedo tube to launch you out of," she retorted. "Genos said that all we have is the main cannon, and he's trying to get a shot."

"I don't think I'll be able to accomplish that," the Tsuna huffed. "I can only catch glimpses of our pursuers. It doesn't appear to be a fighter, but their ship is much faster and more agile than ours. I would say that it would be more likely that an errant asteroid would crash into it and take it out before we have a chance."

"Well, that's unfortunate." Kaiden grinned. "So, back to my plan?"

Chiyo closed her holoscreen and looked at the ace. "I tremble to ask, but what is it exactly?"

"You drop me out of the back of the ship, and I'll board the other ship and take it over."

Both Chiyo and Genos—who should have been focused on the need to dodge the other ship's attacks—looked at him incredulously.

"Friend Kaiden, even not taking into account that it is a very odd and dangerous plan, even by your standards, this is space. There is no gravity. You would simply float in space until you either suffocated or the enemy took pity on you and blew you apart."

"Normally, yes," Kaiden conceded before he drew his rifle and primed it. "But I found a new toy below that I want to try."

Kaiden stood impatiently in the bay and waited for Genos to open the door. He was decked out in the astrosuit and a jet pack he had found. An excited smile settled his face when he heard Genos over the comm. "Are you sure about this, Kaiden?"

"Hurry up and open the door already!" he demanded. "Even if it doesn't work out as I plan, I could be enough of a distraction for you to get the shots you need. Let's do this."

"You sound so jubilant," Genos commented. "Very well, I'll open the doors. I hope you have fun."

"No doubt about it." He braced himself as a light flickered overhead and a warning siren wailed. The doors began to part, and the force dragged him slowly toward them. When the gap was wide enough, he vaulted up and was immediately whisked away. He activated the jetpack as soon as he was clear of the ship.

He set a direct course for the enemy craft. It was slightly smaller than their shuttle and had been painted in pirate colors—the red and black of the DSC. Another idea popped into his head when he saw that, but he would let that wait. He raised Sire and charged it to full, then retrieved one of the seeker grenades he had found and activated it. The seekers erupted from the container and soared toward the enemy ship, attached themselves to the craft's shields, and drained them. The shields briefly became visible, a shimmering blue color, before they faded along the front hull. Perfect.

Kaiden aimed carefully a few seconds before he and the ship collided and fired a blast. He could have sworn he saw the bewildered looks of the crew in the cockpit as they drew closer together immediately before his shot created an opening in the front of the vessel. With his weapon held tightly against his chest, he cut power to the jetpack and cruised through the aperture he had made. Surprised shouts and worried yelps came from the pirates as they either reacted to their unexpected visitor or to the hole in their damn ship.

He dropped Sire, drew Debonair, and scanned the room as he moved his free hand to his belt for the grenade he had previously turned to the heat setting. Seven, by his count—a cinch. As emergency hatches covered the hole in the cockpit, he threw the grenade and spun to fire at the two pirates closest to him. Both were eliminated in four shots. He rolled to the side as a weapon charged behind him, and the pirate's shotgun blast missed him by inches.

By the time he turned again, the grenade had blown and three of the other pirates had been swarmed, including the one who had fired on him. He shifted his attention to the remaining pirate, who scrabbled for a gun on the underside of the console. Chief alerted him to the doors opening behind him, and Kaiden whirled and fired and, at the same time, flicked his wrist so his blade ejected into his hand. Two more pirates rushed in to help their comrades, only to be greeted by Debonair's assault. They fell to seven shots, but Debonair was tapped. The final man had managed to latch onto the pistol he had tried to retrieve, but as he turned to fire, his eyes wild and a yellow, toothy grin smeared across his face, he had only a split second to see the tip of a knife as Kaiden's blade pierced his skull. He stumbled back for a moment as if his body were too shocked to realize what had happened before he finally fell and joined the rest.

Kaiden vented Debonair as he hurried to turn off the ship's engines. "Chief, take a look around and see if there's anyone else. I'll contact Chiyo and Genos."

"Gotcha. On it."

He removed the jetpack and retrieved Sire before he closed Debonair's vent port and holstered it. With a final look around the cockpit, he placed a hand on the side of his helmet. "Genos, Chiyo, are you there?"

"Indeed, friend Kaiden. I assume it went well?" the mechanist asked.

Kaiden grinned. "Very well."

"I see that the ship is powered down now. If you're clear, we can come and get you, or you could fly back using the pack if you prefer."

"Although that sounds great, I'll do it another time."

"I see that the ship is flying Dead Space colors," Chiyo stated. "I don't know if they are looking for us specifically, but I would guess we've lost the element of surprise."

"Yeah…about that. I had an idea that I wanted to run by you two." Chief reappeared in his visor and flashed green to give him the all-clear. "Why don't you two come aboard our new ship? That one was getting a little stuffy."

CHAPTER FIFTEEN

A massive dark shape floated up ahead in the distance. It would have been almost hidden in the blackness of space if it weren't for the illumination of large lights that shone along its hull.

"Is that the station?" Chiyo asked as she donned the Dead Space crew helmet.

"It looks like it," Kaiden replied as he adjusted his own stolen uniform and closed the visor. "It's not shooting at us on sight, which is both nice and a sign that my plan has worked so far. We should be good—"

"We're being hailed," she interrupted.

Kaiden's head dropped as he sighed. "Unless they want to identify us personally. There's that too."

"Should I bring it on screen?" Genos asked.

Kaiden nodded. "Make sure to send the codes you recovered, so it looks authentic. Activate voice modulation, Chief," he ordered, then stood and walked to the center of the bay.

A holoscreen appeared and displayed a balding man

with a salt-and-pepper beard in a black and red uniform and beanie on screen. "What are you doing back so soon, BAT-3? You're still supposed to be on patrol. What happened to the ship that came into our borders?"

"We took it out," Kaiden stated, his voice rougher and shallow as if he had spent the last two weeks smoking and yelling his lungs out every night. "Was able to recover some goods, too, but we were pegged in the front hull. Emergency shutters were activated, but we need repairs."

"I thought you said that thing was a hunk of junk?" The pirate chuckled. "Yet it was still able to get a shot at you. How the hell did a jackass like you get a ship?"

"You have my files. Look up my list of accomplishments," Kaiden retorted and folded his arms. "Keep yapping and I might make you a footnote."

The pirate sneered and looked at Chiyo. "Can you vouch for this guy?"

She nodded. "There were some difficulties, but nothing that we couldn't handle," she explained, her own voice raspy and brittle. "We were caught off-guard by the firepower, but like he said, we have some loot to show for it."

The man placed a pinky in his ear and wiggled it as he thought. "Fine, opening hangar eighteen. Get in there, and be ready for someone to debrief you."

"Hop to it," Kaiden ordered and glanced at Genos, who nodded and deactivated the holoscreen.

"Go ahead and get ready," Kaiden said to Chiyo. "I'm not sure how long we can fool them like this. If that guy is one of their best, I wouldn't be too worried, but let's pretend they aren't all that lazy and prepare to fight if need be. I'll handle the debriefing while you and Genos take notes and download schematics or whatever you can do in the meantime." Kaiden looked at the Tsuna. "How far to the bay?"

"Usually, in stations like these, the repairs would be done on the lower decks. But they have either rearranged the hangars, or they don't know what they are doing," Genos said. "The designated hangar is toward the middle, where they would usually keep the fighters and ships ready for departure or battle. I'll let you know if there's anything suspicious."

"Appreciate it." Kaiden placed Sire on the back of the Dead Space armor. "Remember, if they ask about the weapons, pirates work for shares and they are our cut, so don't let them spook you or take them."

"Acknowledged." Chiyo nodded. "How far do you think we can get?"

"It depends on where we need to go, really." He shrugged. "Since we don't have a bomb that can take this place out, it'll probably fall to either one of you. My guess is that there's an important system you can override and disable or, failing that, we can have Genos do one of his favorite hat tricks and blow the core."

"Perhaps I should try something new?" Genos suggested and looked up from the controls. "I am beginning to feel that I'm predictable."

"Normally, I would be all for that, but considering that this is an important test and all and we're about to be in the base of the enemy and surrounded on all sides, maybe stick with the classics," Kaiden stated. "From what I know, the Dead Space Crew are technically pirates but act more like a tribe. They got their start as settlers who simply said fuck it for one reason or another and became scavengers and eventually grew too big to be mere marauders. They were then classified as pirates, and the name came with the distinction."

"Perhaps, but we shouldn't underestimate them. They are infamous for their raiding skills, and I'm sure they've amassed plenty of weapons in their stocks," Chiyo warned. "This won't be easy."

"I would imagine not, considering what we've accomplished so far." Kaiden chuckled. "By now, the academy staff have numbers on us, so I would guess they tailored the difficulty of the mission to what they believe we can accomplish."

"The objective is to infiltrate the pirate base and destroy it or compromise it," Genos recalled. "Looking at it now, most of it seems derelict, but many parts are active. On the positive side, that means whatever is powering the remnants of the station should be isolated and quicker to disable than if we had to deal with a full power station."

"What are the negatives?" Chiyo asked.

"From a rudimentary glance and an estimate from Viola, we're still looking at dealing with roughly a battalion of pirates. Four to eight hundred, leaning closer to four."

"They were able to take a station with only that many?" Kaiden asked.

She shook her head. "I doubt that's their full number. Plus, this place was probably only a science or small colony station. There aren't many signs of heavy fighting. They probably ransacked it and took over."

"I guess when you're the big dog, you get to say you own the place." Kaiden smirked.

Genos drifted the ship slowly to the side of the station. Kaiden stepped beside him and looked out. "The DSC aren't as bad as some of the other pirates I've heard of, or even some of the merc groups in the area. But they make up for it by being tenacious and ruthless, especially to the military. Apparently, they harbor a grudge due to all the fighting between the two. I would suspect, though, that it simply comes with the territory."

"I suppose I can't blame them for being…annoyed, considering what led to their creation. However, becoming pirates seems to be a rather extreme reaction," the Tsuna commented. "I don't suppose a peaceful solution is somehow obtainable?"

"This all happened a long time ago, Genos. I'm sure that if a peaceful solution was available, the Animus wouldn't have them as an option," Kaiden reasoned. "But hey, if this works out, we could potentially be done with this mission in a few hours."

"There isn't enough time," Chiyo admitted, and he gave her a quick look. "You remember that there is a time limit due to the influx of students. We have a little under two hours left."

He looked at Genos for a moment before he turned to her. "That's good to know. I guess we're not in the home-stretch yet. We'll have to see how far in we can get and hope we make it to a good stopping point before we're kicked out."

"I don't think they'll kick you out if you are in the middle of a firefight," Genos protested. "If we are constantly fighting, we could potentially extend our time for the day." He froze when he realized what he had suggested, and Chiyo stared at him. He could feel her anger even behind the visor. "Or it could end up being a disaster if we alerted the entire station."

"As much as that appeals to me, I'd rather not, for the time being," Kaiden admitted. "We don't know the layout, but I can tell that there'll be a lot of tight spaces in there. Without field advantage, they can keep throwing grunts at us until we are tired and are overwhelmed. This time, you will need to flex your brains instead of your muscles, for the most part." He went silent for a moment. "Or at least, that's the hope. Usually, bad things happen when we get too optimistic."

As they approached the hangar, Chiyo looked around. "I suppose you have an explanation as to why there are fewer people on board than when we set off?" she asked.

He folded his arms. "Of course I do." He pointed a finger at the hole in the cockpit. "That's why I splashed blood around that. I'll tell them a few ended up getting spaced. Not that I would think these guys would have a hell of a lot of common sense, but you would think that when you have the reputation of being a pack of raving lunatics from the stars, a little collateral damage will occur."

"To be fair, it wouldn't really be a lie." Genos drifted the ship into the hangar. "We're about to dock. Are you ready?"

Kaiden knocked his fists together "Of course."

The dropship of Dead Space pirates flew up to the front gate of their stronghold. The leader, dressed head to toe in crimson heavy armor and a rounded helmet with a full-face visor, carried a modified Reaver shotgun when he strode up to the console of the ship and pressed a key to hail the station.

A holoscreen appeared. A woman with a passive gaze and pink and blonde hair looked at the leader. "Password?" she asked, and stared at him for a moment. Her eyes widened when she realized who she was talking to. The leader grunted as he raised a hand and placed it on the scanner.

"I should simply say open the damn gate, but I'll be cordial. It's 'black hole sun,'" he responded brusquely, earning a small nod from the woman on screen. She quickly pressed buttons on her terminal.

"Good to see you, Captain. What brings you back to the station so soon?" she asked.

"Hurry up and open the gates. We have a shipment of chems and loads of Stardust from one of the puppet colonies here, and I want to have a chat with Walker." The captain's gruff voice was accentuated with a crackling voice modifier in his helmet.

The woman onscreen nodded one last time before the screen deactivated. The large doors of the main hangar began to open and slid into the walls around them. The captain turned to the group of pirates in the ship and nodded at them as the ship began to dock, their cue to get moving.

One of them in the front nodded. He turned to the two dozen others behind him and waved them forward. Pirates shuffled around quickly and gathered equipment and goods as the ship stopped and exit doors opened.

The grounds of the DSC base were comprised of the remains of the science station Antarctica. The captain looked around and recalled when they first took the base over. Somewhat ironically, it had also briefly been the base of a company of Red Sun mercs, who had maintained it fairly well. Unfortunately, they didn't do as much when they ousted the mercs from the station. The fading color on the walls and the fact that three-quarters of the place didn't even work properly could attest to the neglect. No one had come to look for them yet, neither the mercs nor the WCM to avenge the scientists. The captain decided it was either because they were too afraid to deal with the Dead Space Crew personally or they knew there would be nothing left of their people to find.

His men filed out of the ship with a caravan comprised of twelve floating storage units holding all the chem and drugs from their haul from the nearby planet of Koma, a planet that seemed to be only good for making powerful recreational drugs. The WC thought it useless, but enterprising men such as he found many uses for it.

The crew maneuvered their way through the hatches and headed to the holding dock attached to the hangar where they could be examined and processed. They entered the building, which was mostly empty. A random tech sat in the corner they had yet to go through. The few crewmen sorting through some items on the other side of the room dropped everything to run over and help with the new shipments. Several Handy droids walked around the floor, cleaning or moving objects into place. These humanoid-design robots were approximately six feet tall, with long limbs, rounded heads with a single large, blue glowing eye, and white bodies that were dirty from their work and lack of maintenance.

One of the bots approached the captain. *"Good day, sir. Anything I can help you with?"*

He drew his shotgun and placed the barrel against the droid's chest. "You can get the contents of these containers ready for processing. Until then, get out of my face." He sneered and pushed the bot back with his gun for emphasis.

"Of course, sir, right away. Sorry to be too close to your face," the droid acknowledged and apologized. The containers stopped in the middle of the warehouse and rotated so they were side by side with each other. The pirates began to sort through and organize the packages within the crates. Two men with the highest rank besides the captain followed him out of the warehouse and to the center of the station.

"Hey, Mick," one of the station pirates hissed, catching the attention of one of the crew pirates. "What's happened with Captain Swarn?"

"What do you mean?" Mick asked. "You know he's not exactly the nice sort."

"Well, sure, but he's mostly only indifferent or snarky. He's coming across like he's bitter. Usually, he would order the bots to leave him alone. There's no point in shoving his gun in their faces when they can't feel anything."

"Ah, right, that." Mick sighed. "That would be one of the reasons we came back early. Turns out one of the deals Walker made went sour. No big fight or nothing, but it was a hell of a lot of wasted time for no payout, the captain hasn't had time to blow off steam for a while, so I'd guess that things will get a little rowdy in the office once the two have words."

"Oh, that's not good." The crewman sighed. "We'd best hope nothing else is out of place. If anything else goes rotten, the captain will probably start on a bloody warpath."

CHAPTER SIXTEEN

The trio left the shuttle and warily observed a group of pirates nearby. The man they had spoken to stood among them, and he pushed past the others and approached them. "Is this all that's left? Weren't there about ten of you?"

"Good day to you too," Kaiden greeted sarcastically. He held out the stolen ID chip and motioned for Chiyo and Genos to be on their way. "I thought you said someone else would debrief me?"

"So I did," the man grunted as he inserted the chip into a tablet. "But we had a sudden change in plans. Captain Swarn arrived at the same time as you did, and all the boot-lickers ran to the main hangar to meet him and get to groveling."

"You aren't a fan of the captain?" he asked as he took the chip from the man.

"He earned his title, and he'll probably keep it until the end of his days. I don't doubt he's earned respect, but I could do without all the toadies who suck up to him whenever he comes back. There are other things to do than kiss his arsehole until it shines."

"I guess I can relate." Kaiden shrugged and gestured behind him with his thumb. "How long till we can set out again?"

The man gave the craft a cursory glance. "What's the damages?"

"The obvious big-ass hole in the front, for one. Besides that, damage to the shields. They aren't charging right. They used some sort of tiny machines to wear it down."

"Probably seekers, although I didn't realize they'd started using them in torpedoes."

"They didn't. They sort of dropped them on us."

The man guffawed. "Seriously? I'm surprised they didn't target their own ship—although, if they've developed something like that, we could make some serious creds if we had a sample to show the markets."

"I think most fell off or were destroyed in the fight, but if you want to get some scrubbers up there to have a look, be my guest." The ace peered to the side to confirm that Genos and Chiyo now wandered around. They acted like they were simply killing time, but he knew they were both focused on the situation.

"Where are the goods?" the man asked, dragging Kaiden's attention back to him.

"Storage bay one. I took all the items they had on board, and anything that could be repurposed or scrapped. Otherwise, the ship was too damaged, so we blew it up before we headed back."

His attention moved to the group of pirates behind the man, who all seemed to scrutinize him. He shifted slightly and snaked his right hand closer to Debonair's holster. "Can I help you guys?"

One of the larger men smiled deviously and walked forward with his hand out. "Your weapons—give them here," he demanded, and two others came up behind him for support.

"Hell, no." He balked, and his hand now gripped Debonair's handle. "This is my cut. You ain't taking a damn thing."

"Come on now, buddy. Are you really gonna be like that?" the tall man asked. "You lost most of your crew. This is, what—your twentieth patrol in the lead, right?" He prodded Kaiden's chest plate. "You BAT guys are all about going out into space and finding the big catch. There'll be more in the future. Some of those guys were my friends, so I feel I deserve a little recompense."

"Really now? What were their names?" he responded.

The man made a fist and held it up to Kaiden's visor. "We had a lot of nicknames. My favorites were 'Fuck' and 'You.'"

"You need to work on your material, dumbass," he muttered as he drew Debonair and held it at the ready.

"You boys stop your bitching!" the first man demanded. He apparently had more clout than Kaiden realized since the tall pirate and his friends backed off. "And you, Doma." It took the ace a moment to realize he was talking to him.

"What now?" he asked, feigning exhaustion.

"I'm answering your question, so show a little gratitude, punk," he warned. "The repairs will take anywhere from sixteen to twenty-five hours unless the shielding really is dead. The minute this thing is ready, you and what remains of your crew will be back on patrol, with an extra shift to make up for your fuckup."

"Fine, fine," he said with a wave, anxious to move on so they could continue with their mission to blow this place to hell. "Do you need anything else?"

"Only to say that I'll take my cut if there happens to be one of those seekers left on the ship."

"Sounds all right." He nodded and strode toward Chiyo and Genos. "Let me know when it's fixed.

"All right." The older pirate looked at the group. "The rest of you get in there and fight each other for the scraps. Get moving!"

Water, oil, and several liquids they couldn't identify dripped from the grates above the canal. Angry shouts and the fizz of overheated electronics from above were muffled but audible. The trio wandered slowly through the tight corridor and hugged the side as they tried not to step into the puddles and keep their noise to a minimum.

Several shots were fired above, followed by laughter and snarls that seemed to indicate pleasure in the violence. In front of the group, a tiny stream of blood trickled through a small hole in the left wall. Genos, who was closest to the drips, inched away to avoid the tainted liquid.

"Hey, Chiyo, out of curiosity, why did you choose the creepiest destination for us to go to?" Kaiden hissed, his annoyance evident over the comm.

"Because I do not have a full map of the station," she explained. "Using what I do have, this was the path that would lead to the central chamber and arguably be the safest."

"Well, at least you thought it out," he mumbled. "It's that door up ahead, right?"

"Yes. That should lead to the western chamber, and from there, we should have a direct route to the center."

Genos approached with his cannon aimed downward and turned the handle, while his teammates held their weapons at the ready. There was nothing behind the door but a longer, darker hallway that offered no visibility.

"I've only now realized that this DSC gear doesn't have night vision." Kaiden sighed and tapped around his helmet before he pressed a button and a small light flashed on. "Well, that's something, at least. So, who's first into the deep, dark hole?" he asked. Chiyo walked up beside him and opened a miniature holoscreen. "My access is extremely limited. It doesn't look like they use a base-wide system, but rather issue commands from one location. It's rudimentary but more effective than most security systems, ironically. That being said..." She pressed a few buttons, and small dots of light brightened the hallway. "There are a few things I can do to make our lives a little easier."

The group made their way along the now-illuminated path, the amber light of the glow strips their only means of guidance. They reached a split in the corridor. One continued directly forward, and the other led them to the left. Chiyo stopped them, pointed down the left hallway, and beckoned them to follow.

"Do you have a map?" Kaiden whispered over their comm link.

"No, not a complete one. I'm filling it in as we go. If I can find a console, I could get a clearer picture, but for now, Kaitō takes what we have and uses the topography to fill in the rest as we go along to make a path."

"That's useful," Genos commented. "What exactly do you suggest we do once we get to this location, Chiyo?"

"Right now, the only objectives are 'destroy the station' and 'don't die.' There should be an important device we can exploit. I hope it's the command system, since I would be able to gain access and set off a destruction order or a deactivation sequence as needed. If we have to go with Genos' traditional route, it means we would have to send the core into meltdown and then run to the hangars before we are also caught in the explosions." They continued moving, and Kaiden remained alert for enemies, cameras, turrets, or anything that could be a potential danger. So far, they had encountered nothing of concern. The hallway was devoid of anything but intersecting corridors and the low lights of the glow strips.

"I don't like this. I know it's cliché and everything, but it's too damn quiet," Chief grunted, his eye peering around in Kaiden's HUD as if he scanned the surroundings.

"It doesn't look like an area they use often. I can't imagine there would be many guards down here," Kaiden reasoned.

"Agreed, although I must admit I would actually like to see something come through here," Genos huffed. "There is something rather unnerving about walking around in such a dark, empty space."

Chiyo raised one of her hands and rubbed the top of her opposite arm as if to dispel goosebumps. "It's uncanny,

I'll admit, but it's better than laser fire and bullets coming at you from all sides."

"That's become our native element," the Tsuna jested.

They came to another split in the path and the infiltrator continued directly ahead, so the others followed. "The less of a mess this is, the quicker we can finish and the higher the score. Like Kaiden said, it's best to use tactics as long as we can, especially with our time running low."

"While we're on the subject, what happens when we run out of time?" Kaiden asked.

"What do you mean? It's self-explanatory," Genos stated.

"Immediately booted out? Do we start in the same area or at the exact same moment when we begin again?" he questioned.

"Indeed, the exact same spot," the Tsuna confirmed. "You would even have the same ailments you did when you left, as Julius explained about Otto yesterday."

"That's a potentially costly mistake." Kaiden chuckled. "I'll do my best not to lose an appendage before we leave."

Chiyo raised a hand, and a hush fell over the group. She pointed above and toward the catwalks. Several droids with jagged bodies and large round heads that illuminated their surroundings paced above.

"Oh, well, that's different. I don't think I've done a mission with those before," Genos admitted. "A first."

"Those are Watchbots," Chief stated. *"They aren't a mortal threat, but they make one hell of a noise if they see you. I suppose they had to have something down here to look around."*

"Can we take them down from afar?" Kaiden asked, holding up his rifle.

"Only if you want to set the rest off. They have good audio sensors too, so you would definitely not want to make a big explosion around them."

"Aren't you helpful?" Kaiden snarked.

"Like I said, they usually aren't well armed, but it'll probably bring this whole place down on you very quickly," the EI warned. *"I'm not sure you can get past all of them without alerting a few, and it only takes one."*

He sighed and exchanged glances with his companions. "Okay, we have a ways to go before we're directly beneath them, and maybe there's another of these hallways that will take us around. Let's keep mov— Genos, Chiyo, get ready."

"What is it?" the Tsuna asked as he drew his cannon and scanned the area ahead.

"See the shadows on the wall over there? Something is waiting for us or coming this way."

"Should we run or wait to engage?" Genos asked, his cheerful demeanor switching quickly to a serious one—a habit implanted by his training.

"Let's leg it. We can cover more ground while we aren't under fire and make it as close to the central chamber as we can get. If we have to fight the rest of the way there, so be it, but it's better to increase our chances as much as possible."

Genos nodded. "All right, I'll take point. Chiyo, tell me the directions over the comm."

"Understood." She nodded and raised her sub-machine gun.

Kaiden followed quietly behind him and tried to identify what lay ahead. They paused at the next corner and peered around it to see a group of Havoc droids—not in the greatest shape—wandering along the bottom path only a few yards from them.

"If we stay here, we have no choice but to engage," Chiyo stated. "What do you want to do?"

"Do we have another option? I'm all right with a fight, considering how far we've already come, but any shot down here will definitely alert those Watchbots, and then every pirate in this place will know we're here."

"I saw a hatch a few hundred yards back," Genos mentioned. "We could see if that leads to an alternate location and go from there."

"It would be better to try that than have to go all the way back and start from square one." Kaiden placed a hand on the Tsuna's shoulder. "Lead the way, Genos."

They raced down the hall, the mechanist moving much faster than one who spent most of his time flying instead of fighting would be expected to be able to. The metallic clacks and shifting figures of the Havoc bots faded behind them. At least they didn't have to worry about pursuers for now. They turned into another hall that led away from the approaching enemy. Genos pointed to a small hatch on the side of the wall.

"Allow me." The ace approached the hatch, twisted the valve, and grunted as he forced it open. A stream of water sounded from deep within. "It's a steep drop," he advised them as he looked down the hole. "I can't tell if it's a slide or a tube or literally only a hole."

"The shocks in our armor should be enough to disperse the fall as long as it isn't over a hundred feet," Chiyo advised.

"Do you guys wanna risk it?" he asked, glancing at his

teammates. "The other options right now seem to be to double back and try to find a different way around or barrel through the droids down here and almost certainly alert some or all of the bastards above."

"This seems to lead to a waterway or sewage system," Genos noted. "I don't think there would be anything of great concern in there."

"I'll be sure to keep an eye out for surveillance," Chiyo promised.

Kaiden glanced at his teammates once more, and both nodded quickly. He placed his rifle on his back and peered into the hatch. The rush of water now competed with heavy marching treads behind them. The Havoc droids had obviously followed, but whether by accident or because they knew there were intruders was anyone's guess at this point.

"It sounds like the droids are coming this way," she warned.

To hell with it. He leapt into the hatch and allowed the water to carry him as his companions followed suit, and they ventured deeper into the station.

CHAPTER SEVENTEEN

When Genos exited the waterway, he fell into a pool of water and muck and climbed out quickly, his visor blurry and armor heavy. He grimaced at the sludge that covered him and tried to remind himself that he was in the Animus. What a disgrace to allow something so vile to coat him. For a moment, he missed the waters of his home.

"Are you all right, Genos?" Chiyo asked and helped him to steady himself.

"Yes. Just give me a moment to get my bearings." He tried to clean off part of his armor, at least. "Where are we?"

"Some sort of facility. Most of the lights are out, and there's leakage everywhere. I assume this was used for tests or monitoring the station's systems, but that's only a guess."

"Where's Kaiden?" he asked.

"Right here." Kaiden grunted, coming over and shaking himself off. "This place is disgusting. Is this the trash area?"

"Feeling a bit ill after the ride, as it were, friend Kaiden?" Genos asked.

Kaiden looked around. They were in another chamber of some kind, the walls a faded red, which stretched on for hundreds of yards. There were halls running everywhere, offering them the opportunity to go in almost any direction. "I think I would have preferred fighting my way through the station at this point. This looks like where they dump the bodies." He sniffed the air and retched. "Smells like it, too."

Genos nodded. "It is certainly a change of scenery."

"I'm not sure if this is better or worse than where we were," Chiyo mused. "How vast do you think this place is?"

"Chief, scan it, please," Kaiden ordered.

"What are you looking for?" Chief inquired.

Kaiden shrugged. "Anything other than muck and parts. See if you can find an exit."

"Scanning... Done. There are a couple of options, but one looks to be covered in debris, and the other will require you to splice your way in."

"Better to go to that one than try to move the debris," Chiyo suggested.

Kaiden nodded. "Agreed. I guess we'll take that one and see where it leads. After that, we'll— You hear something?"

The trio froze as a shriek split the air, and Kaiden caught something out of the corner of his eye. He quickly took aim and fired, hitting something flying through the air and causing it to crash to the ground.

The three ran over to it and discovered a small creature that resembled a tiny pterodactyl with pink eyes and flesh that had yet to fully develop scales.

"It's a...baby mutant of some kind." Genos picked the carcass up and studied it. "Could this be a devil bird?"

"Oh, sweet Jesus." Kaiden sighed. "How are there devil birds down here at what might be the bottom of a space station?"

"This was a science station. They could have run a study on mutants, among other things. When the scientists were driven out, whatever specimens they had may have been set free." Chiyo looked at the others as a small snapping sound echoed in the large space.

"We're in a hunting ground." Kaiden cursed, and readied his weapon.

Genos drew his new rifle and activated it. "We need to move."

"What do you want, Swarn?" Walker hissed, and tried to stare the other man down as his bodyguards paced the room.

"I want to know when I'll be paid," the captain answered. He stormed into the DSC leader's room with open contempt and impatient growls. "Me and my men have run your little scams for months, and now we were screwed by one of your clients, which left us high and dry."

"I would hardly call them scams," Walker growled. "They have brought in a considerable amount of money for us, but we are pirates. You can't expect a warm reception every time you go out."

"I've left the operations to you because I expected

results," Swarn shot back, and slammed his hands on the table.

"And I've kept the position because I get them. I also have time scheduled for potential mishaps like this one," he retorted, and brushed his white locks out of his face. "If you're that strapped for cash or lust that badly for blood, I could—"

The conversation was interrupted by a tiny light that flashed on Walker's desk.

"What's that about, Walker?" the other man asked.

"It's from a tracker we implanted in one of the mutants down below," Walker muttered and stared at the screen. "Normally it would simply stop moving, which would mean the creature died. But this one has been obliterated, so it seems that the beast might have been killed by an energy blast or at least deliberate fire."

As the team raced through the chamber, a sharp buzz echoed off the maze-like surroundings. Kaiden spun instinctively and grimaced at two orbs that rocketed toward them. "Get down!" he shouted, and fired at the globes. He hit one, which exploded and made the other one erupt along with it. The liquid within spattered and melted through everything it touched. Genos dove toward Chiyo to shove her out of the way of a falling beam.

"Chief, scan for hostiles," the ace ordered, the butt of his rifle against his shoulder as his gaze searched the area.

"*I don't need to. There's one above you—nine o'clock,*" Chief warned.

Kaiden's eyes widened when he saw a spotted brown creature that resembled a Bayou Stalker, which peered back at him with large, sickly-green eyes. It was smaller than stalkers he had faced before the Deathmatch, but it was at least seven feet tall, with broad shoulders and long, muscular arms and legs. The body was mostly covered in scales, with hardened flesh along its neck and underbelly. Several large, deep scars traced its arms, and chips in its claws made it look like they had serrated edges.

It roared at them and leapt from the pile of metal it stood on. The ace rolled back before it landed, but the claws sliced his coat and armor. He pushed to his feet and fired several shots in a quick burst. The monster's skin crackled and seemed to glow and burn for a moment, but it simply hissed in response and charged. Kaiden, who was used to this dance by now, sidestepped the stalker's downward swipe and switched to ballistic rounds. He fired two shots to the chest that knocked the reptilian alien back, and it shrieked in anger. He smirked.

"Kaiden, two more!" Chiyo warned. He glanced back as two more stalkers barreled toward them on all fours. One was black with a white chest and the other a murky red, colors he'd not seen before. He fired a few partially-charged shots, but the beasts serpentined around them. The group had to get away. Kaiden knew they were at a disadvantage, fighting these creatures in such a confined space.

"Get out of here!" Kaiden yelled as another stalker came up next to others. Kaiden fired a few shots at the ground around them, which caused them to step back, but more importantly kicking up water, dust, and metal to create a makeshift screen. He took out a thermal and tossed it at their feet, sprinting away as the stalkers recovered. The grenade went off, flinging debris all around, and the beasts shrieked.

Kaiden saw Chiyo and Genos getting closer to the door. He pushed himself to run faster, placing his rifle on his back and taking out Debonair.

He felt something snag his foot, and he was flung to the side. The black stalker had wrapped its tail around his foot.

"Kaiden!" Chiyo called, fear in her cry. Genos turned and fired his cannon at the creature, and Chiyo added to the volley with her sub-machine gun. The monster hissed and spat acid globs at them in response, and the duo was forced to take cover as the area around them began to melt.

Kaiden pushed himself up, running up to the stalker and leaping onto its head as it thrashed. He raised Debonair and aimed at the stalker's eye to fire a direct shot, and as it cried out in pain, Kaiden took out a second thermal and shoved it into the mutant's mouth. As he jumped off, the blast went off behind him, the force nearly knocking him down along with raining the beast's guts onto him. He began to sprint again, checking his armor as he went to make sure nothing was damaged.

The other stalker landed in front of him, halting his escape, and looked down at him, its mouth twitching as it bared its claws.

Kaiden backed up and took Sire out, but before the beast could strike, it was knocked down from behind. Genos now atop it.

"Now is not the greatest time to be taking pointers

from me, Genos!" Kaiden said, trying to aim at the mutant but not hit his teammate.

"Just winging it!" Genos called, trying to keep his hold on the stalker, "The underbelly! Shoot it!"

"Going for the stomach! Hang on!" Kaiden got to one knee, and, taking careful aim, he pulled and held the trigger, waiting for it to charge. The beast had finally gotten a claw into Genos and tore the Tsuna off him.

"Gotcha!" Kaiden shouted as he let the bolt fly. It slammed into the stalker, drilling a hole through it before exploding, which flung all of them back.

Genos and Kaiden landed hard and looked over to see the beast lying on its back, a claw weakly reaching out for them before it fell back to the floor. When Kaiden took a closer look, he could see clear through the stalker. "Don't think we'll have to worry about that one."

Stomping, thuds, growls, and shrieks could be heard in the distance.

"More are coming," Genos muttered. He was trying to keep himself steady, but panic was creeping into his voice.

"Chiyo?" Kaiden called. He glanced around and saw the infiltrator working on the door.

"I've almost got it!" she replied, punching buttons on the terminal. "I'll need your help, though. I can unlock the door, but you'll need to force it open!"

Kaiden and Genos looked at each other, nodded, and ran over to her, They each took one of the edges and waited for Chiyo's signal, and she finally nodded. She took out her gun as the two began pulling, creating a small gap that slowly grew wider.

The sounds were growing louder.

"Get inside, you two!" Kaiden demanded, continuing to pull.

"Chiyo, you first," Genos stated, and she backed through the narrow gap, keeping her gun at the ready. Genos glanced at Kaiden, who nodded, and the machinist let go of the door and took out his weapon. When he turned to the area in front of them, he saw more stalkers and other mutants headed their way.

The stalkers spewed acid at the trio as Genos ran through the doorway. Kaiden took out Debonair and fired at the acidic orbs, but couldn't manage to hit them. He dodged what he could as he dove after Genos and Chiyo, who started to force the doors closed.

Kaiden dropped his pistol and took out Sire, covering them. The orbs hit the closing doors, splattering the liquid all over, and Kaiden jumped back to avoid the burning saliva.

Chiyo and Genos finally got the doors closed.

The ace couldn't help but laugh when he realized that they had survived the sudden attack. He glanced at his teammates. "No one the worse for wear?" he asked.

Both shook their heads, and Chiyo stated, "This won't hold them long" as Genos walked up to the door.

"Maybe not," he mused, activating the pointer finger on his gauntlet. A small flame appeared, and he dragged it from the bottom of the crack in the door up to the top, sealing it.

"Better, I think," he offered, looking over his handiwork.

A reply came in the form of something pounding on the other side of the door.

"You sure about that?" Kaiden asked.

"Yes. Well, mostly," Genos admitted, putting his cannon away. "It is enough to keep them out, but I still recommend we move with haste."

"Happy to follow that order!" Kaiden said, and the three ran down the dim hall and farther into the station.

CHAPTER EIGHTEEN

He was perched on a ledge at the far right of the hangar. The Tessa laboratory wasn't as breathtaking as some of the other squats he had stayed in. There were few ways to traverse the building aside, from a couple of catwalks and an upper level that mostly seemed to function as storage. The few system ducts were too small for him to crawl through, something he had noticed more and more throughout his adventures. He wondered if it was his gear or his girth, and slid a hand down his smooth chest and stomach. Satisfied, he snapped his teeth a couple of times before he left them open in a toothy smile.

Nah, he was fine. A man had to stay lean when his sport of choice could be so demanding.

He watched as the technicians, engineers, guards, and designers walked around the lab and briefed one another on their findings, their latest projects, and their theories. It must have been so much fun.

His focus moved to the party of four that had caught his attention when he had first snuck in, and specifically to a blonde-haired woman who seemed to hold a special place among them. He could sense something similar among those scientists, something akin to how he felt whenever he and Magellan were in the same room. It was an undertone of barely constrained animosity and amusement, of excitement and hate. He somehow knew that while they joked and amused one another, they all harbored grudges.

It's sweet that they think they can hide it. It was doubtful that anyone in that group was fooled. He certainly wasn't, and he was far away and unable to listen in. For a brief moment, he wondered why he took the time to observe the people below when they wouldn't be around much longer. Well, most of them wouldn't. He had to admit, for all the building rage and wrath he had felt as he made his way there, he had cooled rather quickly.

Which wasn't to say that he wouldn't stain this place with as much blood as possible. That was necessary to leave Zubanz one last reminder of who Gin really was. The chairman was fond of telling him that he was less than he was and always seemed so proud to have found and played with him as if he were a toy.

He'd therefore break every other toy the man had, not because he was angry necessarily, but because he needed to set an example for potential future customers.

No, that wasn't right either. He probably wouldn't have any new customers in the near future. Word traveled rather quickly on this planet.

Gin shook the thoughts from his head for a moment and studied the apparent comradery below him once again. To some degree, it made him recall moments from his life before—like those bastards in the Star Killers. The generic name for a merc company should have tipped him off, but the Red Suns didn't align with his interests, and the Omega Horde wouldn't bite. That was ironic, considering they were the reason for his old company's downfall. Nah, it wasn't fair to put all the blame on them. The SK's weakness—that pitiful, infuriating weakness—was in all of their blood. That was why he'd had to get it out of them. Even in the ones who weren't there, it was obviously inherent. Perhaps it was something in the bottled water they drank.

He watched as the denizens below continued to make the rounds. It seemed that everyone there was in some sort of gathering or party. Not much work was done right now, he could safely say, but that worked for him just fine.

The killer activated his cloaking tech and leapt from the ledge to the top of a stack of crates, climbed down quickly, and sprinted to a dangling crane in the middle of the room. He vaulted up to it, balanced the middle of his left foot on the point of the hook, and looked down and around the room. Sentries paced underneath and cameras literally focused directly at him. The merry little workers continued to talk and drink. This was always a favorite part for him—to take the time to bask in the irony of it all. Humans, himself included, always wanted to live life like they had complete control, thinking that nothing happened without consent.

A foolish notion, unless there was a load of people determined to get sick, go broke, or have any numbers of miseries befall them. The best you could do was train, prepare, and be willing to accept the things that came your way, but also have the courage to defy them. Some, such as him, were simply better at that than others. There he was in the middle of a crowded room, and yet no one knew.

A lone man in a black coat sat in a corner and focused on a tablet. Gin felt an odd urge to move closer to see what he was reading and what kind of person he was.

Perhaps he was one of the broken ones? He sensed melancholy begin to swirl within him—one less person to play with—but the apathy left him quickly, replaced by nonchalance. He didn't enjoy playing with broken toys, and as upsetting as it was to see one that looked so shiny and promising fall apart like this, it meant he could focus on what he had *actually* come there to do.

He jumped gently from the crane, landed on the point of a machine's seemingly superfluous pyramid-looking top icon, and launched off that to land on a beam a few feet ahead. This enabled him to jump up back to the ceiling and wend his way through the bars and beams to the other side of the lab and the private offices.

Gin smiled and wondered why they would take a device of such potential and hide it in a drawer. He remembered not believing something like it existed when he first heard of it, and to a point, he had been right. It had never had an effective test, but even as a so-called defective item, possibilities were astounding. Many scientists and technicians had tried to use the device to its full capacity, and many great minds had applied everything they knew to it without success.

Now it was his turn.

A trio of lab techs ran beneath him, and the killer instinctively stood as motionless as possible. Without the proper equipment, they shouldn't be able to see him, but they were three supposedly experienced scientists. That was why he would never remain too long on a crane, for example. A squeak from a lonely hook that swung in a room with no breeze would look rather suspicious, and maybe someone was superstitious, too. In any case, the one with the wavy red hair looked like he wanted trouble, and it would be rather embarrassing for him to be discovered right now because of his own mistakes.

Gin waited for the men to move away and finally crossed the entire length of the lab. He surveyed the surprisingly simple-minded group of geniuses and allowed himself another moment to take it all in. His gaze shifted to his transparent hand. It was almost completely clear, only a slight haze visible. The stealth generator was fantastic and had a long energy span, no notable dip when he moved, and no traceable emissions. When he'd heard about it at the Kioto Station, he knew he simply had to have it. It wasn't as hard to acquire an experimental piece from a station far out in space as one would think, at least not there. And as his previous outings had proven, it wasn't that difficult on Earth either. A station that focused on scientific pursuits screened all their employees and onboard passengers. He had made his way in on a distressed shuttle, one he was responsible for distressing. He'd planned to simply restock when they brought him in, but had found an even greater prize. Things sometimes worked so beautifully in the great abyss.

Gin lowered his hands and tapped a finger on Macha. What was he doing again?

Ah, yes—the BREW device. He almost had it, and once it was his, he would be free to begin the second part of his night. As he prepared to make his way into the wing with the private offices, he allowed the screen on his visor to change. It displayed the lines of energy that fueled the area, the small orbs of personal equipment humming on the guards, and all people.

He loaded Vinci's program. While he wouldn't begin his spree just yet, it might be all right for him to initiate a panic. He thought it over carefully. They might see it as a possible attack—and they would be oh, so right—but they would also ruin his evening if they decided to evacuate or simply leave the area. On the other hand, in corporate labs like this, malfunctions certainly happened, more often than they would admit in their reports. He could have his fun, but he would have to make it seem like an entire generator had gone offline.

And with his new toy, that wouldn't be a problem.

Gin watched as the waves and beams of light in his visor turned black and crept through the trails of energy until they all pooled around their main target. With a snap of his fingers, he killed the power in half the facility.

Someone shouted, and people scrabbled and grunted to force a door open below him. The security guard hustled his four partners through the doors and moved to meet the scientists in the middle of the lab. The killer waited to see if the doors would close before he hurried after them.

He flicked the fingers of his bionic hands, and small spikes emerged from the ends of his fingers. He used them to cling to the wall, and quietly but quickly he made his way down and into the hall. Once there, he climbed the wall once more and made his way along the ceiling. Two men peered at a box farther down and tried to restore the power or determine why it had gone offline.

The killer found a place above them and observed them for a moment. It would have been no problem to take them here. No one else was around, and it would afford him a brief interlude of entertainment. His finger slid across Macha, but he calmed himself with the reminder that these weren't his normal targets. They were simply the unfortunate sheep who had to be sacrificed because the wolf was a rabid, snarling idiot.

Gin continued to the lead scientist's office. He finally found it at the end of the corridor, far from the other staff offices. After a hasty glance confirmed that he was still alone, he dropped from the ceiling, crouched, and made his way to the door. He remained alert for the traps or devices he was almost positive littered the entrance. Even with the power out, the lead tech would surely still have a few toys that would be effective. He studied the wall and the entrance, but there were no devices that he could see. Apparently, the answer was no, which really was disappointing, to be honest.

He pushed the door open slowly and entered. It was rather sparse and drab for a lead scientist's office, with only a desk, one chair, a monitor, and two tablets haphazardly strewn on the desktop. He scanned the room for the BREW and found nothing, but he hadn't expected it to be in plain sight. Once he checked the desk and drawers, he turned his attention to the walls. As he approached one, an oddly darker patch showed a faint flash of light on his screen.

The killer knocked on the wall a couple of times and

grinned at the unexpected clang. He pressed his fingers against it and confirmed a metal surface. With his blade, he cut quickly through the thin material that covered the wall to reveal a metal cache behind the canvas wallpaper. The man hadn't even bothered to put a painting up. How boring. He shifted a little closer and pressed a hand to the cache to obtain a reading of its materials, then nodded. A plasma blade would do. Deftly, he flipped a switch on his Omni-blade to change the cutter out for the necessary blade. When he drew and activated it, the blade hummed with a soft red light.

He dug the blade into the cache to make a small, circular hole, turned it off, and held it in one hand as he reached into the cache for his prize with the other. It looked like nothing more than a cylindrical drive not much wider than his hand, but he knew what the device was capable of. He wondered if he should pay another visit to Vinci and have him examine it. The man would be most appreciative.

But that was something to think about later. He had someone else he needed to see first, and something else to do.

As he grabbed the device, he noticed that it was attached to a wire. Gin studied it for a moment and an amused smile formed on his face. It was a simple little alarm system—when the wire snapped, it would send out a silent alarm. How quaint. He wondered if it still worked. Something that small might have been missed by the program.

Gin ripped the BREW device from the wire and gave it

a final glance before he placed it in the compartment on his left leg.

A beeping from his wrist warned him that his generator needed to recharge. So be it. He wanted to be sporting anyway, he decided as he deactivated his cloak and walked back to the entrance to the room. His primary purpose accomplished, he wondered how he should begin the second part of his night. Should he be loud and boisterous? He intended to send a message, so perhaps something more subtle—more like an assassin, since half the lab was dark already. No. He'd played stealthily far too much, and he wanted a change. His gaze drifted back to the wire, and he wondered if the silent alarm had indeed gone off. If it had, he hadn't detected anything, but it would be a nice surprise to have him waiting there. He could enjoy a little of both options in that case.

The killer shut the door to the room and withdrew into the darkness as he readied Macha and flipped his Omni-blade in his hands. The silence and darkness stretched into minutes, and he began to feel rather silly. He wondered if they would come at all. Had he been *too* deceptive? He felt that perhaps he should have left a trail of corpses. It would probably have been a significant clue.

He had all but given up his vigil when the silence was broken, although only slightly. A skitter was followed by the pounding of boots on metal from the lower floor. They seemed to circle, and Gin smiled. They were coming, and quickly too, with much enthusiasm to retrieve their sacred device. He readied both Macha and his Omni-blade and waited for them to burst through the doors.

What a wonderful night this would be.

CHAPTER NINETEEN

The trio continued down the hall, and Kaiden and Genos ripped open any malfunctioning doors in their path. From what they could tell, however, they had simply moved to another part of the sewage system. All of them groaned almost in unison.

"On our next mission, my orders are that we simply go through the middle." Kaiden sighed and took point as they pressed on. "It worked for me in the Division test."

"True, but may I make the point that we had multiple lives during that test?" Genos reminded him.

"And from what you told me, you were down to your last one," Chiyo added.

"I also took down a giant warbot," the ace muttered. "A hell of an accomplishment for one life."

"We are in our second year," Genos said tentatively. "Perhaps we should make resolutions?"

"That's typically for a new calendar year, Genos," Kaiden explained. "And they aren't exactly hard and fast rules, either. I've already broken mine."

"What was it?" the infiltrator asked.

"I don't recall specifically, but it was something about going to the medbay less due to injuries sustained because of Wolfson. That happened before this year even began." He held a hand up as they approached a corner and walked forward to peer around. When he saw that the coast was clear, he motioned for them to follow.

Genos tapped his neck. "Well, either way, I wanted to suggest that maybe you should focus on dying less? We are training for future conflicts, and there isn't a reset button once life is lost in reality."

Kaiden chuckled. "Not yet, anyway, and when they do make something to fix that, you can bet they will charge an arm and a leg for it."

The two humans looked at the Tsuna, neither expecting him to understand the metaphor. In response, Genos simply looked at each one in turn. "That means it will cost a lot of credits, correct?"

The ace nodded. "Indeed, you are learning. Ah, dammit to hell."

The group approached a chamber that was sealed off and barricaded by a large grate. Kaiden knocked on the exterior. "I can probably blast through it, but it would make a hell of a racket. And without my souped-up helmet, I have no idea what's behind it. Although, considering our little tussle a few minutes ago, maybe stealth isn't in the cards anymore."

"It doesn't look like they are pursuing us, neither mutants nor pirates," Genos stated.

Chiyo opened a holoscreen. "I can't say for sure, but it

doesn't appear that any alarms have gone off, at least not in the systems. The best we can hope for is that if they did hear something, they chalked it up to the mutants. If we still have cover, we should continue to use it to our advantage until we find out exactly where we are."

The ace rested his gun on his shoulder and examined the grate for any possible weaknesses before he shrugged and turned to the others. "There was another path back there. Let's see if it leads somewhere different or at least to a hatch or exit of some kind. Otherwise, we will probably have to go loud."

She closed her screen and nodded. "Agreed. At this point, we're burning time, and having to backtrack would mean that we risk fighting any remaining mutants in that maze-like area."

Kaiden nodded and set off back the way they had come, with the others close behind. Genos tapped the rim of his helmet again. "Chiyo, you mentioned before that much of this station isn't in use. Should we be worried that we might end up in a section with no life support?"

She shook her head. "No, the main systems of these colonies are programmed to feed all sections of the station with the minimum energy and LS necessary to function, with back-up systems in place in case of power failure. The only time that would be a concern would be if there was significant damage to a part of the station."

"Hey, we are dealing with pirates," Kaiden interjected. "They might have gotten bored or drunk enough to spend a few nights blasting apart a few of the unnecessary sections of the station for their amusement."

"Despite their reputation, there is some semblance of order in pirate groups," the infiltrator argued. "Otherwise, no one would really fear them, and they would simply be a problem that would eventually take care of itself. Besides, it's not something we need to worry about. If such a thing did happen or there are massively damaged parts of the ship, they will be sealed off."

"We'll keep a lookout," the ace promised, adding casually, "Did I ever tell y'all that I could have ended up in a pirate group?"

Genos looked surprised. "Really? How did that occur?"

"Well, when I was about sixteen, I took a trip to Baton Rouge and—" He stopped, shook his head, and sighed. "Another dead end, guys."

The others stepped up beside him and stared morosely at the obstacle—no grate blocked their path this time, only a metal wall. They glanced at one another and turned their attention to the walls around them in the hope that they would see something they might have missed.

Genos brightened. "What about this hatch?"

He hurried to a circular valve and gripped it in his hands. With a grunt, he forced it to turn and spun it a few times before the hatch opened to reveal a dark tunnel. Kaiden activated the light on his helmet, and the beam reflected off something ahead. "Is that water?"

"It must be a ravine of some kind," Chiyo guessed as she crowded closer to peer into the semi-darkness. "There is a chance that there would be a maintenance entrance or tunnel somewhere in the area, but it could be a fair distance away."

Kaiden patted himself down. "This armor is basic. It has nothing to assist with swimming."

"But this could potentially lead right where we need to go. A ravine in a station like this has many uses, but one is to act as liquid cooling for the power source. There could be a path that leads to the core, or at least a physical map we can use to find the location that the maintenance crew would use."

"That would be grand," the ace said, but he still looked doubtful as he scowled down the tunnel. "But if there's a possibility of us failing this, I'd rather die in a firefight than by drowning."

"Are you not a strong swimmer, Kaiden?" Chiyo teased.

"I'm wearing nearly a hundred pounds of gear and weapons. Anyone in this kind of gear wouldn't be a strong swimmer unless you were spliced with a dolphin or—" His train of thought ended abruptly, and both he and Chiyo looked slowly at Genos.

The Tsuna returned their stares quizzically. "I had intended to make a suggestion, but it appears you came to the same conclusion."

The duo nodded.

Swarn paced as Walker and a couple of his men studied the security footage. "Are you sure you sent no men into that area, Swarn?"

"You're supposed to be the smart one. I guess that says nothing about wisdom," he grunted. "I just got back. I don't hand orders out the second I set foot on the station."

"I'm merely being thorough," Walker muttered in return. "This would be easier if you would use some of the earnings in the war chest to update the interior security systems."

"I'm not sure if you noticed, but most of the rats we deal with don't make it aboard," the captain growled. "In fact, I'm beginning to wonder if you're simply using this as an excuse to not finish our conversation about your idiotic—"

"I have something, sir." One of the men pointed to the screen in front of him.

"What is it?" Walker asked and leaned in to focus on the display.

"It looks like a group of our guys. The cams caught them looking around section E—the area with all the Watchbots—but another cam picked them up in the maintenance tunnels a few minutes later. It looks like they got in a scrap with the stalkers down there."

"What the hell are they doing anywhere near there? We forbade anyone from going into those hellholes," Swarn demanded angrily. "How the fuck have those things survived so long? Are those fools mincemeat yet?"

"I don't know, sir," the man said apologetically, "Most of the cameras down there are damaged or not hooked up anymore. Maybe try calling them?"

"Do you have their IDs?" Walker asked.

"Uh…it looks like Doma, Skan, and Devi, sir."

Walker straightened thoughtfully and tapped his chin. "Aren't those members of BAT-3?"

"BAT-3 came in for repairs about an hour ago," another guard informed him.

The leader tapped his earpiece in an effort to establish communication with the group. "They don't answer," he said, took a tablet from the table next to him, and skimmed through it. "They don't show up on the board either. Obviously, they are blocking their signals."

"Spies?" Swarn asked.

"That, or they are trying to pull off a three-man mutiny," Walker retorted.

"Maybe they got drunk and on walkabout?" the man at the console suggested, which earned glares from both superiors. He sheepishly fixed his attention on his screen.

"You two!" Swarn exclaimed, and two guards in the corner snapped to attention. "Get a group together and get your asses down there. They are either spies or three idiots who decided my words have no meaning. Either way, they deserve death. Got it?!"

They both nodded and ran quickly from the room to follow their orders, and the captain walked up to the guard at the console. "And you find out who cleared them into the bay and bring him to me. Now."

"Yes, sir!" he said, pushed to his feet, and hurried out of the office toward the hangar bays.

Walker looked at Swarn and frowned. "There's no need to chop heads off for such a petty annoyance."

The captain walked past him and over to the desk, where he opened one of the drawers. "This ain't some white-collar gig like you had before you joined this little enterprise, Walker." He drew a pistol out and primed it. The weapon had a long barrel and was dark-black. Notches and nicks covered the body, and a red light now glowed on the underside. "You have to back your rank up with grit. When I say something, it gets done." He raised the pistol to the side of his face and aimed it toward the ceiling. "And what I want right now is heads."

Genos removed the last of his armor and stood in front of Chiyo and Kaiden in nothing but his underlay and gauntlet. "It is actually something of a relief to be out of that armor. Certainly, it makes me appreciate the suits we get from the academy."

"Unless you land a job with the military or a big corporation, the pirate duds might be closer to what you can expect when we graduate," Kaiden warned him.

"Are you sure about this, Genos?" the infiltrator asked, anxious. "Hopefully, there isn't anything to worry about down there, but if you're caught unaware…"

"I'll be fine, friend Chiyo. And don't worry. I'll only be gone a few minutes." He turned away and looked into the tunnel. "It is more like my native element anyway."

"As close as you can get outside of those special beds they give you," Kaiden agreed. "But remember, only look around for about a klick or two. I don't know how big this ravine is, but there is no use getting lost down there."

"I'll be back as soon as I can."

Chiyo handed him the device she had given Kaiden on the ship. "If there is a drainage valve or system we can use in there, Kaitō will be able to get into it faster than Viola. He will also act as a comm since you don't have your helmet."

"Much appreciated, Chiyo. But are you sure this won't be a problem in the water?"

"It'll be fine, although it is somewhat fragile, so try not to break it."

"No issues there." The Tsuna opened the neck of his underlay and slid the device inside. "I'll be back momentarily." He grabbed the top of the hatch, used it to push himself down the tunnel, and slid into the water. Within seconds, he had vanished beneath the surface.

"Hopefully he doesn't have *too* much fun," Kaiden joked. "I didn't bring a deck of cards with me." His companion looked serious, however, her arms folded as she stared down the tunnel. She didn't seem to have even heard him. "Is something on your mind?"

"Nothing in particular," she said with a shake of her head. "I'm worried, that's all. I don't like that he has no backup in case something happens."

"Have you seen a Tsuna swim? They are like rockets." Kaiden leaned against the wall. "Besides, if this ravine is supposed to carry water for the station, it's like a giant pool, right? What would be down there?"

The water was murky, even to Genos' eyes, and there were glow strips along the walls, but they offered little illumination. He decided he would swim for a while before he surfaced to look around for anything he could use. Arrows were painted along the walls, one marked as Central Station, and he decided that was the best area for exploration.

He swam easily along the ravine in search of his target, and finally reached what appeared to be a central chamber. When he broke the surface, he examined his surroundings quickly and noticed a console on a catwalk above. He retrieved Chiyo's device, looked at it, and shrugged. "Kaitō?"

"Yes, Mister Genos?" the fox EI responded, appearing on a small holoscreen that beamed from the side of the device.

"There is a console up there. Can you get into it while I look for a ladder?"

"I am within range, but this drive is meant for physical connection, so the range is rather limited. If you could do your best to remain in this area, it would be most helpful."

He nodded. "Certainly. I should be up shortly, hopefully."

"Very good, I wish to request what you want me to look for."

"See if there's a way to drain the system. If not, see if we can obtain a proper map of the station, if nothing else."

"Understood. Beginning now." The screen disappeared, and Genos saw a small blue light begin to glow on the other side of the device. He put it away and searched for a set of stairs along the wall. Seeing nothing, he peered up at the catwalk for a ladder or a rope, saw something on the far left, and swam toward it. It was, in fact, a ladder but it was out of his reach. He wondered if the ravine was deep enough for him to build up speed and leap up to it.

The Tsuna dove down and swam to the bottom. Once he reached it, he spun and prepared to ascend. As he planted his feet on the ground for leverage, a noise from farther down the ravine caught and held his attention. He looked up, but the dark water offered nothing. Tense and expectant, he continued his survey until he noticed that the glow strips on the left side of the ravine now flickered. No, he realized, not flickered. Something swam past them.

A chill shafted through him at the truth that he was not alone. As if to confirm this, the figure turned in front of one of the lights to reveal a large silhouette with outstretched arms and a rounded head with four glowing orange eyes that stared directly at him.

CHAPTER TWENTY

"It's been about ten minutes. Has Genos hailed you yet?" Kaiden asked Chiyo, who was hunched over a holoscreen.

"No, and I don't know why. He seems to have found something. I'm linked into Kaitō and he's working to access the controls for the ravine, but Genos doesn't respond."

"Maybe that device isn't as waterproof as you thought." The ace pushed himself off the wall and walked over to look at the screen, which might as well have been written in hieroglyphs as far as he was concerned.

"If that were the case, Kaitō would have been kicked out of the system," she explained. "Genos has him accessing it remotely, which is why this is taking so long. It's not a very complicated defense program, but without a direct connection, Kaitō has to work much slower."

"It might be out of reach for some reason," he suggested, trying to remain hopeful. " As you said, your EI is top notch. I'm sure it could multitask enough to tell us if Genos had died."

She looked at him for a moment, then shook her head and focused on the screen once more. "Not funny."

"Eh, boredom. My bad." Kaiden said with a shrug and a hint of apology. "I'm sure he would tell us if something is wrong. It's not like—"

"Kaiden, Chiyo, are you there?" Genos asked, his voice low and distorted.

"What's with the voice-masking?" the ace asked and looked hopefully at the screen, although it still offered nothing remotely understandable.

"He's talking using Tsuna sound-speak. It's being translated by Kaitō, so he must be underwater," Chiyo informed him. "We're here, Genos. What's wrong?"

"There is a being in front of me—well, above me—and it is staring at me and doesn't move. I do not know what it is," he explained. His words showed concern, even if the translation was barely better than monotone.

His teammates' heart rates rose. "Get back here," Kaiden ordered.

"How much longer until the console is hacked, Chiyo?" Genos asked.

"Genos, we'll find another way. You don't have to—"

"How long?"

She paused as she studied the information. "Approximately four minutes and eleven seconds."

"I'll hold out, then. We've come too far to turn back."

Kaiden balled a fist. "Genos, we have other options. They haven't discovered us yet!"

He had no sooner said that when loud splashing and the

thumping of boots echoed from the direction of the sewers. The duo shared an anxious glance. "I might have misinformed you, Genos."

"They found you?" the Tsuna asked.

"Someone or something is coming," Chiyo confirmed as she drew her weapon.

"Then it appears we both have our problems." He went silent for a moment. "I'll contact you again when I have drained the ravine. Unless you can take them all out, this will be our only escape path."

"I'm sure as hell going to try," Kaiden said grimly and readied his rifle.

"I shall do the same. Stay safe."

"It may be a little hard to do that at the moment, but I can promise to take a few down in your honor. But stay alive this time. I don't want you sacrificing yourself during tests to be a tradition now."

"I can't promise that," the Tsuna said before he signed off.

"How many do you think there are?" Chiyo asked. She moved closer to the opposite wall as shadows appeared ahead of the pirates, who would shortly come around the corner.

Kaiden lifted his weapon, charged a shot, and fired as soon as the first red and black suits came into view. The blast slammed into one and hurled the first batch of pirates back.

"A couple less now."

Genos drifted slowly along the ravine floor. The creature continued to stare at him, and he couldn't tell if it was merely curious to see something other than itself down there or it observed potential prey.

As he floated, his gaze still fixed on what might be his enemy, something struck the bottom of his foot. Distracted, he looked down to see some sort of hatch. It was embedded into the ground and had a circular attachment on top. When he looked up once more, he was shocked to see the creature now only a couple yards away from him. It made no aggressive movements, and still merely stared at him, but Genos was caught off-guard by how fast and silent it was in the water. While he hadn't run into many large aquatic creatures in his time on Earth, he definitely hadn't met or seen anything like this.

The Tsuna planted his feet on the ravine's sandy bottom and prepared to push off to put some distance between himself and his odd companion. He was worried that he had trailed too far from the console. He couldn't risk that since they no longer had an option to turn back. Still, he had no weapons to fight if this thing became hostile. He shifted his foot for better purchase and encountered another of the hatches beside him. Quickly, he looked at his gauntlet, then at the creature, and a plan formed in his head.

The light was still low, but he did see it open what amounted to its jaw to form an ovular hole and reveal sharpened teeth all around the inside. The creature waved its freakish arms from side to side before it grew still again. Genos wondered if this was defensive behavior, having read that some creatures tried to make themselves look bigger to appear more intimidating to what they perceive might be predators.

He was hopeful, but the generous thought wasn't reciprocated.

The creature dove straight at him. He kicked off the ground and rocketed up to the surface. The beast kept pace, flapped one arm quickly to change direction, and lost a little speed. Genos broke through the water and upward. He activated his gauntlet, and drills formed on the fingertips he jammed into the ceiling to hold him in place. As he swung there and heaved a sigh of relief, he twisted at a splashing sound. The creature leapt out of the water after him. Its white skin was dull and dirty from the water, and gray pads with rough and jagged indentations along them lined its arms.

Genos wrenched himself from his perch and kicked off the ceiling toward the water as the creature soared past him. He thought he'd escaped, but it slapped his side with one of its flippers. Something ripped, and pain sliced through him as he crashed back into the ravine. The left side of his underlay under his ribcage had been torn, and blood seeped out into the water. Whatever lined the pads of the beast's arms had sliced into him. He ran an exploratory a hand over the wound and winced, but realized it had created grooves in his skin, almost like it had shaved the flesh off him.

As he swam deeper, the Tsuna fumbled for Chiyo's device. "Kaitō, is there a drain function for the ravine?"

"There is, Mister Genos. One minute and forty-three seconds until it can be activated," the EI responded.

"When it is ready, activate it immediately and allow it to drain as rapidly as it can," he ordered.

"If you are still in the water when that happens, you will be swept away."

"I know, but I have no plans to be. Just follow my command, please."

"Understood, sir."

The creature crashed into the water above him. Its mouth opened and closed rapidly. He had no doubt that it was hungry.

Certainly, he would feed it.

He surged along the ravine floor, and the creature gave chase. By now, he'd guessed that its arms were its primary weapon. The small hooks along the pads were meant to injure and tire the prey so it could feast on them, but their length was a disadvantage because the arms provided obvious warning for its attacks. He would exploit that until he could get into position.

The monster came up behind him and immediately thrust one of its arms forward to try to grab him. Genos rolled out of the way and stopped swimming to allow it to move past him. It turned swiftly and dove for him again while it raised one of its flippers. He kicked to the left as the arm came down. It missed him and dug into the ground, and for a moment, the creature struggled to free itself before it turned to pursue the Tsuna again.

Genos searched the bottom of the ravine for his target, and when he located another of the hatches, he dove toward it.

"Thirty seconds until activation, Mister Genos," Kaitō stated.

"Acknowledged," he replied. He switched his gauntlet into the grip-claw and turned to face his attacker. It torpedoed toward him and raised a flipper to attack again, its mouth agape. He got as close to the bottom as he could as the creature approached, then pushed back with his hands as it moved to attack.

The creature struck his foot, but slipped off it and smacked the rocky ground once again. Genos ignored the pain and launched directly toward its face. The monster looked at him, its mouth open as it made a whale-like moan. He seized the opportunity and clamped one side of his claw into its mouth before he used all his strength to force the head down. It struggled against him, but he managed to thrust the claw into the hatch. The grip ripped through the creature's face to connect and latch it to the hatch, and it wailed in pain and fury.

He unlatched his gauntlet from his arm and swam away as the beast thrashed in place in an effort to escape. The Tsuna held his side and forced himself to increase his speed when he heard Kaitō announce that the drainage would commence.

Far behind him, something opened with a massive grinding sound, and the water began to move. He thrust himself above the surface and up to the side of the ravine, managed to take hold of the railing, and hauled himself up as the once-still water slowly transformed into a raging river. Genos looked back as he lay on the hard floor and gasped ragged breaths as the water level dropped.

For a moment, he saw the creature. It now seemed disoriented and unsure whether it actually wanted to be removed from the hatch, but it had no choice against the force of the water. With one final cry, it was ripped from the gauntlet and carried away downstream. Its arms flailed wildly as it tried to right itself against the current before it vanished.

"Chiyo, my shield won't last much longer," Kaiden stated calmly as he fired uncharged shots at the pirate group that attacked them.

"Hopefully, we don't have to hold out much longer. I think I can hear water rushing from the tunnel."

He listened intently. In the raging battle, he hadn't paid much attention, but now he too could hear the water drain with all the force of a waterfall. Genos had done it.

"Toss me Genos' cannon," he demanded.

Chiyo ran over, snatched the weapon up, and tossed it to him., and he closed the vent hatch and began to power it up. "What are you doing?" she asked.

"Improvising," he responded as he dropped the cannon and charged a shot with Sire. "Gather what you can of his armor and get in there. I'll be right behind."

She nodded, hastily recovered as much of Genos' equipment as she could, and opened the hatch. Kaiden's shield failed as she slipped down the tunnel. He fired one last blast from his rifle to scatter the attackers before he placed Sire on his back and drew his blade, dashed for the hatch, and closed it behind him.

"After them!" one of the pirates barked, and the remaining grunts rushed forward.

"Um…bastard locked it!" another yelled.

"Then unlock it!" The leader drew his heavy pistol and shot the seals on either side of the hatch. "Open it!"

The grunt turned the valve and forced the hatch open, and instinctively stepped back, his mouth open in silent horror. A cannon greeted them, held in place by a knife through the trigger guard. Its core was on the verge of overheating.

"Oh, *shi*—" The weapon blew and the explosion, funneled by the tunnel, enveloped all the pirates around the hatch.

———

"Genos!" Chiyo ran up to the Tsuna, who leaned against the wall and clutched his side. Kaiden set down the equipment she had passed him and knelt beside them. "How are your wounds?"

Both were caught off-guard by the clicks and other sounds coming from the Tsuna and had to wait for the translations from their EIs. "Painful, but not too deep," Genos explained. He rolled his head to face them and pointed behind them. "Infuser, please."

"Oh, right!" Chiyo gestured to Kaiden, who handed her the Tsuna's breather. She checked the lining to ensure his infuser wasn't broken and put it on him. The effect was almost immediate, and the Tsuna's chest swelled as his breathing normalized. "Thank you. It's much easier to breathe."

"And to understand you. Hearing that joyless monotone from you was kind of depressing," Kaiden joked and rested a hand on his shoulder. "Let's get you some serum, eh?"

"I will certainly take some if you have it," Genos said. Chiyo nodded, retrieved a small vial of green liquid, and applied it to his wounds. He leaned his head back. "Much better, thank you."

"You know, depending on how the oscillation is for you, you might feel rough when we get out of this. You might get a chance at Dr. Soni's blue stuff."

"Kin Jaxon told me about that. He said it doesn't work for Tsuna, and that we have to use something devised by the Mortis for heavy wounds."

Kaiden thought back to the blue blob and grimaced. "Ah, right. That's a damn shame."

"You did a good job, Genos, but what happened?" Chiyo asked.

The Tsuna stood and stretched. "The creature attacked me. I don't know what it was—probably a mutant of some kind. I'll have to research it with Viola once we return." He walked past his teammates to his equipment. "But do not worry. I took care of it."

"Damn straight you did," Kaiden said and thumped his friend's chest cheerfully.

"You brought almost everything. Very kind of you considering you were under fire," Genos said appreciatively as he began putting on his stolen DSC gear. "Although, may I ask what happened to my cannon?"

"I used it as a bomb to finish our pursuers off," the ace stated, and rubbed the back of his head. "I didn't have any more explosives on me, so I needed to improvise."

"A trick of mine?" Genos asked.

Kaiden gave him a thumbs-up. "I learned from the best."

"I have a map. Kaitō was able to get one from the console," Chiyo informed them.

"So we're in a good place." The ace looked around the canal. "How much time do we have left?"

"Probably only a few minutes— Wait, there's no more timer. That's odd."

He folded his arms and shrugged. "Maybe there's no more influx. We did have a late start, so maybe most other students have turned in for the night."

"And you also mentioned that it doesn't log us out in the middle of a fight," Genos reminded her.

"True, but we aren't in a fight at the moment. We should be considered out-of-combat." She gave it some thought, shook her head, and looked at her teammates. "Should we continue?"

Kaiden and Genos exchanged quick glances and nodded. "We've come this far. How close are we to the core?"

The infiltrator looked at the map on her HUD. "It's actually quite close—two klicks that way." She pointed down the canal. "But you have to understand that even if they don't know what we're here to do specifically, someone will put two and two together eventually."

"We might still be able to reach the core quite easily, but fighting our way back to the ship will probably be an issue."

"I actually think it may be the opposite," Genos suggested as he checked his heavy pistol and holstered it quickly. "Once I send the core into meltdown, it will cause various malfunctions throughout the station, along with overloading numerous systems and devices before they implode. I'm also sure the central systems that control any defenses will be located in the same area. Chiyo should be able to access those to assist us the rest of the way. But now that we've let them know they have enemies aboard, I'm sure they will mount defenses all through this part of the station."

"That about sums it up," Kaiden murmured as he considered all the ramifications. He snapped his fingers and looked at his teammates. "Well then, since we've already kicked the hornet's nest, why not stomp on it a few times for good measure?"

CHAPTER TWENTY-ONE

"What do you mean, they are all dead?" Swarn roared and threw a bottle that Walker evaded with a tilt of his head. The captain completed his tantrum with a brutal kick at the corpse of the supervisor who had let the spies on board.

"There isn't much to offer beyond that," Walker replied dryly. "They no longer breathe air, their hearts have ceased to function, and they cannot obey your orders due to not being able to hear anything. Do you need more specifics?"

The captain looked at the other man for a moment, and his good eye flared with angry menace. He went to a cabinet in the back and slammed a fist against it so that it opened to reveal his armaments.

"What are you doing?" Walker asked.

"Sound the alarm and start the entire station on a search for them. I'm going hunting."

"Do you think you have the ability to find them now? They escaped into the ravine. It has paths all over the station. You should rally the others and lead the—"

The other man turned and fired a shot from his pistol that skimmed Walker's cheek. He didn't flinch but slowly raised a hand to wipe the blood off a wound that had already been cauterized by the laser bolt.

"I cut my teeth as a bounty hunter, Walker, exactly as my father did. It's in my blood, and is my primary talent."

"Clearly patience is not," Walker muttered and twined his fingers together. "Even so, why should I send everyone into a panic when you seem so confident you can find them? One man against three is not good odds. Three against more than three hundred is even worse. It would simply be in your favor."

"I'll find one, at least, but they won't remain huddled together now that they are aware we know they are out there. My guess is that at least one of them will run a distraction while whoever is left continues to pursue their objective."

"That's suicide, no matter what decision they make. Running around this station alone is foolish. To run around and draw attention to yourself by causing havoc is asking for—"

An alarm blared shrilly over the speakers. Walker spun and stared at the remaining technician, who looked feverishly from one screen to another and scanned the reports. "Section B! There was an explosion in section B. I also have a report of hostile activity from section A."

Walker looked at Swarn, who placed a blade in his belt and took a shotgun from the cabinet as he put his pistol in its holster. "I told you," he grunted, with the first hint of satisfaction in his voice since he had barged into the office.

The other leader looked at the technician. "Send a signal to all troops. Give them the stolen IDs of the BAT-3 crew, and tell them to eliminate them on sight. After that, try to figure out what their plan is so we can cut them off."

The technician nodded and immediately hunched over the console. The captain made his way to the doors. "Swarn!" Walker called, and the man stopped and looked back.

"I'll give you the credit for your strategic guess, but let me tell you something in return that you might find interesting."

"Hey! What's going on? I received a report that—*gurk*." The pirate was knocked cold by the butt of Kaiden's rifle a second before the ace spun and fired a charged shot at two unprepared guards who entered from the hall that blasted them apart. Kaiden searched the unconscious guard and found some fragmentation grenades on his belt. Rudimentary, but they would help, regardless.

"According to the info Kaitō is sending me, they're still running around in a panic. My guess is, it won't take long for them to get their shit together. You have maybe five or six more minutes before they come for you like a bullet train," Chief informed him.

"I won't try to take them all on. I don't know how many it will take to kill me, but I know how many they have." He took the pirate's curved blade to replace his own and shoved it into the compartment on his wrist. "I don't think

I can handle that many. All I have do is keep them all from heading toward Chiyo and Genos."

"They gotta owe you a couple of beers by now, right?" Chief asked.

"Eh, most of these plans are mine, so it kind of negates that." Kaiden opened the vent of his rifle and hurried to the next section. A pirate ran up to him from his left, and as he was about to pass, he drew Debonair and fired a shot into the side of the man's head before he replaced it and closed the vent of his rifle.

Genos pulled the lever and opened the hatch above them. An alarm wailed as he poked his head out. "It would appear Kaiden has already begun."

"He is punctual in that regard," Chiyo reminded him. "Do you see anything?"

"No, but the doors above have all shut. I think any guards in here went to look for Kaiden." He opened the hatch fully, climbed out, and helped the infiltrator up. They were in a small alcove on the side of the room. Cautiously, they snuck along the wall and looked out to confirm that they were alone before they made their way quickly across the room.

"Take a right. There should be a pair of doors that lead to the central station," she directed.

Genos sprinted forward and stopped at the doors beside which a terminal stood. Large windows on either side allowed him to look inside while Chiyo unlocked the door. "There seem to be interior defenses here," he advised her as he noted at least four turrets on the ceiling. "A few droids, as well."

"I suppose they had to have some sense to keep those active. What kind of droids?"

"Guardians. About six that I can see, but I can make out a few bots in the back. They are hidden in all the wires and poles, but they look to be older-model Battle droids, maybe Havoc or Assault?"

"It looks like I get to finally do my job." Chiyo unlocked the doors with a wave of her hand. "Being navigator is interesting and all, but I prefer to live up to my division."

Genos nodded and gestured for her to enter. "After you, then."

"Sir, there was a breach in the central station," the tech informed Walker.

"With the core? So *that's* their game." He clenched his teeth and considered the thoughts racing in his mind. "Send whoever is closest to intercept them and have my shuttle prepared."

"Sir?" the tech asked. "Are we abandoning ship?"

"We are being prepared for potential fallout. A word of advice…Jesse, was it?" The tech nodded. "You'll live longer if you follow my plans rather than Swarn's. Issue the commands and grab a gun. We'll head to hangar seven."

"Understood. Should I inform the captain?"

Walker shook his head. "Even that thick-skulled brute

will understand what is happening here. If they compromise the core, he'll see the explosions and power failures. If he wants his pound of flesh, he'll be delighted by tons. For now, do as I say, and I'll take you along with me. Would you like that?"

"Indeed."

Kaiden fired three shots with Debonair and finally eliminated the large bastard who tried enthusiastically to cave his head in with a sledgehammer. He turned to the wall and kicked the grate in as he holstered his pistol. Quickly, he crawled inside the shaft and into the ducts.

"So the work of an ace is fifty percent ass-kicking, ten percent giving orders, twenty percent planning, and twenty percent crawling through ducts?"

"I would call it fifty percent ass-kicking, forty-nine percent making it look good, and one percent incidentals," he joked. "Crawling through these things has become something of a hobby."

"I've heard stranger." Chief chortled. *"It looks like they are finally regrouping and looking for you in earnest. You might wanna ditch the ID if you still have it. They are more likely to avoid shooting at a no-name than at the guy they are looking for."*

"Aw, hell, you're right." He squirmed an arm behind him to retrieve the ID chip from his helmet and crush it in between his fingers. "It's a good thing Chiyo blocked them or whatever it was she did when we left the hangar, or this would be a canned hunt."

"It would make for a great Darwin Award."

"Do you think we should contact them and tell them to do the same?" Kaiden inquired.

"I wouldn't risk it. The comm link might be intercepted. Besides, they've made it to the power core. Chiyo's doing her thing now while Genos is taking a metaphorical crowbar to it."

"You know, for all the grief they give me for my tiny degree of ultraviolence, they seem fairly apt in that regard themselves."

"You've noticed that too, eh?" The EI laughed. *"Maybe it's only semantics, and you simply prefer a personal touch."*

"I think it is most gentlemanly," Kaiden agreed, continuing to crawl along the shaft. At a fork, he looked one way to see he was blocked by a spinning blade, but the other side was clear.

"So, since we have time to kill, how do you feel about this mission compared to all the others?"

"It's been bumpier than normal, but I guess that's to be expected with a new year and all. Things *should* be harder. Otherwise, I'll continue to make everyone look bad."

"It looks good on the eventual contract."

"I remember telling you that I take the outside jobs so I can buy myself out of my contract."

"You did, but I have plenty of time to think between games of solitaire and throwing and catching a ball against your cerebral cortex. What's the point of buying yourself out of the contract if you'll simply continue to do merc gigs?"

Kaiden stopped for a moment as he thought it over. "Well…I won't be working for someone else."

"You mean besides the person who hired you to do the job, which would by definition be working for someone?"

"It's in the details. I can choose not to do it, and how to do it. That's not the same in a chain of command," he countered, resuming his uncomfortable and slow journey.

"Is that the best you got?"

"I know your favorite pastime is ribbing me, but what brought this on?"

"Like I said, I was thinkin'. I mean, I have a rep too, you know. One of these days, you'll eventually wither and die while I keep going. I would like a better rep than 'Super-advanced EI who was previously partnered with gig drifter.'"

"We've only been together a year and a half, and you're already thinking of replacing me?" Kaiden asked. He tried to sound sarcastic, but a trace of genuine anger tinged his voice.

"Kaiden, baby, please don't be like that," Chief mocked. *"I'm merely a future planner. Plus, with all the shit you get into, the reaper's gotta be creepin' up on your ass."*

"Yeah, and I'll blow his bony ass away, too," he challenged. "Besides, isn't that part of the reason I have you? To make death less likely?"

"And I've done that quite well, don't you think?" Chief inquired. *"But I ain't a miracle worker, man."*

"So you choose this moment to show some humility?" he jeered, and hesitated as he looked at the drop ahead. "Hold onto your encouragement for now. Let's see where this goes."

Kaiden grabbed the rim of the end of the shaft and peered down into a darkened room filled with boxes and parts of ships and robots alike. It appeared to be a storage area. He eased out and dropped to land on the balls of both feet.

As he stood to examine his surroundings more closely, a large arm smashed into his neck and knocked him back several feet. He skidded, but used the momentum to flip himself and stand as he took Sire in his hands and aimed into the darkness

"I figured you would come this way," a guttural, growling voice stated. "I was able to get a bead on your ID for a while. You didn't hide it, only switched the codes around. Otherwise, it would have been obvious that you weren't who you were supposed to be."

Kaiden pulled the trigger to charge a shot.

"Rats always like this room, damn little pests. It figured you would end up here."

"Have we met?" he questioned. A large figure stepped into the light. He was almost as big as Wolfson, with long, matted hair, tanned skin, and thick eyebrows. While he scrutinized Kaiden, the ace saw that the left side of his face was traversed by two long scars and no pupils were visible in his eyes. He wore a red and black coat with black pants and boots, and held a shotgun in one hand.

"You are making a mockery of my colors," the man rasped. "I'll have to peel them off you if you won't take them off yourself.

Kaiden raised his weapon. "First off, *your* colors? I'm fairly sure the Red Suns, the WCM Hell Diver Division, and at least five hundred colleges back on Earth would have something to say about that." He took a step forward. "Secondly, if you're propositioning me, I don't think you quite grasp what a pirate means when he says 'booty.'"

The man aimed his shotgun and fired in an instant. The ace returned the shot, ducked, and rolled to the side. He fired several quick uncharged shots at the man after his first blast sailed past his target. The pirate deserved some credit. For someone as big as he was, he could move damn quickly.

Fortunately for Kaiden, he had trained with Wolfson, and he moved quicker than this bastard.

The ace aimed one last shot directly in front of his attacker and fired. The man saw it coming and threw a container up in an effort to block it. The energy shot merely drilled through the flimsy barrier and struck home in the side of the man's arm. Kaiden smiled for a second before the shot simply slid off and slammed into a pole behind him, and his face dropped.

"What?"

His adversary smiled. "Barrier threading in the coat," he explained as he straightened. "I don't much like all that heavy armor stuff—it's too restrictive—but I have tricks." He aimed his shotgun. "My name is Captain Logan Swarn, and it's my turn now." He released a volley of rapid blasts at Kaiden, and kinetic shots whipped around him as he tried to dodge but was hit in the shoulder, left arm, and right knee. He felt the impact, but his armor blocked the bullets from entering at the cost of it shattering.

The ace took refuge behind a large stack of boxes tied together by a rope. His opponent threw the gun aside, but when Kaiden looked out, he had already drawn a new one and now fired to push him back under cover.

"Tell me why you're here and I won't bother with torture," the captain offered as he strolled toward him. "I'll kill you either way, but I'll be generous enough to let you decide if it's today or when I finally get bored."

"Power core at critical level. Please engage safety measures."

"What in the blazing hell?" Swarn roared.

"I guess I don't have to tell you now," Kaiden said cheerfully as he drew his blade, cut the rope, and shoved the crates violently toward the captain.

CHAPTER TWENTY-TWO

"They're destroying the core. Are they fucking insane?" a pirate yelled as he and a group of more than fifty others rushed into the central station.

"Someone, get it open."

"To hell with that! We should abandon this wreck."

"Can we even shut it down now?"

"Everyone, stop your blathering and take them down!" The group of men ran to the door, and one of them set up at the terminal to force the doors open. "There's no way they will survive all of us. Even if they did somehow make it past the turrets and bots, they gotta be tuckered by now. We have them by the—"

The doors swung open, and the group was immediately greeted by a hail of gunfire from repurposed droids that waited for them within the chamber. Some of the pirates tried to retreat, but several turrets descended from the ceiling of the central station and annihilated them before they had even moved a few yards.

"Well played, Chiyo," Genos complimented his infiltrator teammate from where they stood on the far side of the room. "How much longer?"

"I'll use the droids as a distraction. I've charted a path to the hangars from here. I don't have any resistance to my hacking, so I guess whoever is in charge of cybersecurity has more foresight than this group."

The Tsuna nodded and chuckled as the droids left the room and continued their assault. "I doubt the ship we came in on will be ready. To finish this test, I assume we would have to get far enough away to not be caught by the blast."

"That would be in the 'not dying' part of the objective," Chiyo agreed.

"If we can pile into a fighter, or at the very least a mid-tier shuttle, we should be good." He glanced at her. "Can you find anything in the stations' inventory or directory to tell us if we have something?"

"I'm sure there are plenty of fighters." Chiyo moved her hands as she looked around the map on her holoscreen. "It would all depend on whether we can get to them in time, and before they are all taken by others trying to flee."

"I would assume that those higher up the chain have their own personal vehicles," he said thoughtfully. "They would certainly have something with enough power for us to get out in time."

"Agreed. Let me see…" She continued to scroll, and her eyes lit up after a moment. "Here. There's an AA-class shuttle in this hangar. It's closer than going for the main hangar bays."

"Should we expect trouble?"

A blast from overhead shook pieces of metal from the

walls and knocked some of the railings out of place. "I think we're already in trouble. How much longer do we have?"

"A conservative guess would be about fifteen minutes." Several wires near the console sparked alarmingly. "I would prefer we leave in ten if we can manage that."

"Let's move. I'll contact Kaiden." Chiyo turned her screen off, and the teammates hurried away as she opened her comm. "Kaiden you there?"

"I'm a little busy," he shouted as the captain threw another box at him, fired the last two shots in his shotgun before throwing it to the side, and yanked the machine gun from his back.

"You come to my station, kill my men, and then blow it up?" Swarn yelled. "I'll tear your guts right from your stomach!"

"I don't think this guy will let up anytime soon, Chiyo. We've had something of a misunderstanding." Kaiden dropped Sire, drew Debonair, and fired at the captain's gun and hands in an attempt to make him drop his weapon.

"This isn't the time for you to fight for sport, Kaiden. You have five minutes to get out of there and make it to a hangar. We'll pick you up." With that, she signed off.

"We have five minutes to kill this guy, Chief."

"That's essentially what I took from that," the EI agreed. *"That coat is almost impenetrable, so killing him will take a headshot."*

"I tried, but he hasn't exactly given me a lot of room to

aim properly." He snatched Sire up and dashed across the room as the captain fired a stream shots from his machine gun. "That coat can deflect moderate laser blasts. What about a charged shot?"

"That'll definitely break through, but he's already shown that he can dodge them. You gotta get close."

"Intimate. Got it." The ace fired a few more shots at Swarn from Debonair before he holstered it and closed Sire's vent. He released a couple of half-charged shots to rocket past the captain and hit parts and boxes. Hopefully, the shrapnel would help to disorient him. He held the trigger to charge the weapon as he closed in, then retrieved his blade as he saw the man reach for his pistol. He threw the blade instinctively. It struck the gun as his adversary fired, and a powerful round whizzed overhead. Kaiden held Sire up and fired when he was only a few yards away. The recoil from firing a shot with only one arm pushed his aim slightly off-center, but at that range, it didn't matter.

The captain saw his intention, but he was too close to leap out of the way. His eye glared at Kaiden as he whipped his coat off and held it in front of him to contain the blast. The discharge of energy blew up the containers and any parts around them and hurled the ace back even farther. He crash-landed, and sparks, steam, and metal fell around him as he looked around, but he couldn't find Sire. His ribs felt like they were broken, and he wheezed as he checked his body. Most of his armor was intact, so he had that at least.

As he looked around for an exit, heavy boots thudded behind him. He cursed and moved a hand to his belt as he spun on the floor. Swarn, covered in blood and burns and his face a mask of rage, walked toward him with a large cleaver in his hand.

"I'll give you respect for being a fighter," the captain growled as he stopped a couple of feet in front of Kaiden. "But that won't excuse you from my wrath."

"Do you really want to die in the middle of one of the seven deadly sins?" the ace asked as he pushed himself onto his elbows and fixed his adversary with a hard look. "Although I guess by this point in your life, you ain't much of a one for repentance, huh?"

"Choose your last words and say them," the captain ordered, and brandished the cleaver at him. "At least the ones that won't be screams."

Kaiden flicked his thumb to remove the pin from the device in his hand as he sat up and threw it at his attacker, who caught it in his free hand. "Are you trying to go out fighting?"

"I'm going out of here in a ship," he responded. "You'll go out in pieces."

The frag grenade in the captain's hand exploded a split second after a surprised and angry howl. Shrapnel from the explosion embedded in the ace's armor and a shard almost blinded him as it pierced his visor. Chief's avatar looked at it in the HUD with a wide eye before the display went static and disappeared. Kaiden removed his helmet and stood to remove the other pieces of his armor. Swarn appeared to be very dead. His left arm had been blown off, and blood dripped from his head and chest.

"The coat may have given you style points, but you still should have had armor," he remarked snidely, and threw his chest piece to the ground beside the corpse.

The body shifted, and Kaiden immediately drew for Debonair and aimed it at the man's head. Swarn looked at him and sneered before he shook his head, confusion on his face. His laugh sounded wispy and almost inhuman. "So Walker was right. You are one of those damned siks."

"Sik? The hell is a sik?" Kaiden asked.

"I think that blast knocked out the Broca's area of his brain," Chief volunteered.

"To think...that Swarn...captain of the...Dead Space Crew...would...be felled..." His voice became thinner and thinner, his breathing ragged as it slowed until Kaiden could barely hear him over the flames and electrical static. "By a damn...doll." The captain's head fell to the floor, his body finally motionless in death.

Walker and his two assistants made their way to the ship—a sigma-class shuttle, and one of the few luxury items Walker had amassed. He had, in fact, wrenched it from Swarn's clutches. He tapped a button on his tablet and the shuttle ramp lowered. "Quickly, now. I'd prefer to be in a safe harbor before this place blows up," he ordered.

One of the assistants turned to take the case he carried. He looked over the leader's shoulder and lurched for his gun, but a laser shot pierced his head and caught Walker off-guard.

The leader spun as the other assistant was gunned down in a hail of laser fire. Two other DSC members walked up to him. Now would be the opportune time for a mutiny, but he could deduce who these attackers were.

"I assume you are two of the three people we can thank for this current situation?" he asked as they approached, their guns at the ready.

"We're taking this ship," one of them stated.

"I'd rather you didn't, but considering the circumstances, I'll not argue." He retrieved his case that had fallen to the floor. "My name is Alfred Walker. Might I request that I accompany you?"

The two looked at each other, each seemingly as surprised as the other. "Is this part of the mission?" Chiyo asked

"I don't see any bonus objectives. Maybe it's a secret one? In these situations, you would want to bring back high-ranking men like this for a bounty or to stand trial, right?" Genos questioned.

"Maybe there's something wrong with the Animus? It might have to do with the upgrades. This could be a secondary option of some kind."

Animus? Walker noted that word. He had heard of this device and what it was capable of. He thought back to what he had discovered earlier, put the pieces together, and smiled. So that's what they were doing. He would play along.

"I am unarmed, and while I'm sure at least one of you is a brilliant hacker, I can activate the ship with the press of a button," he assured them.

"Trust me, my EI could get it running just as fast," Chiyo said.

"I'm sure it could, but I should let you in on a little secret, albeit an open one. To keep some of my men from taking my precious ship for joyrides, I installed a proximity mine." He held up a hand with a bracelet on it. "Should it be activated without me on the ship, it will explode."

"Can you confirm this?" Chiyo asked and glanced at Genos.

He studied the ship, and his visor shimmered in purple light. "Scan the ship, Viola, and look for— Oh, it's not well hidden, is it?"

"That would be the point, yes," Walker noted dryly. "I'll submit to any restraints or injuries you feel are necessary, but I would prefer a shot in the leg to being obliterated."

The duo talked among themselves. Genos said he could disable it, but it would take at least twenty minutes. By that time, the bomb would be the least of their worries.

"Get on, activate the ship, and find a seat. No talking to either of us," Chiyo ordered.

"As you wish," Walker said and turned toward the ship again. "Much obliged."

"Chiyo, Genos, where are y'all?" Kaiden asked as he raced through a station that was rapidly falling apart around him.

"We had a slight hold up, but we've taken off," Chiyo explained. "Where are you?"

"The hangar bay next to hangar twelve."

"Most of these hangars are sealed, and the loss of power is depleting the shields. You have to find one that is still active unless you wanna be spaced."

"Any suggestions?"

"*The closest is hangar fourteen, but that could go at any moment. Hangar eighteen is your best bet.*"

"Back to the start," he huffed, "Chiyo, meet me at hangar eighteen."

"On it."

He quickened his pace and covered more than half a mile in two minutes. As he raced toward his destination, the entire station shook. "My guess is we're low on time. Something big just fell off."

"*That would be about a quarter of the station.*"

"Great. Chiyo?" Kaiden entered the hangar. A few pirates remained, obviously seeking to escape. "How close are you?"

"Coming in now." A silver shuttle floated into the hangar, and he ran toward it. When the other men followed suit, he yanked out another frag grenade and hurled it at them. The group scattered and cursed vociferously. The ramp lowered, and the ace flung himself on board. "I'm in. Take us away," he shouted as he took a few shots with Debonair at the pirates who had recovered and resumed their rush to get aboard.

He entered the cockpit and greeted Chiyo and Genos. A man with thin white hair and a goatee sat in the corner. "How long do we have, and who the hell is he?"

"One minute and thirty seconds exactly, and he's the guy who owns this ship. I'll explain when we're done," the infiltrator informed him from where she sat across from the DSC leader with her gun in her hand.

"I assume you are the one Swarn attacked?" Walker asked. Kaiden simply glared at him in response. "Since you are alive, I would guess that he is not."

"Yeah, he's gone. He really couldn't wait a few more minutes to go down with the ship," Kaiden deadpanned. "You gonna miss your buddy?"

Walker scoffed. "Did you talk to him for more than a minute?"

"I have reached the top speed of this ship," Genos said fretfully.

Kaiden crossed the cockpit and sat in the co-pilot's chair. "Is there any way to give this thing more juice?"

"I've had Viola turn off all non-essential systems and reroute the power to the boosters," Genos explained.

"Will it be enough?"

"It should suffice, but that will be up to the Animus. Once the base is destroyed, we should get a mission complete."

The ace looked at the dash and switched a screen so he had a view of the station behind them and could watch it fall apart. Chunks of the station drifted into space, while others exploded or shattered. Finally, once it was almost too distant to see, the station erupted, their mission complete.

Kaiden sat back and grinned at his teammates as the banner appeared in his view. He turned in his chair to Walker. "If you get reused, I hope they don't stick you in as the big bad. You might end up with the same fate as Swarn."

"I wouldn't want that, now would I?" Walker asked, and Kaiden frowned.

"I know they are supposed to be lifelike, but do they have to be so snarky?"

"We're de-syncing," Chiyo warned. He looked over as

the world went white and disappeared around him and waved a cheerful goodbye to Walker.

Once they had left, the man remained and smiled as three bodies slumped over before their suits flattened as dust poured out. He picked a few specks up and rubbed them between his fingers.

Interesting.

CHAPTER TWENTY-THREE

Zubanz strode through the lobby and into the reception area in front of his office without even a glance at his secretary. "Liya, cancel everything for the rest of the evening. I have something I need to deal with." He shoved his office door open and entered, slamming it behind him.

He made his way over to his desk, put down the object in his hand, and activated his monitor to access the list of bounty hunters, mercs, soldiers, and killers—all he could muster who were under the organization's thumb. He sent messages to each of them with one order: kill Gin Sonny. He added all the information he had on him and sent the messages before he opened a compartment on the underside of his desk and removed a bottle of whiskey. Forgoing a glass, he drank straight from the bottle.

It had been barely ten minutes since he had received the report. Everyone at the lab—every guard, scientist, assistant, and anyone else working that night—had been killed and mutilated. Some had tried to escape, but no one on staff had been able to get out of the building. The doors were all locked, and the emergency seals activated.

Forty-seven people gone in a night.

Gin hadn't even been clever or subtle. Zubanz reached for the object he had placed on his desk. It was Gin's knife —the one he'd named—found in the corpse of an engineer near one of the emergency exits.

The chairman, despite himself, felt the loss. That lab was one of the few that had an active staff who knew what they were working on, and, more importantly, who they worked for. They might have been below the people on the board like himself, but they shared the vision.

But what got to him more was the sense of failure and the feeling that he had been made to look like a fool. Gin was a psychopath, but he had worked with people like him before. They always wanted the same thing—their vices catered to and their sick fantasies realized. Do that, and they would do anything you wanted.

But Gin? He was like a child. If he encountered any rule that forbade him from doing something, he did it. What was worse was that not only had he spat in his face, but he had promised the board that he would handle everything when he suggested they use him. He knew he would have to pay, and he could only hope his rank wouldn't be stripped as a result.

They wouldn't do that—risk letting him go. They would be worried he would talk, so they would probably simply have him killed. He looked at the bottle of whiskey in his hand and flung it against the wall with a pained shout before he collapsed in his chair again.

Where did he go from here? He had already sent teams

to the condo he had set Gin up in and sent out over a dozen search parties to comb the area around the lab and city. The killer could have been long gone by this point. He *would* be found. He wouldn't risk leaving Earth right now, not with all the equipment he had stolen. It would prove too much of a risk. He had already sent a tip to the world council about the thefts and they would already be on high alert, knowing that he was on Earth due to the incident in Brazil. He wouldn't get away.

The chairman drew a ragged breath and reminded himself that he needed to calm down. This wasn't something he had to concern himself with now. Instead, he needed to figure out what to do about the organization. They would want answers, but what could he say? He should have acted faster. When Gin first showed signs of being out of control, he should have had him doped up then and there, broken him, and made him follow commands. But that hadn't made sense to him at the time. He'd chosen the man for his talents and skills, and he wouldn't get those with a serum zombie.

He was thinking about Gin again, dammit. *Focus.*

His first consideration was whether he should turn himself in to the organization. Perhaps it would be better to do that willingly rather than have them send an escort. He wondered if they would even bother with an interview or trial. The mission—that was what was important, and despite his loyalty, he had potentially compromised it, even if only slightly.

Gin couldn't be traced back to them, not as a whole. Maybe to Zubanz personally, but he had been careful to cover his tracks. What if that nutcase openly stated he had worked for him? That wouldn't hold up in court. The man was obviously insane.

The chairman checked his messages. Nothing had come back from the people he had sent messages to, and his teeth clenched so hard they could have cracked. They were under orders to reply as quickly as possible when given orders. Was *everyone* defying him now? He began to feel like a joke, and his anger surged again as he smashed his fist into the monitor. It broke and cut his hand, but he ignored the wound and slammed his palm on the desk. Defeated, he rested his head on it and scratched the back of his head rapidly in frustration.

He made a decision. He would head to the manor tonight, prostrate himself before the other members of the Arbiter Organization, and vow to right his wrongs. Even if they didn't demand it, it was his mess to fix.

His choice made, he placed a finger on the button of his call pad. "Liya, call Jorge and have him ready a team and prepare my ship," he demanded, but there was no answer. "Liya? Do you hear me?"

The lights in Zubanz's office flickered. Was there a malfunction? Suddenly, they went out and plunged the room into darkness. When the shutters fell into place over the large windows in his office, he jumped, and his heart thudded painfully within.

"What's going on?" he shouted into the blackness.

"Why soundproof the room if you're going to yell like that, Zubanz?" a mischievous voice asked.

The chairman's heart almost stopped. He opened a drawer in his desk quickly and drew out a heavy pistol. Without hesitation, he fired into the shadows. Brief flashes of light illuminated the surroundings, but he saw nothing and hit nothing but what he owned.

"Where are you?" he demanded as his hands fumbled to vent the pistol.

"Here, obviously," Gin replied. His voice sounded as if he was both in front and behind him, but when Zubanz spun and fired once again, he hit nothing. "I've played with the different settings on the Wormwood device. I like this one—the voice projection. It is rather cinematic, for lack of a better term. Actually, perhaps 'haunting' works better."

"D-do you r-realize what y-you've done?" Zubanz stammered, and closed the vent on his pistol.

"What I normally do—the thing that got your attention in the first place," the killer responded. His voice made it sound as if he had answered a mundane question. "I will admit, most of my actions in the last few hours have been more malicious than usual, but I was dealing with some issues stemming from you."

The chairman crept toward the door to his office. He tried furtively to open it with no luck, then slammed against it in the hope that it would either break or someone would hear him.

"I would imagine you paid top cred for those doors so they wouldn't budge an inch whenever you had to take your frustrations out on them with all that petulant door slamming," the intruder mocked. "I only got in rather recently. Talked to Liya. Lovely girl,"

"What did you do to her?" Zubanz demanded.

"Oh, I sent her home early," Gin stated. "And before you take that to mean I sent her off to the afterlife before her time or something, I'm not so... Well, I would say cruel, but

I think I've demonstrated the ability to be. I've worked my anger out, for the most part, though."

"That wasn't Liya. When I came in that wasn't—"

"To think I spent all that time messing with the setting on this thing for nothing. You didn't even spare me a look. I so badly wanted to know if I had it down." Gin sighed. Silence ensued and stretched for what felt like hours to Zubanz. It was more distressing than hearing him speak.

When Gin finally spoke again, the disturbingly playful tone was gone, replaced by a grim, hissing voice. "Tell me, Zubanz, what did you think I was when you hired me? A potential pet? A fancy toy you could play with because you had the cash? I had hoped that this would be an interesting new direction in my life, the closest I could come to going straight." He drew a long, forced breath. "I would laugh if it didn't piss me off so much."

"This was because of you!" the chairman snapped. "I told you I would let you do what you wanted, that I would pay for anything you needed. You only had to do one thing!"

"We've already had this discussion, Zubanz, and I didn't like how it went the first time," the killer stated in a flat tone. "If you or any of your friends in your little club really had had any sort of plan to deal with your current problem, I would be far away from here, not troubling you."

It went quiet again, but a shocking noise erupted and a searing pain burned into the chairman's leg. He cried out, fell, and immediately tried to stand, but he couldn't find his balance. In the darkness, he fumbled around him to figure out what was wrong and his hand landed on something.

He brought it to his face and recoiled. It was a shoe, one that was filled with his foot.

As the horrifying realization hit him, a boot slammed against his chest. He winced and looked up. Gin stood above him with a glowing plasma blade in his hand. "But you brought me here, Chairman, and had the audacity to not know your place."

Zubanz tried to respond, but only mumbled words formed around his hitched breathing. The killer knelt and held his blade up to his face so he could see it in the darkness. He was emotionless, and stared sharply but blankly at him as if he were staring through him. "I kill for sport, to fill a void, to achieve something I couldn't do as a 'normal' person. That's why I go after those we generally consider warriors of some kind, although I suppose I'm not too picky in some areas. If there is one thing I absolutely despise, it's having to deal with those who believe themselves to be better than they are."

Gin pushed away from Zubanz, who tried to suck in as much breath as possible as the other man walked over to his desk. He picked Macha up and slid it into its sheath. "It was kind of you to bring her back. I was concerned I would have to make another stop to retrieve her if you let the cops take her. At least you proved somewhat useful."

"A-a-are, y-you going t-to—" The chairman couldn't form the words. The killer looked at him and twirled the plasma blade in his hands.

"Speak up. Isn't a proper voice something they teach you in business?"

"A-are you g-going to k-k-kill me?" Zubanz asked, and

tried to compose himself as he pushed up to sit on the floor.

"Eventually...perhaps." Gin admitted coyly. His mouth formed a small smirk as his macabre happiness returned. "I suppose how this all ends is up to you, but you shouldn't really be all that surprised if I do." He held up a few fragments of the broken monitor. "You tried to kill me, now didn't you?"

"I'll call it off," he promised. "I'll call it off. I'll pay you what I promised. You can leave and do whatever you wish."

"How thoughtful. But you know, sometimes the intention is more important than the outcome." The killer took a few steps closer. "Besides, the messages never made it out." He held the plasma blade over his own wrist, a compartment popped open, and the BREW device slid out. "This is my newest little toy, and I've already found that it works wonders." He slid the device back into the compartment and looked at the tablet. "After I deal with that boy, I have a list of other people to meet—another plus."

While Gin was distracted, Zubanz leaned back to retrieve the pistol. He turned and fired at the other man, who simply created a small shield with his palm to block the blasts before he formed the barrier into a ball and hurled it at the chairman's hand to knock the gun away.

"So should I take that to mean you wish to die?" he asked. "You had better come up with a good reason why you thought that was a good idea."

Zubanz lowered his head in defeat, and the killer sucked his teeth. "Disgusting," he muttered, and stepped forward to finish the chairman.

"You said 'that boy.' Do you mean Kaiden Jericho?"

Zubanz asked. "The Nexus Academy student, the one I hired you to go after to begin with?"

Gin knelt and placed the flat of the blade against the man's cheek. He winced as it burned his skin. "Yes indeed, but not out of some debt or promise to you. Even if your mission were different, I have my own reasons for going after him now." He released a cackling laugh. "Funny thing, that. If you had simply kept your mouth shut, the chips would have landed in your favor anyway."

The chairman did something that caught Gin genuinely off-guard. He began to laugh as well. "Have you broken down now, Zubanz? Don't be so boring."

He looked at the killer and, despite the pain, blood, and sweat on his face, gave him a smile. "Then...the mission can still be completed."

The man's joy sent him over the edge. He stabbed him several times in his chest with the blade before he dug it into his throat and glided it across. Blood coated both their faces. Zubanz' body slumped to the floor, and Gin stood over him, breathing heavily as he turned the plasma blade off and placed it in its holster.

"He can't even die right. What a freak," Gin murmured. With a flick of his hand, the lights in the office came back on. He sighed and looked at his latest victim. "I hated your face, and I'll forget it quickly."

"Sir? It's getting late, do you wish for me to drive you home?" the steward asked as he knocked on Zubanz's door. He knocked again when he received no reply. "Sir? Are you in there?" He turned the knob, walked in, and recoiled at the scent of fire and burnt copper. His mouth open, he surveyed the destroyed furniture and antiques and the laser burns that defaced everything. Stunned, he looked down and yelled instinctively at the sight of the mutilated body of his employer on the floor.

CHAPTER TWENTY-FOUR

"Well, that was uneventful." Cameron sighed as the advanced class left the auditorium.

"Nearly unceremonious." Raul yawned. "Almost every test last year had some grand finale. This one had no fireworks or anything."

"Hey, at least we have a feast waiting for us," Marlo protested. "I'll take that any day over pretty sparks."

"It's not like when we head off to our real jobs, they're gonna celebrate every accomplished mission," Silas pointed out. "I'll be happy with a cookie and a bonus."

"The cookie will probably *be* the bonus," Izzy interjected.

"Do we get to choose the type?" Flynn asked.

"Don't let it be raisin," Luke pleaded. "What was your score?"

"Eight hundred and ten out of one thousand," Silas answered. "What about you?"

"Seven hundred and sixty," Raul answered. "We lost

some points because we couldn't find the target fast enough."

"How does that happen?" Amber asked, "You're a tracker, and Cameron is a bounty hunter. That's like your thing, isn't it?"

"It's bullshit. We found the guy, but we had a walking tank with us. Not exactly built for stealth," Cameron chided.

"Oh, you ain't blaming this on me, hothead," Luke retorted. "I recall that you were the one who fired at every dumbass in your way. How is that stealth?"

"What? Am I supposed to let them shoot me?" the bounty hunter retorted defensively. "And it's not like you—"

"Kin Jaxon!" Genos called, and the group waited for Kaiden's team to approach them. "Congratulations on your victory," Genos complimented.

"To you as well, kin." Jaxon nodded. "And to you two as well—a nine hundred, one of the top scores. You certainly keep your reputation up."

"We do our best, but there are a few things we can work on," Chiyo noted and placed a hand on Genos' shoulder. "But at least Genos came out relatively unscathed this time around."

"Yes, although that creature in the sewers was rather unnerving," the Tsuna recalled. "Do any of you know of a mutant sea creature with long arms and four orange eyes? I meant to look it up, but I've been busy since the end of the test."

"Hmm? Did those arms have little ridges on them?" Raul asked as he mentally went over his tracker glossary in his head.

"Yes, sharp enough to cut through skin, and they stick to you as well."

"Yeah, those are samehada. Mostly found in Oceania, but the first was spotted around Japan. I've never seen one myself, but I hear they are nasty."

"Damn fiends, they are," Flynn spat. "They cause about ninety deaths a year back home. Did you take it out?"

"Yes, I drained it," Genos stated smugly.

"Drained it? In the galaxy's biggest sink?" Marlo asked.

"Down a ravine on the station we blew up," the Tsuna explained.

"You guys have the best stories." Izzy sighed.

"It was the first time I saw a Tsuna in the water, albeit only for a split second." Chiyo looked at her friend. "If you guys ever make a settlement down here, it would probably be the closest thing we have to Atlantis."

"We actually have a research station in the Pacific called the Atlantis," Amber recalled. "My mom worked there for a couple of years when I was really young. I don't remember much about it, but I liked walking along the halls surrounded by ocean life."

As the group chatted among themselves, Kaiden was unusually quiet, something they all noticed.

"Hey, Kaiden," Cameron said and nudged him with his elbow. "What's got you in a funk?"

"Funk? Nada, just thinking."

"That's actually more concerning," Luke jested.

"Do you guys wanna head over to the cafeteria? The feast will begin soon," Silas reminded them.

Most agreed, but Kaiden paused and looked at the R&D building, "You guys head on over. I'll be back in a bit."

"Where are you going, mate?" Flynn asked.

"I want to go talk to Laurie. This is usually the best time to catch him before he heads off for either a nightcap or an experiment that's best left unknown. I'll catch up. Congrats on passing!"

As he left the group, Jaxon walked up to Chiyo and Genos. "Is he all right?"

"How do you mean, kin?" Genos asked.

"I suppose I simply mean in general. He seems to be back to his old self, but I worry that he may still be dealing with the aftermath of his near-death experience."

Genos pondered it for a moment, but Chiyo was the first to speak. "He's doing fine. He wouldn't want us to worry," she explained, and received a few surprised looks from the group. "I've been concerned ever since the day he came back, but as he would put it, it's not his style to stay that way. I'm sure if he had problems, he would let us know."

"Your word would be the best in this situation." Jaxon nodded. "Hearing it out loud, I feel the same way."

"Hey, Prof, you got a min—" Kaiden stopped when he saw Laurie, Sasha, and Wolfson standing in Laurie's office. "Do you guys have a book club now or something?"

"That sounds like a fun idea," Laurie said and clapped.

"Feh, I'll stick to the stories I make in my life," Wolfson snorted as he strode up to Kaiden. "How'd you do, boy?"

"Final score of nine hundred," Kaiden stated as he sat in front of Laurie's desk. "Before you ask, I could have killed a few more pirates before we destroyed the ship, we could have tried to access certain terminals to get info, and should have sabotaged ships before setting the core to blow to prevent escape." He held a finger up as he rattled off each point. "All of that is usually bonus objective stuff. I'm a little surprised about the first one, though."

Wolfson stroked his beard. "Same. You usually aren't one to pass up a fight."

"You should consider the usual bonus fodder as natural and common tactics from this point on," Sasha advised. "The willingness to do them without incentive shows both a strategic mind and the drive to go beyond merely the minimum."

"My mission was to blow up an entire pirate station with only a group of three, but I'll certainly make a note of it, Commander."

"Not so tough. I took out three dreadnaughts on my own during my career." Wolfson chuckled, momentarily lost in his memories.

"Are we really dick-measuring right now?" Kaiden sighed. "I'm sure you'll fill me in the next time we spar, but as much as I would like to catch up, I have to do something I don't like to."

"And what is that?" Sasha asked.

"Ask Laurie for information."

The professor frowned and moved a few strands of hair. "You're picking up on Wolfson's bad habits, particularly in regard to me."

"It's nothing personal. Prof, but you're long-winded."

"I prefer 'thorough,'" the professor countered as he settled in his chair. "What can I help you with, Adva Jericho?"

"Hearing you call me by my title is like a parent calling a child by their full name," Kaiden grumbled.

"You've stopped visiting, so a loss of familiarity is only to be expected," Laurie stated, but a sly smile crossed his lips. "Try not to make your being injured the only reason we see each other. Now, what can I do? Is it about Chief?"

The EI popped into the air. *"Nah, I'm doing dandy, Professor."*

"You know, I've wondered why you don't call him something like 'Father.' He is your creator, after all."

"Because then I would get accused of nepotism," Chief said jokingly. *"You may not be able to tell, but I'm obviously the favorite."*

"You *are* the most fascinating, but do remember you are with Kaiden because of a biological abnormality. Otherwise, you would still be sitting in a box."

"So the Gemini thing is an abnormality now? You made me feel so special last year," Kaiden retorted.

"And you still are, but I thought you wanted me to cut down on the things that made you feel like a 'lab rat?'" Laurie teased.

"Take it from me, boy, stay away from the cutting table. If Laurie could get away with it, you might be more machine than man," Wolfson advised.

Laurie scoffed. "I might be a technophile, but I only have a few personal upgrades. I have no desire to turn myself into a cyborg."

"He was referring to Adva Jericho, not you. Could you say the same for him?" Sasha asked.

The professor replied by silently pouring himself a glass of wine and taking a long sip.

"I wanted to talk to you about the Animus and some of its parameters," Kaiden stated.

Laurie lowered his glass and regarded him curiously. "Oh, really, now? What brought this on?"

"During my last mission, I was fighting this big burly pirate. Before he croaked, he said I was a doll or something."

"That merely sounds like he was trying to insult you before he died. It's not an abnormal thing for a blood-thirsty killer to do when his end is coming. The Animus is supposed to replicate personality traits."

"I would have picked up on that," Kaiden stated flatly. "But I had to take my helmet off. When he looked at me, it was as if…I don't know, as if I was something supernatural or alien. He said that someone was right, and I was a doll. I guess it rubbed me the wrong way, but it seemed a weird thing to put in the middle of a mission with no backstory."

Laurie took another sip. Kaiden thought he saw his gaze dart away for a moment, but he closed his eyes as he took a long drink to finish the glass. "True enough. I can look into it, but every mission for the advanced mid-year test is artificially crafted based on the team makeup, skills, and rankings of the students. It may have been done as a test of your mental capabilities."

"How's that?" he questioned. "Do you guys test us to see if we're insane? Or only me?"

"Potentially," Sasha said, moving closer to Kaiden's left

side. "Perhaps not your psychosis, but we do occasionally add random or specific elements to test your mental state." He pushed his oculars up. "We do this because unfortunately, mental breakdowns can happen in this field, especially for soldiers, that lead them to become a danger to themselves and/or others. It's best that we catch them now so we can help them through it rather than have something happen later."

"I'll let you know if I start seeing pink elephants or if I think the vampires are coming," Kaiden said sarcastically.

"If it's the mutant kind, you'd better," Laurie said cheerfully. "Even the ones with capes. I wouldn't want them around. They have terrible taste in music."

"I should probably also add a little detail," Chief interjected. *"Kaiden took him out with a frag grenade that tore off a chunk of his head. I thought it was simply a mental trauma thing."*

"Heh, I can tell you that isn't a sunny day." Wolfson chortled. "I had something like that happen to me, and most of my dome is metal now."

Kaiden looked at his mentor. "How are you even alive right now?" He stopped to think for a moment. "Wait a minute—that time you headbutted me and knocked me out? That's cheap!"

"You use what you have. Do you think an Omega merc with a chain gun for an arm will give a damn if you have a handicap?" Wolfson challenged him.

"It is certainly a possibility," Laurie agreed to bring the conversation back on track. "The Animus was created and designed to replicate a gazillion possibilities." He chuckled. "I am stunned by my feats so often."

"I'm not sure how I feel about one of the top scientists

in the world using a word like 'gazillion,' but keep that ego burning," Kaiden muttered, earning a glare from the professor.

"It's getting late, Kaiden, and your class feast is underway," Sasha said. "Do you need anything else?"

"Nah, I can take a hint." Kaiden pushed to his feet and Chief disappeared from view. "I simply thought something was buggy. I guess I'll see y'all around."

"I should see you tomorrow evening, right?" Wolfson asked.

"Right, right, I'll be there. I'll see if I can't drag a few of the others along," Kaiden promised, and took his leave.

Laurie exhaled a long sigh and poured himself another glass. He offered some to both of his visitors. Sasha declined, but Wolfson snatched the bottle and the professor didn't bother to put up the barest hint of a fight.

"I suppose it was inevitable that one of them would notice at some point," Laurie whispered as he swirled his glass.

"I told the board it was too much of a risk," Sasha reminded them. "If this gets out—"

"It won't. I'll shut the operation down from here on out until we can find a better option." He took a quick sip and put his glass down before he rested his head on his hands. "Everything is piling up—those laboratory thefts, one of the most notorious killers walking on our planet, and now we have to worry about this. We should never have considered it in the first place."

Wolfson, having drained the bottle, placed it on the desk with a hard thud. "I agree with what the intention was, but the fallout that could happen if the news got out or something went wrong with the transference? We'd have the screws put to us, and the entire Academy would be up shite creek."

The two other men nodded. "I agree with you, Laurie," the commander said. "Shut it down. I'll deal with the board if anything arises."

"Thank you, Sasha," Laurie said appreciatively. "Do you ever wonder if we could be the next Arbiter Organization?"

"That's doubtful," Sasha stated. "Everyone knows about us."

Kaiden walked along the coast of the island. The evening was settling in, and he took a moment to look at the sky, where blood-orange hues mixed with blues and violets. The chill breeze of early winter flowed across him, and he buttoned his coat and slid his hands into his pockets.

"Cred for your thoughts?" Chief asked.

"Just taking a moment," Kaiden answered. "Do you remember when I mentioned that I could have been a pirate?"

"During the test? Yeah. You never told me that story."

"I guess I made it sound like a big deal, but it wasn't really. A member of the Lunar Sails saw me shooting at a range and thought to bring me on board. I told him I was already part of a gang and he left me alone. I guess it made me think about the irony that out of all the possible paths in my life, I ended up with the one that'll have me chasing down everything I could have been."

"The dramatic irony is palpable," the EI jested. *"For what it's worth, I like this path, at least."*

Kaiden laughed. "I would hope so. Without me, you wouldn't be the super EI you are."

"That was always going to happen. I merely wouldn't have been as shiny."

He smiled as loud explosions erupted above, followed by crackling and fizzing. Fireworks above the Academy signaled the end of the first semester. He leaned on the railing and watched them set the sky ablaze.

Across the water and high in the mountains, another figure watched the fireworks, but he was focused on the island. A smile graced his lips as he tapped the blade on his hip.

He would have a homecoming soon.

LATE EPILOGUE

THE STORY OF GIN

"Did you ever wonder how it got to this for me?" Gin asked his companion, who listened intently. "I mean, this wasn't the big picture for me when I was a kid. I actually wanted to do the complete opposite! I planned to be a medic and went to the Nexus Academy and everything —the one across the lake. I got to combine my love of tech and my desire to help people."

His companion nodded, but she shifted away slightly. He caught the movement and gave her a curious glance, which made her freeze and move back into place.

"I guess we have some time to kill, ha-ha! Erm, sorry, that was probably a pun, wasn't it? Never mind. I'll tell you about me, starting with the time I left Nexus."

***

Three men exited the Animus pods and limbered up after their prolonged exposure.

"Man, that was intense," the ace declared, and rolled his

shoulder to ease the stiffness. "What was the final score and time?"

"Three hundred and eighty out of five hundred. Total time was four hours and twenty minutes," the decker related. "That's a better score than last time, but we took almost fifty minutes longer."

"It's all right. We'll run another one in a couple of days." The ace placed a hand on the third teammate's shoulder. "I'll probably bring the new guy along. You did amazingly. I was surprised by how well you were able to keep up and help us maintain the advantage. This was my first time running with an exotech."

"I was happy to help," the man said with a small smile. "Although I'm still getting used to using the Nanos in the middle of heavy combat. If the two of you weren't so calm under pressure, I would have had a much harder time. You deserve as much praise."

"Appreciate it." The decker returned the smile. "I gotta admit, the exotech class is fascinating. I've worked with bots all my life, but I've only seen them as helpers with manual labor or as grunts. It's nice to get a new perspective."

The exotech nodded. His voice grew more excited. "The applications are numerous. I spent time in prep school learning traditional surgical skills, but after I watched a demonstration on the extranet, I switched class options."

The decker looked off to the side in thought. "Which one?"

"The Axiom corporation demonstration a couple of years ago."

The ace folded his arms. "Axiom? Aren't they the ones who gave us mutants?"

"Nah. Well, kinda. That was the Fillan conglomerate, and after that fallout from...you know, *that*...it was dissolved. But a lot of the top scientists and engineers split off to form their own companies. It's said that Axiom was founded by three of them," the man explained.

"I see. So does that mean—"

"Well, hello there, Gin."

The ace flinched as his name was called, and the trio turned to see three other students approaching them.

"Who are they?" the exotech whispered to the decker.

"The one with the frayed jacket and long hair is Rick, a battle medic. The one with the red hair and wine stains is Tai, a raider." The decker glared at the last member, the one who had called to Gin. "That one with the blond crop-cut and shit-eating grin is Eddy, who is a dick."

The exotech chuckled but tried to keep it quiet as Eddy and his posse walked up to Gin. The decker moved to his side. "So, how'd you do?" Eddy asked, and tilted his head so that he could look down at the ace.

"We did fine, Ed. What about you?" Gin muttered, and his lips barely moved.

"Does that even need to be asked?" Eddy demanded. "We got the top score possible—five hundred out of five hundred. But I want a little more detail, Gin. Tell me, what was yours?"

The ace flexed his arms in annoyance. "Nearly four hundred."

"Skirting around it? Final score, Gin."

"Three hundred and eighty. You gonna say something about it?" the decker challenged.

"Oh, come on, Inigo. No need to spit," Eddy mocked, and wiped imaginary spittle from his mouth. "Three hundred and eighty, hmm? I guess that's above average." He glanced at Gin again. "Kinda low for the son of a WCM general, though."

The ace's arms continued to tremble for a moment, then he exhaled a sigh and smirked at Eddy. "Maybe, but I guess I have to congratulate you. A perfect score is really impressive."

"Well, at least you know who your betters a—"

"For the son of a disgraced captain."

Eddy's eyes flared at the comment, and he took a swing that Gin ducked. The ace dodged as his opponent tried to hit him again before his lackeys grabbed him and forced him back. "You shouldn't come at me, Eddy, not if you're going to get so pissy each time I say that."

"You don't know a goddamn thing, you pissant!" Eddy roared.

"Ed! Calm down," Tai pleaded, still trying to pin his arms back.

"There are teachers all over the AC, man. If you are caught trying to pick a fight, you could get your rank docked or even be expelled," Rick warned.

Eddy ceased his struggles. "My dad—he was a hero. He would do what others wouldn't, and won plenty of fights because of it," he declared. "I'd rather be like him than some ass-kissing general. The life of a soldier—of all humans—is dictated by who is the most powerful."

"For soldiers, it's about who's strongest, and that's

measured by more than who's a better fighter," Gin stated. "I'm tired of dealing with you, Eddy. If you want to settle this, fight me in a PvP match. Otherwise, get lost."

The man straightened his jacket and smiled. "You know what?" He punched one of his fists into his other palm. "That sounds good. Since we're both aces, how about your group against mine?"

"I'm surprised you don't wanna go mano-a-mano," Gin said, and glanced at his teammates for confirmation. Inigo stepped up and the exotech looked worriedly at him, but he merely gave him a reassuring smile. Gin nodded quickly in response.

"It'll be better like this. See if you have what it takes to command." Eddy pointed to Tai and then to the console. "Set us up, and we'll crush these idiots."

Gin, Inigo, and the exotech appeared on one side of the arena. It was basic—dark, rocky terrain that covered three hundred yards with a few columns surrounded by a dome of blue light. They huddled around one of the pillars.

"Inigo, when the match starts I'll need eyes, so send a scout out."

"Got ya." He nodded. "What about defenses?"

"What do you have?"

"Three scarabs and a rolly," he said and pointed to the large box on his back with treads. "Sorry, engineer lingo. A panzer."

"Use the scarabs to distract them, not for real damage. Keep the panzer nearby in case they circle around."

"You want me to stay put?" Inigo asked with surprise. "What about backup?"

Gin smirked and flicked a thumb at the exotech. "He'll be my backup. You'll be more efficient without having to multitask. Focus on the bots."

"Are you sure you want me with you?" the exotech asked as he checked his equipment. "As I said, I'm still getting used to all this. I was a surgeon until this year."

"Hey, if worse comes to worst, dig a scalpel into them," he joked. "You said you need practice. It might be a little intense, but pressure makes diamonds."

"Yeah, I guess so," he muttered.

Inigo smacked the back of his hand against the exotech's chest. "Don't fret, man. You got this, and already showed what you could do ten minutes ago."

"I'm sorry you were dragged into this," Gin apologized. "But I appreciate you stepping up, Placido."

He nodded but still looked doubtful. "Oh...uh, thank you."

"What wrong?" the ace asked.

Placido rubbed the back of his head. "Oh, nothing. It's just... Most people don't call me by my full name. They say it's too hard to remember or pronounce."

Gin laughed. "The joke's on them. In the field, you wanna know the name of the guy responsible for keeping you alive."

"That's certainly the wise move," Inigo agreed.

"Battle commencing in thirty seconds."

"Are you guys ready?" the ace asked as he drew his rifle.

"You bet." Inigo retrieved a cylinder from his belt and opened a holoscreen.

"You stick with me. I bet we'll be done with this in ninety seconds." Gin glanced at Placido, who nodded in response.

"Are we taking bets now?" Inigo asked, and drew his arm back to throw the device.

"Do you wanna risk the creds?" Gin asked.

The decker thought about it for a moment. "Nah, ninety seconds seems about right with you taking them on."

The signal to begin the match sounded. Inigo threw the cylinder into the air, and it unwound and launched an airborne scout. Inigo turned as the bot on his back dropped. The treads activated and allowed it to roll around. Three orbs popped out of it that extended four legs apiece, and a single red eye lit up on each as they landed on the ground.

"Your cover's in place. Do your thing." Inigo knelt and controlled the bots using his screen.

"Let's get out there," Gin ordered. He ran off with his rifle at the ready. Placido clicked a button on his gauntlet to open the tube on his back that contained his Nanobots. They scattered and formed around him.

Laser blasts issued from the other side of the field. The raider stood atop a large rock and fired down on them. The exotech created a barrier using his Nanos. "This isn't like a vanguard's barrier. It won't hold up for long."

"Can I shoot through them?" Gin asked as he took aim.

"I can open a path."

"On the left. I have a shot."

A clear space opened in the barrier and Gin fired three quick shots. All of them struck the raider, and his shield disintegrated after two. His armor saved him from lethal damage when he was hit in the chest and knocked off the rock.

"Ed is probably trying to flank us," the ace surmised.

"You have that right, and Rick is heading to Tai's aid. He'll get there before you," Inigo informed them.

"He won't heal him," Placido stated. He took a launcher from his belt, put a small grenade in it, and fired. The explosive arced over the rock, landed at Tai's feet, and erupted.

"I heard a boom, but I didn't see an explosion?" Gin asked and flashed a hasty glance at Placido.

"It's a grenade filled with bio-sabotage Nanos. If the medic tries to heal him with a stim-ray or serums, they will cause infections instead."

"Nice. Let's finish them off." Gin readied a shock grenade and activated it when they drew close to the rock. With a grin, he lobbed it to one side. Two loud yells gave a warning a split second before a shield burst.

"Got 'em!" The ace rolled past the boulder, dropped to one knee, and fired several shots. Their two opponents disappeared in a flash of light.

"Two down!"

"Gin, Eddy took out my scout and the scarabs. I have no eyes. Shit!" Inigo cried.

"Inigo! What happened?" Gin asked as he vented his rifle and ran back. Placido followed closely behind.

"The bastard got me in my arm and chest. I tried to chase him off with the panzer, but it went dark on my holo."

"Where are you?" the exotech asked.

"I made it to the pillar across from where we started. I don't think I'll celebrate the victory with you."

"Hold on for a few more moments," Placido instructed. He threw a volley of Nanos at Inigo's location, and they immediately set to work to close the wound and inject him with healing serum.

"Wow, I'm feeling better already. Gin, he's coming for you! Behind the rocks."

Eddy leapt from his hiding spot and hurled two grenades. They rolled and stopped, but were still too close. Placido slammed a spike into the ground near Gin's feet and surrounded himself with his remaining Nanos to create a weak barrier. The grenades exploded a split second after the spike formed a personal shield around the ace. Placido was thrown back, but thanks to his Nanos, survived the blast. Eddy followed up with a barrage of machine gun rounds at Gin, and although the barrier continued to protect him, it began to break apart.

The ace closed the vent on his rifle and jumped back. As the shield split, he fired two shots. One pierced Eddy's gun and the other impacted in his shoulder, but not enough to fully deplete his shield. He dropped his gun and spun to throw his last grenade at Gin while he fired his heavy pistol.

Gin avoided the blast, but the force knocked him down and depleted his shields. Placido hastily switched the types of Nanos on his device. He activated the second canister on his back and sent the Nanos directly at their opponent. They emitted electrical charges that effectively weakened the remainder of his shields and pushed through to connect with the armor. Eddy's muscles spasmed and his shots went wild.

This gave the ace enough time to snatch his rifle from the ground and fire at Eddy. The impact threw him to the ground. Gin walked up and looked down at him.

"This is...bullshit," Eddy blustered, his voice strained from the shocks. "I have better...scores than...you do!"

"You also supposedly have some of the top students of our year to support you, but none of that did do you much good," he retorted. "Anyone can be great when they have the advantage, but that's not our job. We're aces. We help others and lead them, even if it costs us top scores. I see the potential in Inigo and Placido." He pressed his rifle against his adversary's head. "And they help bring out the best in me."

With that, he fired, and his opponent disappeared from the arena. Victory was declared for their team, and Inigo ran up and gave Gin a high five. The ace turned to Placido, who pushed slowly to his feet. He gave him a smile and a nod, and he felt a warmth in him at the kindness the ace had displayed as the area turned white and they were de-synced.

G in sat back and spun Macha in his hand. "Gin… He was my first real friend in a long time—the first one I really counted back at the Academy." He continued to twirl his blade and stared down at it in silence. "I imagine you think I'm a little crazy, talking about myself in the third person and all, eh?" He grinned at his companion. "Not at all. Gin isn't my real name. I…borrowed it when I joined the Star Killers, but we still have a way to go before that."

The killer looked up and checked the time in his HUD before he resumed the motion of the blade in his hand. "We still have time to burn, so I guess I'll keep going. I have nothing better to do. I had to delete solitaire from my apps to make room for other stuff." He studied his companion in silence for a moment. "I should let you know, this is where it gets…dark, even for me." He frowned at his blade as it rotated in his fingers

"Is that a nervous habit or something, Placido?" Inigo asked from where he leaned against the Animus pod.

The exotech stopped spinning the scalpel. "It's a dexterity exercise, something I picked up when I was a boy."

"I've seen you do it a few times over the months. Do you use that scalpel in your work?"

Placido chuckled and held it between his thumb and forefinger. "It's not exactly sterile now, is it?" He placed a cap on the blade and put it in his pocket. "It was part of the surgeon set I received on the first day of initiation. I keep it with me as a token of sorts."

"To remember where you started and all that? I can see that. It's good to remember what you did before you were got whisked away by the new shiny thing."

Placido folded his arms. "Speaking of starting, Gin is rather late. He's usually the one waiting for us."

Inigo took a tablet from his jacket pocket. "No kidding. He did tell me he had to go somewhere about a half-hour before I left to come here, but I thought he'd be done with whatever it was by now."

"I don't see him on the network." Placido checked his friend's list on his oculars.

"Do you think he's meeting up with a special someone?" the decker asked.

The other man shifted slightly and shrugged. "He *has* become much more popular in the last couple months since we took the top spot in the mid-year master exam." He rubbed the back of his head. "It's possible. We probably shouldn't bother him if that's the case."

"Jealous?" Inigo teased.

Placido shook his head "Of Gin? No, no. I would be happy for him. I'm far too busy to consider a relationship that intense right now."

The decker frowned before he shrugged. "It wasn't what I was implying, but I can see that." He looked at his tablet again before he put it away. "I say we give him about fifteen more minutes before we go out to look for him."

"I'm sure he'll show up well before then. I bet he's coming up the stairs right now."

"So much for that," Inigo muttered as the duo exited the Animus Center. "Where should we start?"

"I think we should split up. I'll check the gym and tech department," Placido suggested.

"Then I'll check the plaza and library."

The exotech tapped a few fingers nervously on his chest. "I'm a little worried."

"About Gin? Who's gonna mess with him? The only guy I can think of is Eddy, and he's already in hot water. If he even gets within a hundred feet of Gin, his ass will be kicked out of here," Inigo stated and lapsed into thought for a moment. "If you do find him and he is with a hook-up, let me know and we'll all reschedule. I'll do the same."

"Right." Placido nodded.

With that, they split up and went to their respective search areas. Placido spent at least twenty minutes looking around and asking the few remaining students who still loitered around in the late evening if they had seen Gin. He finally caught a break when someone told him they had seen him talking to someone near the engineer's dorms a little over an hour earlier.

They didn't know what they had discussed or who it was, but it had looked like a girl. He thanked them and headed that way while he thought it over and wondered if he should inform Inigo. It seemed the right thing to do, so he opened his network list and called him, then placed his transmitter in his ear.

"Calling Inigo Alamo," his EI, Sigmund, confirmed.

"Hey, Placido, did you find him?"

"Another master student said that they saw him talking to a girl near the engineering dorm. They didn't catch the conversation, but he said they headed toward the docks afterward."

"The docks? That's a weird place to get busy."

"You shouldn't be so crass," he chided.

"Ah, come on. I'm only being real." Inigo laughed. "How about this? Let's go see if we can catch him."

"What?" Placido asked, flabbergasted. "What if he is actually—"

"That would be even better. He made us wait all this time, so we should have a little fun, don't you think?"

"What if he gets mad at us?"

Inigo scoffed over the comm. "Come on, that ain't like Gin. He might get a little ruffled, but he'll probably only be as apologetic as you usually are when you mess up."

"Yeah, yeah." The exotech sighed. "I am reasonably close to the docks, actually."

"Cool. I'll meet you there. See if you can find him." With that, they ended the call. Placido retrieved his transmitter and sighed. How did he constantly get dragged into Inigo's little pranks?

Hopefully, Gin wouldn't be too mad at him.

The exotech walked down to the warehouses at the end of the pier. So far he hadn't seen him, and he wondered if Gin had already returned and was now waiting for them. No, that didn't make sense. He would have turned his visibility on in the network by now if that was the case.

As he walked up and down the rows of warehouses, storm clouds formed above. He realized that he should probably quicken his pace. If it got too bad, he would have to hope Gin would contact them later.

He heard something, but couldn't make it out. It seemed quick and dull and sounded like it came from inside one of the storage units. Placido jogged over and leaned against the side of the unit to listen. Was it a malfunctioning machine or something?

A thump was followed by another sound, this one clearer, and it sounded like a pained grunt. Two more thuds were followed by muffled words. Something was definitely going on in there.

"Have you had enough yet?" a voice rasped, low and menacing and barely audible. The unmistakable sound of someone crying punctuated the short silence that followed. "Stop your bitching! You're in on this now too. If you don't want those pics to get out, keep your mouth shut."

What the hell was going on?

"Ed, we have to wrap this up." Placido knew that voice.

It was Rick, one of Eddy's flunkies. "We've been here way too long. I think Gin's gotten the point, man."

Gin. They have Gin.

"We could get caught," Tai added, and he sounded nervous. "This is way more than you said we would do, Ed. This won't only get us expelled, we'll all go to jail."

"Shut the hell up. That will probably happen anyway once—" Eddy's retort cut short and transformed into a haunting chuckle. The tone was ominous, and Placido trembled involuntarily. "You want to wrap this up? Fine. I'll wrap it up for good."

Collective gasps confirmed the man's intent. "Eddy! Don't!" Tai yelled.

"What the fuck, bro!" Rick protested. "Don't kill him!"

Kill? No, no, no!

Placido ran to the side of the storage unit, shoved the bar aside, and dragged the door open.

"Stop!" he and the others shouted.

Blood sprayed in the air—Gin's blood, released by the knife in Eddy's hand.

"Do you feel strong now?" Eddy sneered. Tai, Rick, and a girl with auburn hair stared at the entrance of the storage unit and Placido, who stood there in shock. Gin winced, and his eyes fluttered as Eddy twisted the blade deeper.

The exotech grew silent, and his hand moved mechanically to his pocket. Eddy finally looked over his shoulder. "Hey, look, it's one of Gin's buddies," he mocked. "So you came looking for this pissant? Well, take a good last look. This'll be the last time he ever talks down to—"

Placido ran forward, and both Tai and Rick seemed too surprised to stop him. He flicked the cap off his scalpel and drew it out. Eddy's eyes went wide as he straightened and yanked the blade out of Gin's chest. He wasn't quick enough. The exotech rammed the scalpel into his throat, and his adversary's shocked gasp became a guttural gurgle as he dropped the knife. Placido simply stared at him and dragged the blade across his throat. Once the scalpel slid free, Eddy's body subsided into a heap.

"W-what the h-h-hell…" Tai stammered as he backed away from the newcomer.

"Why didn't you stop him?" Placido asked, his voice monotone and eyes downcast as he held the scalpel up.

"We couldn't, man. Eddy was…he was losing it, man," Rick said, his voice trembling.

"You should have tried. Look at what he did!" the exotech roared, and tears formed in his eyes as he looked at his friend. "You didn't stop it."

Without any warning of his intention, Placido launched himself at Rick, who didn't seem to register the danger he was in. Too late, he tried to scream, but it was cut off when the scalpel stabbed viciously into his jugular. He staggered back against the wall of the storage unit, and the girl shrieked, covered her mouth, and scrambled away. Rick leaned against the wall for a moment before he slid down, his hands clutched around his throat.

Tai tried to fight and attacked Placido before he could turn on him. The exotech slammed his knee into his attacker's groin, and the medic doubled over. He raised the scalpel, drove it viciously into Tai's head, and dragged it down his face as the man screamed. The agonized cry faded, and Placido released the scalpel and let the body fall. He looked at the girl.

"You brought him here," he said, his voice low and venomous. "You were the one who brought him here, weren't you? You trapped him."

"I-it wasn't m-my fault," she pleaded. "Eddy made me. H-he threatened me."

"Gin is… Because of you, he is…" His voice began to break and he shook his head, walked over to her, and moved his hand to her throat.

"Placido…please stop," a weary voice said behind him. He turned, and Gin stretched a shaking hand toward him.

"Gin!" he cried, and clasped his friend's hand. "I'll call the medbay. They'll fix you. I promise I'll—"

The ace gave him a small, soft smile, then his eyes closed and his chest stopped moving as his hand went limp in Placido's grasp. He tightened his grip on Gin's hand before he released it. Numb and resolute, he picked Eddy's knife up, stared at it for a moment, and then looked at the girl.

"Placido…" He turned. Inigo stood at the entrance, face pale and mouth agape. The next moments were a blur. He pushed past the decker and sprinted to the edge of the dock. The only thought that drummed in his brain was that he couldn't be there anymore. A red flash in his oculars confirmed that his EI had sent an alarm to the faculty. He whipped the device out and removed the EI chip from it. Poised on the edge of the pier, he held it briefly in his hand before he let it fall and crushed it under his heel.

Placido leapt into the bay and swam maniacally toward the forests that surrounded it. He made it to shore and turned to see several scout ships take off. They were coming for him already. He ran deeper into the forest.

After several hours, his body gave out, and he collapsed near a tree to drag in deep breaths as his muscles tensed up. Something dug into him when he sat, and he fumbled in his pants pocket to pull it out. His heart thudded as he stared numbly at a knife—the one used to kill Gin. He must have pocketed it when he ran away from Inigo.

Placido traced his fingers over the bloody blade and flinched when he cut himself. He hurled it into the underbrush and curled into himself. The rain began to fall as he trembled and rocked on the forest floor.

CHAPTER THREE

"Worst fucking day of my life," Gin muttered and slid Macha back into its sheath. "I had a few bad ones before then and a few after, but nothing comes close to that."

His companion placed a vape stick in her mouth.

"Do you like those things?" the killer asked, regarding the device with mild curiosity. "I never touch them myself. I knew a guy who always seemed to have one in his mouth. He was the one who set this whole ball rolling for me."

It had been three months since the incident, and Placido had been able to make his way back home. Well, at least to Los Angeles, the city he was from, although he couldn't go to his actual home. They would definitely be waiting for him by now; he'd seen enough to confirm that he was a wanted man. He moved the brim of his hat down as he walked out of the market, a few bags in hand as he made his way back to the building he currently squatted in.

Wearily, he placed the bag on the nightstand he had found in the alley and sank into a rickety chair to hold his head in his hands. What could he do now? He had been like this ever since his return. The disguises wouldn't protect him forever. He had buzzed his hair down to almost a shaved look, wore contacts and sunglasses, and even had his ears pierced, but he couldn't run forever, could he?

He took a pear from the bag and bit into it. His prospects were bleak, to say the least. He contemplated turning himself in, but that was pointless. Honestly, he felt no remorse. They all deserved it. Eddy, Rick, and Tai had all deserved to die for what they did. They were all responsible.

Frustration ate at him, as always. He should have been there. Gin should have told him about...whatever it was. Placido took another bite of the pear before he stood and hurled it at the wall in anger. He walked to the nightstand and opened the drawer to retrieve a knife with a five-inch blade. His gaze dispassionate, he studied it for a moment before he raised it slowly to his neck. It scraped against his throat, and he held his breath as he tried to will himself to slice it through his flesh. He had done it to Eddy but couldn't do it for himself.

Frustration mixed with disappointment as he lowered the blade and exhaled before he stepped back and dropped into the chair. He sat motionless for a while before he raised the knife slowly, ready to throw it down.

A commotion outside distracted him. He first thought he should simply ignore it. The building was dilapidated, and it was probably only scavengers. They wouldn't bother him once they saw he had nothing to steal. He glanced at the bags from the market and remembered that he did have food. That might be enough for them to start trouble.

Placido pushed quietly from the chair and walked over to the doorway, where he knelt and peeked out at a trio of men across the hall. They didn't seem to have any intention of ransacking the little that was left, which was interesting since he had been able to sell some of the items he had found for a few hundred credits.

Instead, they seemed to search for something in particular as another man emerged from one of the rooms and shook his head. "I'm not sure he's here," the newcomer muttered.

"We've only checked half the building. He couldn't have gotten far," another stated as he turned quickly. The flashlight on his helmet almost caught Placido, but he managed to duck back behind the wall in time.

"We still have a few rooms left. Should we split up?"

"Against that crazy bastard? Hell, no," one of them spat. "That's asking for a blade to the eye."

"Then let's move on to the next. Keep your eyes peeled. He might try to vanish while we're looking around."

Placido moved to the corner of his room and gripped the knife tightly in his hand. He looked at the broken window across the room. Maybe he should try to get away? He wasn't sure who these men were, but they didn't seem to be looking for him. From the sounds of it, they were already in pursuit of someone, but he was a wanted man now. They would probably see it as a bonus, especially if they didn't find their target.

He froze and looked up as loose rubble fell from the ceiling, and his heart skipped a beat. A man was attached to the ceiling of his room—how had he gotten there? He was clad in dark armor, but pieces of the suit were cracked and visible indents covered the chest, shoulders, and legs. He looked down and placed a finger where his mouth would be, except that the bottom half of his face was covered by a mask. His gray eyes were visible, however, and stared at him in cold warning.

One of the mercs walked into the room and looked around for a moment before he caught sight of Placido.

"Who the hell are—"

The man on the ceiling dropped, caught the merc around the neck, and snapped it in one swift movement. He laid the body down and drew a blade as a second merc stepped through the doorway. The stranger drove the knife into the merc's neck, and the victim made a rough gurgling noise before he collapsed.

The killer walked away from the body and exited the room and Placido, shaking in shock, focused on the sounds of a scuffle. The third merc was likely the next victim, although he seemed to at least be fighting back. Placido simply froze. He didn't know if he should consider himself lucky or not and supposed it would depend on whether the man came back to finish him off, so as to leave no witnesses.

A boot slid over the floor, and a gun clicked. He dragged his gaze to what he assumed was the fourth merc, who stood directly outside the room, his gun at the ready but not aimed at him.

"Hands up, Kilian," he ordered in a tense growl.

A laugh sounded before something heavy dropped. "It's gonna be like that, eh? I'm not sure if you wanna look around, but no help is coming."

"I don't need help. I have enough right here." The merc waved his gun. "As for them, I'll hire a new crew with what I'll get once I turn your head in."

"Ain't that ironical? I'm probably worth more than I actually have," Kilian mused. "But you won't get a cred today."

"You won't escape."

"I had no plans to. After all, you need to be chased to escape." He chuckled again. "No one will follow me tonight, boyo."

The merc fired, and a red light hurtled from the barrel of his gun and struck something Placido couldn't see from his vantage point. "Do you think you can dodge that? This is one of the fastest guns on the market," the bounty hunter threatened. " You come with me, and I'll only wing ya a few times to keep you in line. You are worth more alive than dead."

"Ain't that the truth?" Kilian smiled. "I would be right grateful should I get a bit of a hand here."

Placido startled as the insinuation took root. He looked at his knife as the merc took a couple of steps forward. "You don't have the creds to offer to get me to help you out."

"That wasn't my thought at all," the fugitive retorted. Placido gripped the blade firmly in his hand and peeked around the corner. The merc stood with his back to him. He wore a helmet, but his neck was exposed. Still, Placido hesitated. The reality was that he was in enough trouble and should stay out of it, but against his better judgment, he glanced at the stranger, who smiled at him. To the merc, it would look like a cocky smirk, but to Placido, it seemed warm.

He straightened and snuck forward as the merc reached one hand behind him to retrieve a pair of cuffs. Placido shoved his hesitation aside, grabbed the man by the neck, and pulled back. The bounty hunter yelled in surprise and fired his gun into the air as the blade sank deep into his neck. The man continued to fight with all he had left in him and tried to strike at his assailant with his free hand. Kilian joined the fray and thrust a long blade into the flesh beside the one that protruded, Placido's hand still gripping the hilt. Blood poured down the merc's chest, and a few droplets splashed on the attackers. He went limp, and they released the body as one. Kilian freed his blade casually, but Placido let go of his in shock as the body tumbled.

The fugitive laughed and wiped his blade with a handkerchief—one that seemed to be nearly useless now since it was covered in dried blood. Placido looked from the bodies to Kilian, who simply grinned and took a drag on a vape stick. A small white light glowed at the tip. "Good moves there, sonny," he complimented, and exhaled a stream of vapor. "Do you have a name?"

"P-P-Placido" he answered, his voice a choked whisper.

"Hmm? Speak up, now. No one else will hear ya." Kilian kicked the merc's body. "Obviously."

"P-Placido, sir," he answered again. His heart beat rapidly, and yet, strangely, he didn't feel like he was in any danger.

"Plah-see-dough? Hmm, a bit of a twister, I think. I'll

stick with 'sonny' for now. I'm sure there's no need for formalities and all."

Placido looked at the bodies. "This...does seem like it's not a very civilized environment, I suppose."

The man laughed boisterously. "You have that right, sonny, but even without the bodies decorating the place, it's not exactly the height of comfortable living here."

"I suppose you are right," Placido conceded.

"Eh, sorry. I didn't mean to make fun of ya."

He waved a hand. "It's all right. It's not really my place, just the closest thing to home I have for now."

Kilian stroked his chin. He took out a glowstick and snapped it, and after it lit, he raised it to better illuminate the room. Placido could see his face properly now without the mask. He was pale-skinned, and the suggestion of a beard had formed around his face like he hadn't shaved in a few days. His hair was long and brown and caught in a single braid that started from the middle of his forehead and wound to the back of his head.

"Hey, you look familiar." He studied Placido with his piercing gray eyes.

He tensed instinctively. If he figured out who he was, would he turn him in?

The older man snapped his fingers. "You're that kid they're looking for, aren't ya? The one who killed some of the kids at that fancy school in Washington?"

Placido didn't answer, simply focused his gaze on the floor.

"I knew there had to be something. That strike wasn't a fumble or a lucky trick. You've had a little practice."

"That wasn't what... I'm not..." He looked at Kilian and

scowled. He didn't have to defend himself to this man, who was probably worse than he was. "They deserved it."

Silence descended between the two of them for a moment. Kilian walked up to Placido, who immediately tensed, expecting an attack. Before he could move, the man placed an arm on his shoulder. "I'm sure they did. I've learned that there are a few too many people in this world who stay breathing when they shouldn't. I don't see any lies in your eyes. You didn't do it for pleasure." He leaned in. "I'll bet it felt that way, though."

Placido didn't know how to feel. Did he really want to relate to this man? But a part of him did agree. When he'd looked back on it over the months he had been in hiding, the shock of that day had eventually gone away. The sadness of losing Gin had dulled, but a new emotion—joy —replaced it. A new feeling, satisfaction, had settled in since then.

"You know, I wasn't lying when I said I would be grateful for some help. I'm glad you picked up on that," Kilian stated, stood back, and stroked his chin. "I had planned to offer you a bauble you could sell for some creds, but I see something interesting in ya." He looked away for a moment as if debating with himself. "This might be a bit of a leap, but I have needed a little help and looked for a project of some kind."

"What are you talking about?" Placido asked, now at ease, his tension replaced by confusion.

Kilian smiled and nodded. "My guess is that you used to be a student at that academy?"

"Not anymore."

"No doubt." He laughed and shook his head. "But that

means you had planned to go into a trade. With that out of the picture, you could be in the market for a new line of work. How would you like to join me?"

Placido frowned. He felt that he should yell, 'No!' but seemed unable to voice the protest. Instead, something stirred within him as he considered the proposal. "What... What do you do, exactly?"

The man's smile widened. "Something that will let you have that feeling much more often." He extended his hand for Placido to take. "So, will you join me, sonny?"

"I took his hand and never looked back. That was probably the beginning of how I came to be…well, *me*. If the events at the Academy were the fuse, this was the bang." Placido looked at the device on his table and sighed. "Wow, this was supposed to be in a completed state? Good God, how are you supposed to do anything efficiently when it takes this long to work?" He looked at his companion. "Thanks for being so patient. I didn't expect it to take this long."

She simply nodded nervously and took another drag of her vape stick.

Placido sighed once more. "I mentioned that I never touch those things. Despite the claim that they are safe, it all depends on what you put in them." He leaned forward. "I spent a few years with Kilian and learned from him when we went out on gigs. I was able to not only learn a new craft but get a new life. In time, I broke out of my shell —metamorphosized, you might say."

He looked at a painting of Earth on the wall. "But all

good things come to an end. My time with Kilian was probably the last long-term relationship I had. Well, at least where the other person didn't want me dead. And for all the good things he taught me, and all the help and wisdom he gave me…" Placido tapped his fingers on the desk he sat on. "He was also the one who signed me up with those imbeciles, the Star Killers."

Kilian coughed into his handkerchief and tossed it on the desk as he took another drag from his vape stick.

"So, for all the people after you, it's the Megafire company that claims your head, huh?" Placido challenged as he cleaned his blade.

"I think I liked you better when you were quiet," Kilian muttered, only partially joking.

"Hey, you were the one who said I should find the brighter side of things," he countered with a smile. Satisfied that the blade was clean, he set it down and walked over to Kilian, who was seated in a large chair.

"Yeah? And you've found the bright side to this?" the older man asked.

"I've found the irony, at least."

His mentor chuckled and shook his head. "Are you finished with the blades?"

"All sharpened and polished, at least the ones I can do that with." He looked at another desk. "I guess I can go over the plasma blades and electric batons if you want."

"Nah, I've given you enough busywork." Kilian leaned

back in his chair. "I've actually got something for ya if you're interested."

"Another gig?" Placido asked and sat opposite him.

"Of a sort, but more a new position, actually." He pointed to the tablet on the small circular table in front of them. Placido picked it up and turned it on. "I have a contact, an old friend of mine, who put together a pirate outfit a few years back. They are doing good business now, but he's looking for some neck-cutters. You have a penchant for that."

"Are you trying to toss me out already, Kilian?" Placido challenged as he read the message on the tablet. "Is this because I'm starting to surpass your tally? Are you scared that the student will become the master?"

"Ha! You may be catching up, but you still have a ways to go there." Kilian took another puff. "Besides, I'll still get the majority of the cut. I win either way."

"You should treat me to more meals," he muttered and held the tablet up. "What do you think about this?"

"Well, if I thought it was shite, I wouldn't have bothered to bring it up," he retorted. "I figure it's something with multiple benefits for you. The truth is, you're still wanted down here, so getting up in the great black with several dozen people to guard your back is better than sticking down here with only me. Plus, you keep all these little doodads with you on the occasions we go tripping through a lab or a research center."

"I have to keep myself occupied," Placido said. "Besides, that shield generator I restored for you has helped you more times than you care to admit."

"I don't care to admit that," Kilian grumbled. "But my

point is, think about the haul you'll get while you're with them. They go out and bust far-off colonies and stations all the time. You'll get way more toys to play with out there."

Placido thought it over. "I'm not sure. What about you? Why don't you sign on?"

The older man took another long drag before he set the vape stick down and exhaled a billow of vapor. "I'm afraid I don't have much more time."

"What?" He looked up in concern.

"I stopped at Gilly's med shop after the last gig. Obviously, he's not a real doc, but that machine of his don't lie." He pointed to his heart. "I ain't got much longer to breathe on this planet."

"So go to another," Placido retorted, and his mentor laughed loudly.

"Don't be a fool." Kilian sobered and leaned back in his chair to stare directly into his pupil's eyes. "Listen here, sonny. You're the closest thing I've had to progeny, and I wanna make sure you have something ahead of you when I'm no longer here."

"Why can't I keep doing what you've taught me?" he questioned.

"You can do more than that. Guys like me, we keep to the shadows. Our names will never be remembered, and we're lucky to inspire fear if someone bothers to," the man responded. "But you? I think you could be a rev."

"Reverend? That's a hell of a lot of 'our Fathers' I'm gonna have to say to be considered."

"No, idiot. Revenant. I'm talking about the Revenant List," Kilian chided. "Those are the guys you wanna be like. They are feared across the galaxy. You'd never have to worry about trash gigs ever again, and never worry about being lost to time. Most people may think it's a myth or some sort of unofficial list, but it's quite real."

"Wouldn't that simply make me more likely to die?" Placido pointed out. "I mean, I would imagine that being on a list like that will mean that everyone would be after your ass."

"If you make it on there, I doubt there will be many who could actually do anything about what you wanna do," Kilian challenged. "I'm not saying you have to stay with them, but think about it as a starting point."

Placido looked at the tablet again. "If I'm gone, what happens when...you know?" He tapped his finger against his own heart while he looked at his mentor.

"I never wanted a grand burial anyway. They'll toss me into some landfill with a tiny headstone like the life I led deserved," Kilian huffed. "Or maybe simply send my body up in smoke. But knowing that you're out there doing me proud? I can actually look forward to it instead of wasting away." Kilian drew his blade, Macha, and handed it to Placido. "At least think about it, sonny."

He took the blade and studied his reflection in its sheen. "Strength is about more than who's the better fighter."

"Is that a proverb or something?" Kilian asked. "I've heard you mutter that a few times after a kill. I thought it was some sort of tic."

"It's something someone said to me a long time ago, about power versus strength."

The older man scratched his chin. "Eh, it seems a bit weird, but I guess I can see the wisdom in it, especially in our business." He smiled at Placido. "After all, how many times have we taken out a bounty hunter or captain who was supposed to be unbeatable?"

He looked up and smiled as he spun the blade in his hands. "Every time."

Placido walked through the underground market and searched for the bar listed on the message. Two men tumbled out of a door on his left, followed by another two with gang tattoos who tried to separate them. He glanced at the Warlock's Bar sign on the top. Having found his location, he circled the scuffle and stepped into the bar.

It was filled with smoke, crowded, and smelled of alcohol, blood, sweat, and strangely, citrus. He walked cautiously forward and looked for anyone marked with the symbol in the message. In the far corner of the room stood a man who wore a blue and black underlay with chest armor and greaves. On the shoulder, a star with a blade in the middle was easily recognizable as the Star Killers' logo.

Placido walked up to him and tilted his shades down. "Are you a Star Killer?"

"Yeah. Who are you looking for?" he asked, puffing his chest out. Placido handed him the tablet, and the guard read it quickly. "New blood, huh? Go check in with the boss, but if you have Kilian's backing, I'll call you 'brother' soon."

"Just don't ask for money," Placido joked. "You're more likely to get a knife to the belly."

"So you already know the rules. Good to know." The

man snickered. "Get inside. The boss is in a good mood today."

He nodded, skirted the guard, and opened the door to the private room. It was dark inside, with low red lights. A man sat on a long half-circle couch with two women, and two guards hovered behind them. The gang leader had long white hair and handsome features and wore a long blue jacket with a black underlay. "Well, who do we have here?" he asked. His voice was playful, but there was an edge of maliciousness to it.

The guards straightened and eyed the newcomer, who waved casually at them. "Evening. My name is Placido, and I'm—"

"Kilian's protégé, right?" the man asked, and he nodded in return. "Good to meet you. The name's Vito. Do you want to take the gig?"

"What do you need me to do, exactly?" he inquired. "Kilian said you need people willing to get...intimate."

"Oh, I have those," Vito said and winked at the girls beside him. "But if you're talking with a blade, fist, or gun, that's exactly right. Do you think you— Hold up." He pressed a finger on the transmitter in his ear. "What's going on? Uh huh, tell them to piss o— Actually, hold that thought." He released the transmitter and looked at the new recruit. "Wanna give a quick demonstration?"

———

Placido walked out of the room and paused to study two men who yelled at the guard. "What's going on?"

"That asshole in there is with our chicks," one of them cried.

"That's bullshit! Who knows what he's doing with them?" the other yelled.

"He's currently fondling the breasts of one and kissing the other," Placido stated.

This enraged the men and they shoved up against the guard, who held them back.

"I'll fucking kill him!" the first man bellowed.

"No, you won't," Placido said casually. He drew Macha in a fluid movement and sliced the man's throat. The other backed away, his stare fixed on his friend. His shock gave Placido time to snatch him by his shirt and draw him forward, stab him in the chest several times, and release him with a grim smile. The man tried to walk away, but only managed a few steps before he collapsed.

No one seemed to notice, and the few who did paid him no mind.

"It's not the best idea to start fights in a place filled with thieves, gang members, scavengers, and contract killers," Placido mused and grinned at the guard, who looked at the bodies with surprise on his face. "Do you mind taking care of those, brother?"

The guard relaxed. "You gonna tip?"

Placido smiled, called a waitress, and told her to bring his new friend some drinks. She nodded and stepped over the bodies on her way to the bar. "Something to look forward to after you take these to the dump."

"Physical labor does get me parched." He chuckled. "I'll take them out. I guess the next time I see you will be on the ship."

"See you then," Placido promised and walked back into the room.

"Damn, I said I wanted quick, and you delivered," Vito said approvingly. "You got the gig, kid. It was only a little taste, but Kilian obviously didn't only make you sound good. No hesitation at all."

"It's mostly muscle memory at this point," he explained.

"Silvio here will take your info down." Vito snapped his fingers, and one of the guards produced a tablet. "What do you want your handle to be?"

"Handle?" Placido asked.

"We don't work in the legal business, obviously. Most guys assume fake names or titles as a buffer—or, you know, something that's cool to them for the sake of image. It's something of a tradition. What do you want to call yourself for your new life?"

Placido thought about it for a moment and tapped his fingers on his chest. "Gin..." He looked at Macha. "Gin Sonny."

CHAPTER FIVE

"And there's the big reveal, but you waited with bated breath." Gin chuckled, flipped Macha in his hand, and studied his device. "Ninety percent…almost there." He leaned against the desk. "Thanks for being so patient. I planned to consider this a test run anyway. This thing had a number of options already in it that worked right away. I didn't think adding a new one would be such a slog."

His companion nodded, then reached for a mint in a bowl on the desk, unwrapped it, and popped it into her mouth. After a moment, she picked the bowl up and offered it to him.

"Why, thank you," he said with a smile as he took a couple and followed her example. "You know, I thought my time with the Star Killers would prove more fruitful. That I could work my way up in the ranks and become a leader or something. From what I knew of the Revenant List, most of the guys on there were leaders in big organizations, so it seemed to be the best way to 'make it' in that regard." He shook his head, tossed Macha up, and caught it by the handle. "It was a hell of a nuisance when it turned out they were so damn weak. But it was another important realization, and the final stop on the journey. The beginning of the end. Wait, no, the beginning of the beginning? That seems redundant. Whichever, it began with our little tussle with the guys in the Omega Horde."

Gin breathed heavily. Most of his armor was compromised, and explosions continued outside. The battle had raged in earnest for at least forty minutes, but he had been in this damn base for almost three hours in preparation for the strike. He began to see a hell of a lot of names with the word "deceased" beside them on the network list on his HUD. The Star Killers were apparently confused. That, or they thought they could live up to their name no matter who was dead—including themselves, apparently.

But he was a little preoccupied at the moment. Four bodies lay at his feet, but the beast of a man in front of him clad in jet-black heavy armor wielded a giant hammer that Gin was certain was either a metaphor or compensation. That notwithstanding, the fiend now launched forward for another strike. Gin leapt back as the attacker swung. He had no problems dodging him, but he was actually there to kill him. Unfortunately, that thick armor and the shielding device he used to block his shots made that difficult.

"Do you think you pests can come onto our planet and claim it so easily?" the leader of this sect of the Omega Horde challenged. "You're scavengers. You should have stayed in your lane and eked out whatever measly life you could." He activated a bounce jet on his armor and flung himself at his opponent, and his shield activated as he closed in. Gin vaulted upward and dropped a flashbang as he jumped over him. The leader landed, and his shield condensed into a ball that he flung at Gin. It slammed into his stomach, and he tumbled awkwardly along the ground.

The man yanked a rod from his belt and clicked a switch, and it transformed into a rather pointy spear. He had just cocked his arm to throw it when the flashbang went off and blinded him. With a curse, he stumbled back and shielded his eyes until they adjusted. He grinned when he saw that Gin hadn't recovered and was still trying to push off the floor. With a triumphant snarl, he snatched the spear up again and flung it at him. He gaped when the projectile passed through his adversary without pause. No blood covered the point of the spear or spurted from the target. Instead, his adversary became intangible and disappeared. The man cursed when he realized it was a hologram.

Gin came up behind him with Macha in his hand, shoved the blade into the center of the leader's bounce pack, and cut through it. The damage to the systems inside caused electricity to spark and shock them both, but Gin had a mod in his armor that enabled him to resist it for the most part. The leader was not so lucky. Although his shields were able to absorb some of the shock, the blade had dug deep enough to strike the core. This, combined with the surge of electricity, overloaded the core, and it exploded and hurled them both away in the blast.

Sonny scrambled to his feet and readied himself to continue the fight. His opponent slammed the staff of his hammer into the ground to help him stand. Without the power core, most of his systems would malfunction until reset or the remaining power was manually redistributed. He would have a hard time moving in all that weight.

Victory was within reach when Gin received a call from Vito. "Gin, this is Vito. We have to retreat. We're being overwhelmed."

"What?" He sneered. "I'm about to finish—"

"It's taking way too long, Gin. We've already lost more than half our men. There are lots more guys in this base than we thought."

"You were responsible for intel," he yelled into the comm. "You told me that the leader wasn't a fighter but a logistics man."

"The intel was bad, or I confused it with another base," Vito muttered, too nonchalantly for Gin's taste.

"You damned idiot," he snarled. "This failure is on you."

"Watch your tone, Gin," Vito retorted angrily. "I am the leader of this crew. You will fall into line. Now, if you're not back in ten, we'll leave your ass to the Horde, so get the hell back here." With that, he signed off and left Gin trembling in rage as a timer appeared in his visor.

The Omega Horde's captain, still on his knees, chuckled, which drew his attention. "Your mic is on, you know," he said through heavy breaths. "While it's probably a little unorthodox, considering the men you've killed…" He motioned to the bodies that littered the floor. "You've been able to both catch me by surprise and bring me to my knees. Neither has happened since I was only a grunt."

"My guess is you haven't seen much action in the time since you became captain of this sect," Gin responded and looked at Macha's blade to inspect the damage. It would probably need to be replaced.

"Hardly. All captains enter the field of battle with their men in the Horde," the captain stated. "Where's yours? Your mission was to take me down? Should he not be with you to make the final blow?"

"He said he was 'coordinating,' as always." Gin sheathed Macha and drew a plasma blade.

The Horde captain removed his helmet, tossed it on the floor, and spat. "What a pathetic leader, hiding in the shadows while his men do all the work." He looked up to reveal a toothy grin. "And have all the talent."

"I'm glad you seem so enamored of me. I still have to kill you, though," Gin said unapologetically. He held the plasma blade up and turned it on, and the edge turned bright blue.

"I would be disappointed if a few compliments made you malleable." The captain grunted and heaved himself up. He turned to grab a box on the console behind him, threw it at Gin, who let it fall at his feet, and prepared to back away. "Don't fret, it's not a bomb or a trick. You've earned a reward. All pirates get their cut."

Gin eyed him suspiciously, but against his better judgment, he kicked the button on the front of the case. It opened to reveal a shielding device. "What's this?"

"A shielding mod like my own," the captain explained. "I'm not sure what power unit you have, but it's useable as soon as it's installed."

"You would give me something like that when yours is blown and we're still fighting?" he questioned incredulously. "You *do* understand that I'm here to kill you, yes?"

"That's one way it could end." The captain nodded and pointed to his helmet. "But we were able to hack into your commlink. That's how we were able to overwhelm you so easily. And I heard your leader call the retreat. That must sting after all your hard work."

Gin stared at the captain, unmoving. "We'll have words when I return."

"Or you could kill him for his transgressions," the captain suggested. "Maybe under the banner of the Omega Horde."

"Is this some sort of unorthodox job interview?" Gin inquired. He closed the case with one foot, kicked it up, and caught it in his hand. "After today, if I leave the Star Killers, I don't think I'll throw my lot in with anyone."

"That's a damn shame. I see real talent in front of me." The captain shrugged. "You're running out of time. I may like you, but I'll still kill you if you are dead-set on trying to end this. Our little chat has given me plenty of time to get my armor back to working condition." He took a fighting stance and swung his hammer to prove his point.

Gin tilted his head as he thought things through. "It might be the chat, or the sting of betrayal, or even the real-ization of what kind of weaklings the people in my crew are, but I feel less inclined to kill you." He looked at his blade. "But more people will die today."

"If you leave, I have no reason to pursue," the captain promised. "I still think it's foolish that you'll walk away from us to be with those weaklings, though. They get some numbers and fancy guns and think they can take on the Horde? They confuse power with—"

"Strength," Gin finished as something clicked in his

head. "Either you are a mind reader or I'm precognitive, but I think I've thought of something that'll make us both happy."

"And what would that be?" the captain inquired.

"I'll take your gift but not your offer," he stated and turned away. "I also want to ask that you pull your men back."

"Are you trying to bargain for your crew's lives?"

"Not at all." Gin shook his head firmly as he walked away. "I want some left for me."

"Finally, you made it," a Star Killer grunt barked and closed the hatch behind Gin. "I thought we were gonna leave your sorry ass behind."

"Vito would never do that. Gin is our best fighter!" another grunt said dismissively.

"You know Vito. His whims change on a dime." The other man sighed.

"Strangely enough…" He drew two plasma blades, one in either hand, and activated them. "Mine have too."

Gin made his way to Vito's quarters and slaughtered anyone in his way. His blue and black armor was soon covered in the blood of his former brothers.

He didn't have to make the entire trip. Vito met him in the hall outside his room with three guards in front of him who aimed their guns at Gin's head.

"Have you gone mad?" the leader snarled. "What have you done? We already lost so many, and you come in and kill almost everyone else? What if the Horde follows us? We weren't in any position to fight even if—"

"I find it amusing that you're concerned about statistics rather than the fact that I've killed nearly the entire crew," Gin muttered. He stood perfectly erect, and his hands held the plasma blades lazily. "A great show of heart there, Vito. Maybe I should go for the head instead? Ripping out your heart may not produce dividends."

"You're… You're going to lecture me about how much I care?" Vito shouted, angry and aghast at the same time. "You've killed men you've traveled with for over a year. You showed no mercy."

"None was needed," he responded flatly. "If they were better, they would have killed me. It's as simple as that."

Vito clenched his teeth and pointed at Gin. "Kill him."

The trio of guards fired, but the new shield blocked the blasts. A shimmering purple glow rippled around his suit until their guns overheated. Instead of venting them, they dropped their weapons in shock.

Gin pointed at Vito. "Kill him, and I might spare you."

The guards looked at one another, and their leader stared at them anxiously. One drew his pistol and fired into Vito's head. A sizzling hole appeared as he fell back and dropped without a sound. The other two guards stood in shock until a plasma blade punctured each of their chests. Gin released the blades and shoved their bodies out of his way to approach the soldier who had followed his order.

"And who might you be?" he asked and motioned at the visor. "Let's have a look."

The guard nodded and removed his helmet with shaking hands. Gin smiled at the sight. "Rocco! From my first day at Warlock's Bar," he said when he remembered the guard he had bought drinks for. He put his arm around the man's shoulder and leaned against the wall. "Who would have thought this is how things would turn out, huh?"

"C-can't say I-I did," Rocco stammered.

"Right? Crazy." Gin shook his head in disbelief.

"Are y-you g-gonna k-k-kill me?" the man asked, petrified.

"You know, I was," he admitted, and the guard stiffened beneath his arm. "Of course, I could say something sarcastic like, 'I said might, no guarantees,' but I like you. You have good taste in drinks."

"T-thanks."

"Well, I'm gonna be on my way." Gin clapped the man on his shoulder. "I'll grab what I can and head to the escape pods. Some of them have to be working. A few were able to escape in them, but... Wait a minute." He paused, then walked over to Vito's body to rummage around for his tablet. "Let's see...do...do...do—ah, a list of all crew members and their info." He placed the tablet in a compartment on his left leg. "That'll be useful to hunt them down."

"You're going after all of them?" Rocco asked, and flinched when Gin looked at him. "I mean... Just don't. Sorry."

He walked past the man, stopped for a moment, and tapped his chin. "Wanna do me a favor, Rocco?"

"I won't tell anyone, I swear to God!" Rocco pleaded.

"I'm not sure how much good that'll do. I doubt He likes these kinds of things," Gin said airily. "But actually, I want you to do the opposite." He looked at the bodies. "Tell everyone you can about everything I've done. They might not believe you at first, but trust me…" He chuckled darkly as he stepped over the bodies, leaving the blades jutting out of them. "I'll give them reasons to believe you soon enough."

THANK YOU for not only reading this story but these *Author Notes* as well.

(I think I've been good with always opening with "thank you." If not, I need to edit the other *Author Notes*!)

RANDOM (*sometimes*) THOUGHTS?

So, originally I really hated Gin. I mean, I wanted him dead, and I wanted him dead in the last book.

I was talking with Joshua about the villain, and Joshua (who likes complicated villains) was giving me a bit about Gin's background. So, I asked him to write an epilogue where we got to see a bit more about Gin's history, and what made him...*him*.

Thus, you get the story of Gin in this book.

I hate to admit that now I almost...*almost*...like Gin. Which, is sad cause the fucker has to die.

Right?

I mean...he IS the bad guy here.

Dammit Joshua, you are screwing up my nice black and white worldview here!

AROUND THE WORLD IN 80 DAYS

One of the interesting (at least to me) aspects of my life is the ability to work from anywhere and at any time. In the future, I hope to re-read my own *Author Notes* and remember my life as a diary entry.

NEW YORK, JFK AIRPORT

I'm presently hanging in the British Airways lounge in Terminal 7 of New York's JFK airport. It's 10:04 PM, and I have to finish these author notes in ten minutes and get them over to Stephen Campbell and Lynne Stiegler to get in the book so it publishes really quickly.

I sure hope I make it everywhere I need to.

While I am flying towards London (for the London Book Fair next week) I'll be working on two books, hoping that my crap sleeping doesn't screw me over. I noticed on the flight from Las Vegas to here that I didn't have the emotional desire to do anything.

So I read.

I'm going to save a couple of minutes and get book 03 of the series I'm reading 'just in case' I can't make myself work.

I suppose I could fire myself for not working, but I doubt that I will.

Joshua has the beats for the next ANIMUS book completed and is writing, so I am hoping the next book will be out in April.

Crossing my fingers, since I love these stories!

FAN PRICING

$0.99 Saturdays (new LMBPN stuff) and $0.99 Wednesday (both LMBPN books and friends of LMBPN books.) Get great stuff from us and others at tantalizing prices.

Go ahead. I bet you can't read just one.

Sign up here: http://lmbpn.com/email/.

HOW TO MARKET FOR BOOKS YOU LOVE

Review them so others have your thoughts, and tell friends and the dogs of your enemies (because who wants to talk to enemies?)… *Enough said ;-)*

Ad Aeternitatem,

Michael Anderle

AUTHOR NOTES - JOSHUA

APRIL 2, 2019

(These author notes were added to version 1.01 of this book with the update on April 2, 2019)

I usually prefer to leave this to my father, but I wanted to apologize for the previous state of the book, and thank those of you who were still kind despite the problems.

Because of my delays in writing it, it caused trouble in the editing. I didn't send the right pages either, which made for some of the confusing chapters and poor wording, particularly with one that was an amalgamation that I had previously used as a template and left in, sending it for processing before swapping it out.

Thank you again for all the positive feedback and helpful critique. This one was a bit different—more episodic, since I wanted to get Gin a bit more involved. I'm currently working on book 6, and hope you'll enjoy the wrap up to year two and look forward to going beyond.

Sincerely,

Joshua (D'Artagnan) Anderle

CONNECT WITH THE AUTHORS

Michael Anderle Social
 Website:
 http://lmbpn.com

Email List:
 http://lmbpn.com/email/

Facebook Here:
 https://www.facebook.com/OriceranUniverse/
 https://www.
facebook.com/TheKurtherianGambitBooks/
 https://www.facebook.com/groups/
320172985053521/ (Protected by the Damned Facebook
Group)